Susannah could not help wishing that she and Harry might have had a little time together before all his relatives arrived.

She was trying to accustom herself to the idea that she was engaged to a man she loved—a man she was not sure felt quite the same about her. She knew that Harry felt something for her, but most marriages were arranged for reasons other than love, and she could not yet be certain that she was loved as she would wish to be—to distraction.

* * *

A Country Miss in Hanover Square
Harlequin® Historical #312—July 2011

Author Note

Writing for Harlequin is a constant joy. *A Season in Town,* Book One, is about Susannah and Lord Pendleton. Susannah never expected to have a season because her mama could not afford it. However, Amelia Royston has inherited a fortune, and she wants to spend some of it on young women in less happy circumstances than herself. Susannah is flattered by the attentions of the dashing Lord Pendleton, but overawed by the prospect of becoming the wife of such an important man.

Beneath the story runs a thread of intrigue that continues throughout all three books in this trilogy and may threaten Amelia herself. Look out for Harry and his friends in the next two.

This book is dedicated to
the memory of my mother, who once told me
my books would be enjoyed by hundreds of thousands
of people worldwide. I laughed, Mum, but you were right!

A
Country Miss
in Hanover
Square

ANNE HERRIES

Harlequin®

TORONTO NEW YORK LONDON
AMSTERDAM PARIS SYDNEY HAMBURG
STOCKHOLM ATHENS TOKYO MILAN MADRID
PRAGUE WARSAW BUDAPEST AUCKLAND

Recycling programs
for this product may
not exist in your area.

ISBN-13: 978-0-373-30621-3

A COUNTRY MISS IN HANOVER SQUARE

Copyright © 2009 by Anne Herries

First North American Publication 2011

Printed in U.S.A.

A Season in Town

a new Regency miniseries from Anne Herries

Look for
A Country Miss in Hanover Square
An Innocent Debutante in Hanover Square
The Mistress of Hanover Square

Available from Harlequin® Historical and
ANNE HERRIES

*Banewulf Dynasty
**The Elizabethan Season
†The Hellfire Mysteries
††Melford Dynasty
‡The Horne Sisters
‡‡A Season in Town

Did you know some of these titles are also available
as ebooks? Visit www.Harlequin.com

Award-winning author **Anne Herries** lives in Cambridge-shire, England. She is fond of watching wildlife, and spoils the birds and squirrels that are frequent visitors to her garden. Anne loves to write about the beauty of nature, and sometimes puts a little into her books—although they are mostly about love and romance. She writes for her own enjoyment, and to give pleasure to her readers. She invites readers to contact her on her website at www.lindasole.co.uk.

Prologue

The Spanish Peninsula—1812

Three men lay slumped on the earth, which had been baked hard by the fierce Spanish sun. Harry Pendleton had his back against a rock. Of the three he was in the best shape. Max Coleridge was lying with his eyes closed, his blood-soaked shirt stuck to his chest in this damned awful heat. Gerard Ravenshead was fanning Max with a large leaf, trying to keep the flies from settling on his wound. A neckcloth was wound around a deep cut at the side of Gerard's head.

'I thought we were done for,' Harry said. He was speaking his thoughts aloud, saying what they all felt. 'What a mess!'

'You can't blame yourself for it, Harry,' Gerard said and looked at him. 'They knew we were coming. Someone must have warned them.'

'Ten killed, and the three of us only got out by the skin of our teeth.' Harry stood up and walked over to take a look at Max. 'Somehow they must have got wind that we planned a surprise raid to take prisoners…'

'One of the servants,' Gerard replied and shrugged. 'In this damned war I'm never sure whether we are fighting the French with the Spanish or the Spanish and the French.'

'I wouldn't trust their generals as far as I could throw them,' Harry growled. He looked at the blood trickling down Gerard's face. They had wrapped a kerchief round his head, but it wasn't doing much good. 'Your wound is still bleeding. Do you want me to take another look at it?'

'You saved my life once today,' Gerard said and grinned at him. 'You don't have to nursemaid me, Harry. I'll manage. We have to get Max back to the village, and by the looks of him that means carrying him between us.'

Harry pulled a wry face. 'The way you've been behaving out here, I've sometimes felt as if you meant to throw your life away…' Gerard had gained a reputation as something of a daredevil.

'There were moments when I didn't much care if I died,' Gerard admitted. He took a swipe at a fly buzzing about his face. 'But when you're facing death things come into perspective. I intend to live and return home and one day….'

Gerard left the sentence unfinished. Harry nodded. He knew something had been eating at his friend. He suspected it was to do with a young woman Gerard had been courting—and the tiny scar at his temple that he'd noticed when they first met in Spain after a year of not seeing one another. Gerard often rubbed at it when he was thoughtful, and the look in his eyes told Harry he was remembering something that made him angry.

'I know what you mean,' Harry said. 'Soldiering is blood, sweat and tears—and that is the easy part.' It was listening to the screams of dying men and knowing you couldn't save them that hurt the worst. 'Come on, then. Help me get Max on my back and I'll carry him.'

'I can walk...' Max mumbled. 'Just give me a hand up....'

'Don't be a damned fool,' Harry replied. 'You'll be carried as far as we can make it. When we get near the village, Gerard will fetch help.'

'I could walk with help.' Max's face set stubbornly as he attempted to rise. 'Damn you, Harry. I'm not a baby....'

'But I'm the superior officer here, so you will do as you're told,' Harry muttered. He grinned at Gerard. 'There's one thing, we're bound for life by this day's experience. It's something none of us will forget—and if any one of us can help the other in future, we will....'

Max grunted as they hauled him to his feet, and Harry took him over his shoulder. Gerard nodded, his eyes hard but appreciative of his friend's stubborn determination to take on the burden. He wasn't sure he could have done it himself, though he would have tried.

'Comrades in war and peace,' he said. 'Let's get back. My head is fit to burst and Max needs attention....'

Chapter One

England—1816

Harry Pendleton saw the girl run across the narrow country road seconds before he pulled on the reins, bringing his horses to an abrupt halt. Jangling harness, the sound of snorting horses and the curses of his groom took Harry's attention for a moment as he fought to control the startled beasts. They were not used to being so roughly used! Harry cursed loudly. Another second and he would have knocked the girl down! His heart had been in his mouth for an instant—and it had done his horses little good to have their mouths sawed at in that way!

'What on earth do you think you were doing?' he thundered, tossing the reins to his groom and jumping down to confront her. He hardly noticed her pale face or trembling hands. 'That was a damned stupid thing to do! I could have killed you!'

'Had you not been driving so carelessly, it would not have happened,' the girl retorted, eyes flashing. She tossed her long hair, giving him a look filled with contempt. 'These country roads are not made for such haste, sir. I had no idea that you would suddenly come round that corner like a bat driven out of hell….'

'You must have heard the sound of my wheels,' Harry retorted, though he knew that she had some right on her side. 'What on earth possessed you to dash across the road in that way?'

'I saw some primroses I wanted,' the girl replied. 'This is a quiet road, sir. No one ever drives the way you were driving.'

'Possibly because they are none of them able,' Harry retorted. Even as he spoke he realised that he sounded petulant and arrogant, which was far from his nature. 'You should be more careful when crossing the road near bends in the road, miss…' Harry belatedly became aware that she was rather lovely. Her hair had been tossed by the wind and looked like spun gold, and her eyes were so clear that a man might drown in them. He found himself staring like an idiot. 'Forgive me, I do not know your name.'

'Nor shall you,' the girl replied, giving him a haughty stare. 'Sir, I find you arrogant and rude and I shall say good day to you.'

Stunned, Harry watched as she ran from him, scrambled over a stile at the side of the road and set off swiftly across the fields. He came to himself in that instant, realising that he had handled the situation badly.

'I am sorry…' he called after her. 'I was anxious because I might have killed you. I did not mean to be so harsh.'

The girl did not falter or look back. Harry continued to watch her for a few moments, then he shook his head and climbed back to the driving box. His damnable temper had let him down. It was not often he lost it, but for some reason he had done so this morning. Instead of shouting at her, he should have made sure that she was none the worse for her fright. For a moment he was tempted to go after her, but he was in a hurry; he had promised to meet his friends at a mill held locally at a certain time and was already late. He frowned as he began to drive at a slightly more sedate pace. It was obvious the girl was unharmed, but he had not made the proper enquiries. He ought at least to have asked if she needed his assistance, though it was self-evident that she did not.

A little smile touched his mouth. She had answered him with spirit. Clearly she had not suffered an irritation of the nerves, as most of the young ladies in town might have, had they been subject to such a display of bad manners from a man who was generally considered to be one of the politest men in society. However, from the look of her clothes and the way she had been roaming the countryside without a hat or a companion, she was just a country girl—possibly the daughter of the local vicar. It was unlikely he would ever see her again, and, while he felt a certain regret, the incident was soon pushed to a distant corner of his mind.

Susannah stopped running when she was out of breath. What a bad-tempered man the driver of that phaeton had been! Had he been a little more considerate, a little caring in his manner, she would have apologised, for she knew herself to be partly at fault. However, he had come round the bend at such a pace that it was a wonder he had managed to stop at all. She was fortunate that she had not been trampled beneath his horses' hooves. If she had not felt so startled, she might have admired the way he handled his horses, which were clearly high spirited. However, the way he had shouted at her had put all thought of apology from her mind.

Frowning, Susannah sat down on a fallen log to recover her composure before going home. As her nerves ceased tingling, she suddenly saw the amusing side of the affair and laughed. It had been quite an adventure, and she had often longed for something of the sort. However, in her dreams the gentleman would smile and speak softly, making her heart beat faster. Her heart had indeed slammed against her chest, but from fright rather than pleasure. Now that she had begun to feel calmer, she remembered that he had been rather handsome—if you liked arrogant, rude men! She tossed her head and put the incident from her mind as she approached the cottage they had taken after poor Papa died. She must hurry; she had been out a long time and her mama would be looking for her.

Susannah walked into the cottage, carrying a basket of herbs and wildflowers she had picked in the hedgerow. Her fine gold hair had blown all over the place and her cheeks were pink from the fresh air. She looked beautiful, if untidy, and not quite the proper young lady. Her looks were misleading—she had been taught her manners and was in truth a well-behaved girl, though spirited and inclined to be reckless at times. She took her precious finds into the large kitchen, setting them down on the scrubbed pine table. The smell of baking was everywhere, tantalising and tempting. She felt hungry, her mouth watering at the thought of such a treat. Her hand was reaching towards a plate of cakes that were still cooling when Maisie walked in. Maisie had once been her nurse, and now she kept house for Mrs Hampton, turning her hand to anything that needed doing, because they could no longer afford the luxury of servants.

'Now then, Miss Susannah,' the woman grumbled. 'You leave them cakes alone. Your mama has the Vicar and some friends coming for tea this afternoon, and I've used the last of the butter. At least there's none to spare for more baking.'

'Can't I have just one?' Susannah pleaded, her stomach rumbling with hunger. 'I haven't eaten since first thing this morning.'

'You should have been here for your luncheon instead of wandering about the countryside like a hoyden.' Maisie looked at her with disapproval, which masked the deep affection between them. 'Go and change your gown before anyone sees you. It will be time for tea in an hour or so. You can wait until then.'

'I'm hungry now,' Susannah said and snatched a warm and chewy oat biscuit, fleeing from the kitchen with Maisie's scolding ringing in her ears.

She sighed as she went upstairs to change out of the old gown she had worn for her walk. She had managed to get grass stains on the hem again, and there was a small rent where she had caught it on some briars, so it was a good thing she had chosen this gown. It was important to conserve her best things for special occasions these days. They had just enough money to live on and pay Maisie her meagre wage, but Susannah had no idea what they would do when they needed new clothes.

Everything had changed after her father died, for he had lost his estate by making unwise investments and at the gaming tables. Mama had a little money of her own, which she had inherited from her father, but the income was scarcely enough to keep them.

'I do not know what to do, Susannah,' her mother

had told her when they moved from their comfortable house to this modest cottage. It had seemed bare and poor compared to the comfortable house they had been forced to leave, but somehow they had managed to turn it into a home. 'If I release what little capital I have, we could afford a Season in town for you, but then we should have nothing left.'

'And if I did not take, you would have given up your living for nothing,' Susannah said. She was a good-natured girl and had accepted their downfall into poverty with good grace. 'No, Mama. We shall manage as best we can. Perhaps I shall meet someone—a prince!—who will love me for myself and carry me off to his castle. I shall have jewels and beautiful clothes, and you will never have to worry again.' Her smile was unconsciously wistful.

Mrs Hampton shook her head sadly at her daughter's flight of fancy. 'You are very pretty, my darling, but things do not often happen that way. I dare say someone will offer for you, but he may not be to your liking.'

'You are thinking of Squire Horton, I suppose.' Susannah pulled a face, for the Squire was past forty, a generous kind gentleman, who had buried two wives and had a brood of boisterous children. She appreciated his qualities, but found him rather large and a little too dull for her quick mind.

She flicked her long, honey-coloured hair back out of her eyes. It was always escaping from its ribbons and curling in tendrils about her face. She presented a charming picture, for she was truly beautiful, but she seldom considered her looks, though she knew she was pretty because everyone told her so. However, it had not turned her head, and she was generally popular with both the gentlemen and the ladies she met. Unfortunately, situated as they were, she met very few gentlemen that either she or her mama considered a suitable match. 'Well, if nothing else turns up, I may be forced to such a marriage, Mama—but it is not yet too late for something exciting to happen.'

Susannah lived in the expectation of something exciting happening. She would meet a handsome man, not necessarily a prince, of course, but rich enough to keep both her and Mama in comfort. He would sweep her up on his horse and ride off with her to Gretna Green, where they would be married and live happily ever after, preferably in an ancient castle. Failing that, perhaps a relative they had never heard of would leave them a fortune. Mama said they had no rich relatives, but perhaps there was someone somewhere who might be kind to them.

Her biscuit finished, Susannah applied her mind to the little tea party her mother had planned for friends. She changed her old gown for a favourite primrose-silk afternoon dress and brushed her hair into order, tying it back with white ribbons. A white stole draped over her arms and she was instantly transformed from the hoyden, who had been traipsing the fields to find herbs her mama might use to make lotions and seasonings, into a young lady of some considerable style and beauty.

Susannah had an English rose complexion and sea-green eyes, her mouth soft and attractive. It was the kind of mouth gentlemen found irresistible and wanted to kiss, but she had not yet been brought out into society and could not guess at what might happen if she were. She sighed as she looked at her reflection in the dressing mirror. It was true that she was not ill favoured. If only they could afford a Season in town without ruining Mama! Surely then she could make a good marriage and rescue her beloved mother from the genteel poverty in which they now lived. Susannah did not care so very much for herself that they lived in a tiny cottage, but Mama had found it hard.

With an effort she banished her dreams of romantic love and handsome gentlemen who would beg for her favours. Mama was right: these things did not often happen. She might have to marry one of the gentlemen who called on Mama with gifts of fruit and vegetables from their gardens and looked at Susannah slyly whenever they got the chance, but she would not if she could help it!

She was about to go downstairs to the parlour when her bedroom door opened abruptly and her mother swept in. Wearing a gown of grey silk, Mrs Hampton was still an attractive woman, her colouring much as her daughter's, but she often had an air of sadness, which, her daughter noticed, seemed to have vanished for the moment. Susannah had not seen her mother this animated since Papa fell into a decline after losing all his money and died of a putrid infection some nine months earlier.

'Mama! What has happened?' Susannah's heart raced with anticipation, for she sensed her mother's excitement. 'You have news.'

Mrs Hampton waved a sheet of quality vellum at her. 'I have had a letter from Amelia Royston. You must remember that we met her once in Bath? She was visiting with her sister-in-law, Lady Royston. I felt so sorry for her having to live with that harpy. Her brother is a gentleman, of course, but I am not sure that I like him…' Mrs Hampton looked pensive, for her friend had not said much about her circumstances, but she had sensed her deep unhappiness at the time. 'Well, as you may recall, I asked her to a party and took her to a dance at the Assembly Rooms. She fell into a habit of visiting us every day, and we have kept in touch ever since through letters. I remember she was so grateful for my kindness…it was before Papa—' She broke off with a little choke, the sadness back in her eyes. 'Anyway, she went to live with an elderly aunt soon after that and everything has turned out most fortunately for her.'

'Yes, I remember Miss Royston,' Susannah said. 'What does she say in her letter, Mama?'

'It is like a miracle,' Mrs Hampton said and the light came back to her face. 'Amelia's aunt—Lady Agatha Sawle, I met her once, but you did not know her—well, she has died and left Amelia a fortune. She did not expect it. Indeed, she had no idea that her aunt was so wealthy. She knew she was to have something, but she says she had no expectation of being left more than an independence.'

'How wonderful for her,' Susannah said, her lovely eyes sparkling. 'You see, Mama, exciting things do happen. Perhaps someone will leave us something one day.'

'Amelia is so generous,' her mother said and dabbed at her eyes with a lace kerchief. The scent of her favourite lavender water wafted towards Susannah. 'She has offered you a Season in town, dearest. She knows of Papa's misfortune and she wants to help us. She will pay all our expenses and give you a dowry of five thousand pounds. Five thousand pounds, Susannah! Such a huge sum—and she makes it sound nothing! It means you have a chance of making a decent marriage, my love.' Mrs Hampton was quite overcome. Her hand trembled as she touched Susannah's arm. 'I can hardly believe that anyone would do such a thing, for we are not even family. However, that may be—' She broke off mid-sentence. 'Do you realise what this means, dearest?'

'A Season in town...' Susannah stared at her, disbelief, excitement and triumph warring in her head. 'Oh, Mama, how good Miss Royston is! But what made her think of us?'

Mrs Hampton shook her head. 'I really cannot imagine why she thought of us. She said it was because I was kind to her at a time when she needed friends, but I think she has other reasons.' Susannah lifted her brows in enquiry, but Mrs Hampton merely frowned, clearly preferring to keep her own counsel. 'I cannot tell, but I think she may be lonely. Her family is not kind, though she never complains. However, one knows...' She looked thoughtful. 'To give us so much is extremely generous, Susannah. I know one should not take charity, and I should not normally do so, but it is just what I have prayed for, my love. You deserve your chance and, if we are lucky, we may be able to repay Amelia for her kindness one day. Think of it, my love. You will meet everyone—Amelia is well connected and highly thought of in society. If you are fortunate...who knows what might happen!'

Susannah nodded, her face thoughtful as she looked at her mother. Some of the euphoria faded as she realised that Mama was expecting her to make a brilliant marriage and solve all their problems. She would be happy if that happened, of course, but she could not easily relinquish all her dreams of romance. She wanted to oblige Mama, but she also wanted to be swept off her feet, to fall madly in love. For some reason the picture of the outraged gentleman who had almost run her down flashed into her mind, though she could not think why—he had been abominably rude!

However, her overwhelming feeling was one of pleasure at the thought of her Season in town. It was what she
had longed for, hoped for these past months since Papa
died. If she were fortunate she would fall in love with a
suitable gentleman, one who made her heart beat much
faster, but who was also acceptable to Mama. Someone
who might look a little like the rude gentleman she had
met in the lane, but who was far more romantic!

'I do not understand why Miss Royston is being so
very kind to us,' Mrs Hampton was saying. 'But I shall
write at once and tell her we are delighted to accept her
generous invitation. She has asked us to join her at her
house near Huntingdon next week so that we may all get
to know one another in comfort. Then we shall journey
to London together. She is sending her own carriage to
fetch us.'

'That is very thoughtful of her,' Susannah said. She
frowned as something occurred to her. 'What shall we
do for clothes, Mama?'

'That is all taken care of,' Mrs Hampton said. 'Amelia
says we must not worry about anything, for we may use
her seamstress in town and send the bills to her!'

'Mama! She will buy my clothes as well?' Susannah looked at her mother in awe as she inclined her
head, feeling overwhelmed. 'She must be very rich. It
is beyond all expectation.'

'Yes, my dearest, I imagine she is very wealthy now,
but she knows what it is to live on a small income, and
to be treated ill by one's relations. I think that is why
she has taken it into her head to help us.'

Susannah nodded. Her mother's friend was being
extraordinarily kind to them. They could not have
expected anything of the sort and it was a wonderful
surprise. She could not wait for her adventure to begin!

However, the next few days would fly by—she must get out all her clothes and see what could be done with them. Some of them could surely be refurbished with fresh ribbons. It would not do to impose on Miss Royston's generosity more than was absolutely necessary!

She was smiling as she joined her mother's tea party that afternoon, unconsciously practising her society manners. Soon now she would have the chance to shine in society drawing rooms—and who knew what might happen then! Dreams did come true sometimes, it seemed, for just an hour ago her hopes of a Season in town had been just that...

Susannah looked towards the house as a groom opened the carriage door and helped her down. It was a pleasant L-shaped country residence built of yellowish stone with an imposing front door and leaded windows. However, it was no larger than Papa's house had been, modest by country-house standards, but the gardens were particularly beautiful and there were some graceful old trees. She thought that she would very much like to explore the garden at the earliest opportunity.

Susannah followed her mother into the front hall, smiling at a young maid who came to assist her. Mrs Hampton was speaking to a lady Susannah suspected must be Miss Royston's housekeeper.

'Miss Royston apologises for the delay in greeting you, Mrs Hampton,' the woman said. 'If you will allow me to take you upstairs to your rooms, she will be with you shortly. An unexpected visitor arrived just a few minutes ago...'

'Yes, of course. It is no matter,' Mrs Hampton said. 'Come along, Susannah.'

Susannah hesitated. 'Mama—do you think I might take a little stroll in the gardens? I shall be only a few minutes, but they are rather lovely. Would Miss Royston mind, do you think?' She threw an appealing look at the housekeeper.

'Miss Royston is a keen gardener. She has taken great pride in them since she came to live here,' the housekeeper said and smiled at her. 'You take a little stroll, miss. Riding in a carriage is so confining. If you stay close to the house, I can call you when Miss Royston is ready to receive you.'

'Very well, you may go,' Mrs Hampton said. 'But do not go off on one of your long walks, for that would be very rude.'

'No, Mama. I shall just wander as far as the rose arbour and back.'

Susannah went back towards the front door, which was opened for her by an obliging footman. She gave him a bright smile, feeling delighted to have a few moments of freedom before meeting her hostess.

When the carriage had stopped at the front of the house, she had caught sight of the rose garden. The bushes were well tended and growing lustily, though it was too early in the year for them to be at their best, of course. In another month or so this garden would be a riot of colour and she imagined the scent of roses would reach the house. Besides the roses there were wide beds of lavender, peonies and other perennial flowers. Miss Royston must spend a deal of her time in her garden; it was clearly well planned.

Susannah hesitated as she approached the rose arbour and heard a raised voice. The fencing had hidden the fact that there was anyone there; she was about to turn away when she heard her mother's name.

'Margaret Hampton is a good friend of mine. I made the offer, Michael. Nothing was asked of me, I assure you. I will not allow you to say such terrible things. Margaret and Susannah are not hangers-on. Nor will they take advantage of my good nature.'

'You are a fool, Amelia,' a man's voice answered sharply. 'Upon my word, I do not understand you! You refuse to make your home with Louisa and myself—and you open your home to strangers….'

'I have told you that I shall never live under the same roof as Louisa again, Michael. Your wife does not like me. She never has and she never will.'

'You were pleased enough to take advantage of my generosity before you inherited a fortune,' the man snapped back irritably. 'If Agatha had left it to me, with an income for you—as any sensible woman would!— none of this would have occurred. She might have known that you would not know how to protect yourself.'

'If Aunt Agatha had wished to leave her money to you, she would have done so,' Amelia replied, her voice calm but with an underlying anger. 'She told me that she had done all she intended to do for you or your sons. We share the same father, Michael, but it was my mother of whom Aunt Agatha was so fond.'

'I dare say, but Agatha was Father's aunt and I am as entitled as you, Amelia. I did not fight the will; it would cause a scandal, and I dislike that of all things, as you know. However, you could have put things right. You could help your cousins, at least.'

'I may do so in time if I feel they deserve it,' Amelia said. 'However, that is a matter for me. You may not command me and I shall not be bullied into…'

Susannah jumped guiltily as she heard a twig snap underfoot and realised that she had been eavesdropping.

She moved away quickly, turning back the way she had come, running now because she believed that someone was leaving the shelter of the rose arbour and she did not wish to be seen.

Susannah was overcome with embarrassment and shame. She had overheard what was clearly an argument between Miss Royston and—she presumed, for she had heard the name—Sir Michael, Miss Royston's brother. What a revealing argument! She would not have listened if she had not heard Mama's name, but she had wanted to know what was being said and could not leave when what she heard was so very shocking. Poor Miss Royston! Mama was right to suspect that she had been bullied and made unhappy by her family. It was not surprising to Susannah that she did not wish to live with them ever again.

Susannah stood at the front of the house, looking back at the tree-lined avenue, composing her thoughts. It was uncomfortable to know that Miss Royston's brother had been warning her of hangers-on. Had she heard only that, Susannah might have begged her mama to take her home at once, but she had heard Miss Royston's spirited defence of her friends—and she was quite certain that Sir Michael was merely angry because he wanted his sister's fortune for himself! What a truly unpleasant man he must be to speak to his sister in that tone!

Having made up her mind that she would not let what she had overheard spoil her pleasure in the coming visit to town, she turned towards the house just as the front door opened. The housekeeper beckoned and Susannah ran towards her.

'Miss Royston has come in now, miss. Your mama is ready to join in her the small parlour and I thought you would like to be there too.'

'Oh, thank you,' Susannah said. 'I hope I have not kept her waiting?'

'Miss Royston would not trouble if you had,' the housekeeper said. 'She is too good natured, miss—but you have not, for I cannot think you went far.'

'Just a short wander towards the rose arbour,' Susannah said, a faint blush in her cheeks. 'Does Miss Royston have many visitors, ma'am?'

'She has been living quietly since Lady Agatha Sawle's death, though she entertains now and then… just friends of her aunt…'

'Does her family visit often?'

'No, miss, they do not.' The housekeeper's mouth pulled into a prim line. 'Miss Royston has talked of your visit for days. I can't say when I've seen her so pleased with life…' She smiled at Susannah. 'Here is your mama, waiting for you. Miss Royston is in the front parlour.'

Mrs Hampton looked at her daughter. 'Well, dearest— are you ready?' She looked expectant as the housekeeper knocked, opened the door and then announced them.

Susannah looked past her and saw a woman standing by the window. She had her back to them, but turned as her housekeeper spoke, a smile on her face. Had she not overheard the quarrel, Susannah might have missed the telltale signs of distress. Her mother saw nothing, moving towards Miss Royston eagerly.

Susannah hung back a little, watching.

'Amelia, my dear friend,' Mrs Hampton greeted her with an embrace and a kiss. 'I cannot express how grateful I am for all you are doing for us!'

'I explained in my letter that you will be doing me a favour,' Amelia said and smiled in welcome. 'I do not wish to stay in town with my sister-in-law, and I cannot stay alone. As yet, I have not thought of taking a companion. Besides, it is so much nicer to have friends, is it not? Once we are invited out, we shall meet all our acquaintances, but it will be more comfortable for us to attend the various affairs together, do you not think so?'

Listening, Susannah realised how true Amelia's words were. She had felt that they were very obliged to Miss Royston for her invitation, as of course they were, but what she had overheard in the garden had brought home how very uncomfortable Miss Royston must have been in her brother's home. His angry tone, the unkindness in his words, were hurtful, and she could imagine that Miss Royston had had much to bear in the past from her family. The knowledge made her angry that anyone could be so unkind to their own sister, and it made her wish to protect and help Miss Royston.

'Yes, much more comfortable to have a friend,' Mrs Hampton was assuring her as Susannah's eyes wandered round the room. It was a large room, furnished with important, dark mahogany pieces. Comfortable rather than fashionably elegant. 'You are looking very well, Amelia. I see you are wearing grey. I myself have put on my lilac for the first time today. Shall you go into colours once we are in town?'

'I think grey and lilac would be suitable, and perhaps some dark colours as the weeks pass,' Amelia said. 'I have only just put off my blacks, but I shall wear colours again soon. Aunt Agatha would not expect me to wear black for ever. Indeed, I doubt she wished it at all, but in the circumstances I thought it right to show respect. She has been so very generous to me. I knew she intended to leave me something, but I had no idea how much that would be.'

'Well, I am sure you deserved it,' Mrs Hampton said with a look of warm approval. She turned towards Susannah, beckoning her. 'Come forward, my love. You remember Miss Royston, of course.'

Susannah made an elegant curtsy, smiling a little shyly. 'Yes, I do remember Miss Royston. It is exceedingly kind of you to invite us to stay with you in town, ma'am. I do not know how to thank you—for everything. If you are certain you wish to do so much…' She had to ask, since she had heard what Sir Michael thought of her and Mama, but there was no hesitation in Miss Royston's response.

'You may thank me by being happy,' Amelia told her with a look of such warmth that Susannah's last reservation fled. 'I knew that you must be finding things difficult since your terrible loss, and I wanted to help a little if I could. Besides, as I told your mama, I wish for friends to stay with me in town. You are doing me a great favour by agreeing to accompany me to town.'

'I think you are very kind, ma'am,' Susannah said, glowing with pleasure. Miss Royston was so exact in her manners and did not make one feel one was receiving charity at all. She had been a little nervous of meeting her, especially after hearing the argument—but her charm banished all Susannah's doubts. 'It is so exciting. I can hardly wait!'

'Once it is known we are in town, I am sure we shall be invited everywhere,' Amelia went on. 'You will make many new friends and I dare say you will be one of the prettiest girls of the Season—if not the prettiest!'

Susannah blushed and shook her head. She thought Miss Royston was beautiful with her reddish toned hair and green eyes, though she would not have dreamed of saying as much to her face. For a wealthy woman, her attire was modest. Although still in mourning, Amelia was wearing a stylish gown that owed everything to good taste and nothing to ostentation. Indeed, the only jewellery she wore was a small but pretty gold-and-pearl brooch pinned to the bodice of her gown.

Susannah remembered that she had thought Miss Royston had been a little quiet when they met in Bath, though she knew that their friend had possessed a lovely smile. She had not smiled often then, which was hardly to be wondered at in her situation! She could have had nothing to smile about living in her brother's house, for he was undoubtedly a bully.

'Come and have tea,' Amelia said and indicated that they should sit. 'You must wish for some refreshment after your journey. I am sorry that I had to keep you waiting. My brother came unexpectedly to call…' A look of anger and distress passed fleetingly across her face, but was gone so quickly that it might never have been there.

Susannah glanced around the large, square room. The décor was all in varying shades of green and cream, soft muted colours that gave it a feeling of comfort and ease. She thought that the curtains had not been changed in an age, but liked the homely feeling that prevailed. The room had an atmosphere of having been lived in happily for some years: a book lay on a table, a sewing basket stood by a comfortable elbow chair, and the pianoforte had a well-loved shine that seemed to indicate it was often used. A pretty Canterbury held sheets of music that had been much handled.

Amelia rang the bell and almost immediately a butler brought in a large silver tray displaying a handsome set of plain silver. A maid followed and set up the stand so that he could deposit his burden and another maid brought in an arrangement of dainty cakes and biscuits that she set on an occasional table.

As the tea was poured and Susannah got up to hand a cup to her mama, she observed that Miss Royston seemed more in command of her situation than before, which was understandable. In the past she had been obliged to consult her sister-in-law before making plans. Now she was free to do as she pleased, and it seemed she was full of plans for the coming Season.

'I have written to one or two friends, telling them of the date I intend to be in town,' Amelia said. 'We already have several invitations to dine, and I am certain there will be many more. I shall give a dinner the first week we are in town and I thought we might have a little dance for Susannah once she has made friends.'

'Oh, Miss Royston,' Susannah exclaimed, struck by this extra kindness. 'I had not expected a dance of my own. Do you truly wish to go to so much trouble on my behalf? You have done so much—some would say far too much. We are not even family…' She glanced away, her cheeks heating as Miss Royston's eyes flew to her face. She nibbled at a delicious almond comfit as Amelia sipped her tea and looked thoughtful.

'You are my very good friends,' she said after a pause. 'At one time your mama was the only friend I felt I might trust. To me you are as much and perhaps more than family. Besides, it will be no trouble at all,' Amelia said and laughed. 'I shall employ others to make certain that everything goes well on the night. Besides, I love to dance and to see young people enjoying themselves.'

'You speak as if you were past your youth,' Margaret Hampton said and shook her head. 'You are still young enough to dance and enjoy life yourself, Amelia.'

'Yes, perhaps I am, if anyone wished to dance with

me,' Amelia agreed, and her eyes reflected amusement. She looked at Susannah. 'Please, my dear, you must call me Amelia, at least in private. I want you to think of me as your good friend—an older sister, perhaps.'

'Oh...thank you,' Susannah said, a faint colour still in her cheeks. Had Miss Royston suspected her of over-hearing her argument with her brother? 'Yes, that would be very comfortable, when we are all together.'

'Good. I want you to be comfortable and happy, Susannah.' Amelia assured her. 'Your things have been taken to your rooms, though only the small bags have been unpacked, for the day after tomorrow we set out for London.'

'This will be my first visit to London. I have been to Bath twice. Mama took me to the theatre and the shops. I think London will be very exciting.'

'You will find it strange and new, but I am sure you will enjoy yourself. There are many theatres and excellent shops in town.' Amelia smiled at her. 'Come, we shall go upstairs, for I understand that you have not yet seen your room, Susannah.'

Susannah followed her hostess up the wide staircase, glancing at the portraits hanging on the wall. She felt excited and nervous at the same time, because she understood how lucky she was that Amelia had offered her this Season in town. Amelia's claims to need friends were mere politeness, because she could have employed a companion for far less than she was giving Susannah and her mother. It was sheer good nature on Amelia's part, and Susannah was suitably grateful.

The room she was shown into upstairs was pleasant. Decorated in various shades of blue and cream, it had a cool elegance that she guessed was Miss Royston's doing. The bedchamber had clearly been refurbished recently, and she guessed that their hostess had used her time of mourning to good purpose, ordering the house to her own taste. She had left the parlour untouched, perhaps because it was so very comfortable. Susannah approved of what had been done here and thought how nice it would feel to be in a position to do as one wished. She would love to have the task of refurbishing a large house, but it was expensive. Money was certainly important for a comfortable life.

Left to herself, Susannah sighed. She so longed for romance, but she also knew her duty to Mama. Mama belonged in a house like this, not the cottage she was forced to live in these days. Her only chance of a better life was for Susannah to make a suitable match.

Susannah had finished her examination of the room and begun to change out of her travelling gown when someone knocked at the door. Thinking it must be her mama, she called out that she might enter. A young girl with brown hair and dark eyes came in. She smiled and bobbed a curtsy, seeming a little shy.

'My name is Iris, Miss Hampton,' she said. 'Miss Royston says I am to be your maid for the next few weeks and accompany you to London.'

'Oh...' Susannah was surprised; she had grown used to looking after herself at the cottage, but it would be nice to be waited on again, if only for a few weeks. 'Please come in, Iris. I knew someone had unpacked the gown I wished to wear for this evening—was that you?'

'Yes, miss. I pressed it while you were having tea.' Iris looked at her with interest. 'You have lovely hair, miss. May I dress it for you?'

'Do you know how to?' Susannah was hesitant, for

her hair was so fine and she could never get it to stay tidy for long.

'My mother used to be a lady's maid before she married,' Iris told her. 'She taught me all the skills I need and Miss Royston took me on a few weeks ago. She has her own dresser, but I was allowed to help—and now I am to serve you. It will be exciting to visit London, miss.'

'Yes, it will.' Susannah smiled at her. 'Well, you may put my hair up for me this evening,' she said. 'I have been experimenting with it myself, but it always falls down again. We shall see what you can do, Iris.'

'I think I can manage to make it stay in place, miss,' Iris said. 'You will be surprised at the difference it will make.'

Susannah felt very grand as she went down for dinner that evening. She was wearing an expensive yellow gown Mama had bought her for her birthday a few weeks before Papa died. She had not worn it since, because she had not had reason to do so, but this evening was a celebration and she wished to look her best. Her hair was dressed softly into a double loop at the back of her head, caught back with a silk flower and a few wisps allowed to curl at the sides of her face. She looked elegant and quite different from her normal self.

'Susannah!' Mrs Hampton stared at her daughter in surprise. 'You have done your hair differently, my love. It makes you look older and more grown up.'

'I think it suits her very well,' Amelia said as she came to join them. 'Are you pleased with Iris, Susannah? I thought she would be a help to you; if this is an example of her work, I am well satisfied.'

'Iris put my hair up for me,' Susannah said. 'She says

we shall try different styles and see which looks best. I think she is very clever with her fingers, for I could never have achieved something like this.'

'I think I like it now that I am getting used to it,' Mrs Hampton said, looking slightly pensive. 'I have been used to thinking of you as my little girl, but I must get used to the idea that you are a young lady now.'

'And a very beautiful one,' Amelia said in a tone of approval. 'I believe she will create something of a stir in town, Margaret. I think you must accustom yourself to the idea that Susannah will be much sought after by the gentlemen.'

'Well, I hope she may meet someone nice,' Mrs Hampton said, giving her daughter a fond look. 'She is a good girl and has been a great comfort to me these past months. I am not sure what I should have done without Susannah's support.'

'Yes, of course she has,' Amelia said and laughed. 'But we must stop talking about her, for we are making poor Susannah blush.'

Susannah shook her head. She had always known she was pretty, of course, but with her hair styled differently she was beginning to feel like someone else—a young woman instead of a girl.

'I hope that I shall meet someone I can like well enough to marry him,' she said. 'There was a gentleman at home who might have proposed marriage, but he was some years older and I did not care for him….'

'I dare say you will be able to pick and choose when we are in town,' Amelia told her. 'I was thought pretty when I was your age. I might have married several times, but I hesitated and then…' She sighed, shaking her head. 'It was too late. I wasted my chance, Susannah, but you must make the most of yours.'

'Yes, I shall,' Susannah agreed. 'If I am lucky enough to meet a gentleman I can like.'

In her mind she substituted the word *like* for *love*. She wanted to fall desperately in love with a handsome man, one who would carry her away on his white horse to a castle where she would live happily ever after. As her mother and Amelia turned to walk into the dining parlour, Susannah laughed at her foolish thoughts. It was unlikely she would meet a prince and live in a castle, of course, but she did hope that something exciting would happen.

The evening was as pleasant as any Susannah could recall for a long time. Her mama was so happy, so clearly pleased to be with her friend, and content with the arrangement that Susannah had almost made up her mind not to mention what she had overheard. However, Amelia drew her apart when Mrs Hampton stopped to enquire a recipe from the housekeeper.

'Susannah my dearest,' Amelia said softly, 'my house-keeper tells me that you took a little walk towards the rose arbour earlier.'

'Yes…' Susannah blushed. 'I will tell you that I heard Mama's name mentioned and then…an argument. I did not listen long… Forgive me. I know I should have walked away immediately, but I could not help listening for a moment or two.'

'If you heard someone say unpleasant things of you and your mother, please forgive me,' Amelia said. 'I am sorry if you were hurt and I hope you will not let it spoil your visit—or our friendship?'

'It will not, for you said only good things,' Susannah said. 'I think he must be very unkind to speak to you so! Oh, I should not have said that—but I did not like to think he could speak to you in such a manner.'

'Yes, my brother has been unkind,' Amelia replied, a hint of sadness in her eyes. 'His wife more so. Louisa can be spiteful when she chooses. However, I do not speak of it. I did not wish to be rude by appearing in town without informing my family of my intention, but Michael came down after he had my letter and we quarrelled. I shall say no more of the affair. I just wished you to know that his thoughts were not mine. I hope you know that I am truly happy your mama accepted my invitation.'

'I do know,' Susannah said and smiled. 'You are kind and generous and I think we shall be very happy together.'

'Then that is all I ask for,' Amelia said. 'Run along to bed now, my love. You have had a long journey and you must be tired.'

Susannah kissed her cheek on impulse. 'You are so good! I hate him for being unkind to you,' she said rashly and then ran away because she feared she had said too much. However, when she looked back, she saw that Amelia was smiling.

Chapter Two

Toby Sinclair looked at his uncle and frowned. He was twenty and newly in town, on the brink of his first Season since leaving Oxford. Harry Pendleton had just promised to put him up for several clubs, excluding the one he most wanted to belong to, however, which was the Four-in-Hand driving club. The elite group consisted of a select band of Corinthians who believed themselves to be masters of style and sport, allowing only a favoured few to their ranks. Having met his uncle by chance at a society affair, he seized his opportunity.

'Dash it all, Harry! You know I've got good hands. You taught me to handle a team yourself. Why can't you put my name forward?'

'Because, my young friend, they would blackball me immediately,' Harry replied with a teasing grin. He was very fond of his sister's boy and he had taken him in hand from an early age, teaching him the things his father would have had he been able. Sir James Sinclair had married late in life and was now a semi-invalid, confined to his estate and quite often to his rooms with bouts of ill health. 'For one thing, those clothes you are wearing won't pass muster, not precise enough—and you've a way to go in your handling of a team before they would consider you up to scratch. Coleridge and Ravenshead are pretty strict about who they allow to join. If you keep your nose clean and show that you're up to snuff this Season, I'll put you forward next year.'

'Next year,' Toby said and pulled a disgusted face. 'I know they are your particular friends, but I'd back myself in a race against either of them with your blacks, Harry.'

'Always supposing I would allow you to handle my blacks,' Harry replied and flicked a speck of non-existent fluff from his immaculate coat of superfine. 'Don't look now, but Northaven has just come in. Remember what I told you, Toby. The marquis is received everywhere and you cannot avoid him and his cronies, but be careful of them. The last thing you want is to be caught in their net. Your father asked me to look out for you. He would expect me to warn you of men like Northaven.'

'Didn't you say that you won a hundred guineas from him a couple of weeks ago?'

'Yes. I found it impossible not to oblige him when he invited me to play, but I suspect he may not be completely honest at the tables.'

'You mean, he cheats?' Toby's face showed his disdain as he glanced at the man they were discussing. The Marquis of Northaven was a tall, well-formed gentleman with black hair and very blue eyes. He was generally held to be handsome and the ladies liked him. His progress through the room was causing something of a stir amongst the fair sex, though most looked at him slyly when they thought he was not aware. All the matchmaking mamas were sure to have warned their daughters that he was a rake and not to be trusted, though in some cases that probably only made him more attractive to very young ladies.

'Well, I dare say he may think I am a flat, but, thanks to you, I am up to most tricks,' Toby said, his gaze drawn to some newcomers. 'I say…she's a beauty, wouldn't you agree? I believe she is new. I haven't seen her before.'

Harry followed his nephew's gaze. A vision in white had just entered the room, accompanied by two attractive older ladies wearing grey and lilac respectively. His eyes narrowed, for the girl was certainly very lovely. Her hair was a dark honey blonde, and she stood out by virtue of the simplicity of her attire. Most of the younger ladies had frills and flounces on their gowns, but she had chosen something more elegant, plain even. Her hair was dressed simply in a loop of the back of her neck, yet it suited her perfectly. He thought perhaps she had taken her cue from the younger of her companions.

Harry frowned as he recognised the lady in grey silk. He had not seen her for some years and she had changed a great deal, but she was still beautiful, extremely elegant. Miss Amelia Royston! If he remembered correctly, his friend, Gerard Ravenshead, had once been interested in the lady, but something had gone wrong. Harry did not know all the details, but Gerard had certainly been cut up about it at the time. It was about the same time that a livid scar appeared at his left temple. Gerard had never spoken of the scar or the reason for the loss of his hopes.

'Yes, she is rather lovely,' he said, bringing his gaze back to the vision in white. 'I have no idea who she is, but I know one of her companions.'

'You couldn't introduce me, could you?' Toby asked and arched his right eyebrow.

'Fancy your chances, do you?' Harry asked and chuckled as he saw the younger man colour. 'I do not think your mama would be happy to see you ensnared too soon, Toby.'

'Oh, lord, no,' Toby said and made a grimace of horror. 'I shall not marry until I am at least as old as you and ready to set up a nursery. Far too boring to be married before you've been on the town a few years.'

'You young cub!' Harry said and made a face at him. 'What makes you think I am ready to set up my nursery?'

'Mama said it was time you did,' Toby replied innocently but with a wicked air. 'She says if you leave it much longer, it may be too late.'

'Good grief. I am three and thirty,' Harry said and grimaced. 'I do not think the case desperate yet. Lady Sinclair would have had me married ten years ago if she could, but I had no mind for it. I believe she is more desperate to see me wed than Mama!'

He smiled oddly, for he knew his sister Anne had his best interests at heart. They had always been close and she understood him, perhaps even better than he did himself. Besides, of late he had begun to feel it was time he settled down. Indeed, these days he was as happy with his dogs and horses at home in the country as cutting a dash in town. However, he had not met a lady he wished to marry. Most of the young ladies brought to London by their eager mothers were too naïve and often too timid for his taste. He knew that he would be bored by their company within months and that would be unfair to his wife. If he were to marry, it would be to a lady of spirit, someone who could retain his interest. He was not sure that romantic love existed, but it was certainly possible to admire and care for another. His mother had undoubtedly loved his father, and would never consider marrying again, though she might if she had wished. Harry felt that if he were to marry he would like to be loved in that way, though he knew that most of his friends had married for reasons other than love. Had he been satisfied with a marriage of convenience he might had wed a long time ago, but he was looking for something more.

His eyes narrowed as he noticed that a steady queue of gentlemen were making their way to the side of the beautiful young lady in white. He watched her for a while. Something about her seemed familiar, but he could not think what. He was certain he had never met her before—and yet there was something. She had pretty manners and a nice smile, he observed, before turning away to join some friends in the card room. It was very unlikely that the newcomer would be any different to the other young ladies in the room.

Harry rather thought that when he married, he would probably choose an older lady, perhaps a widow. An intelligent lady, who would fill his house with good company and give him an heir. It was all very well to hope for something more, but in the end he might be forced to marry for the sake of the family.

'No, no, please, gentlemen, you must not fight over me!' Susannah begged, her eyes bright with laughter as the two young bucks argued fiercely over the last dance on her card. 'If you cannot agree which of you should have the dance, I shall promise it to neither of you.'

'But it should be mine,' Tom Roberts asserted. 'I am sure I asked first.'

'I am the elder by birth and therefore I should take precedence over this rascal,' his twin Edgar replied, glaring at his brother. 'You must dance with me, Miss Hampton.'

'I believe this dance is promised to me, gentlemen.' The newcomer held out his hand with a touch of command that prompted Susannah to obey, even though she had not yet been introduced. However, she knew who he was, for she had remarked his progress through the room and asked Amelia.

'Thank you, sir,' she said, smiling up at the Marquis of Northaven as he led her out to join the throng of dancers. 'It was good of you to rescue me.'

'The Roberts twins are known for squabbling with each other,' Northaven said. 'Harmless enough, I dare say, but I thought you needed a little help. This is your first Season in town, I believe?'

'My first dance,' Susannah confided, her smile sparkling at him, because the evening had been far more exciting than she could ever have imagined. She had not sat out once, and the twins were not the first gentlemen to argue over her, in a friendly, teasing manner, of course. It was just good fun and she had thoroughly enjoyed being fussed over. The reality had far outweighed her dreams thus far. 'I have had such a lovely time.'

'Everyone speaks of you as the latest rage,' Northaven said, amused by her honesty. She was very young and he was usually bored by innocence, but she had spirit and an artlessness that was amusing. 'It all seems fresh and new for the moment, but you will be bored within a month.'

'Oh, no, I couldn't be,' Susannah retorted. 'We have been invited everywhere, to so many different affairs. I couldn't possibly be bored in London.'

'Do you not know that it is fashionable to be bored?' Northaven lifted an eyebrow, his expression mocking.

'Oh…' Susannah laughed because she believed he was teasing her. 'I fear that I must be unfashionable then, sir. I have not yet acquired town bronze and you must forgive my country manners—but I refuse to be bored when people have gone to so much trouble on my behalf. It would be rude and ungrateful.'

'Then you will set a new fashion,' he told her. 'Since everyone approves of you, you can do no wrong.'

Susannah looked at him uncertainly as their dance ended. She was not quite sure what to think of him, because he was very different from most of the young gentlemen she had danced with that evening. He returned her to her mother and Amelia, bowed and took his leave. She was conscious of a feeling of disappointment. There was something slightly dangerous about the marquis, and she was not sure she had made an impression on him, though she found him intriguing. He was very handsome, like one of the heroes from her dreams.

'Susannah…' She became aware of her mother speaking. 'This gentleman wishes to make your acquaintance. Lord Pendleton—my daughter, Susannah. Your father was a friend of Lord Pendleton's father, my dear.' Mrs Hampton smiled and moved away a few steps to talk to a lady who had caught her attention.

Susannah turned to look at the gentleman her mother had just introduced. He was tall, though not quite as tall as Northaven, but in his way equally attractive. His hair was not as dark as the marquis's, being a chestnut brown, and with a slight curl to it, his eyes a soft, melting brown. A little shock ran through her as she recognised him. He was the rude gentleman who had almost knocked her down in the lane. He was dressed very differently this evening, but she could not mistake those eyes, even though they were not flashing with temper. She felt hot inside as she wondered whether he would recognise her.

'Sir.' She inclined her head, but kept her eyes lowered. Her heart was racing for she hardly knew how to face him. She was almost sure that he had not recognised her and she hoped he would not. Their encounter had been so brief that he would surely have forgotten her. Her hand curled into itself, her heart beating faster. 'I am pleased to meet you.'

'It is your first visit to town, Miss Hampton?'

'Yes—how did you know?' Her heart raced. Had he recognised her as the girl he had met briefly in a country lane?

Harry hesitated, frowned, then said, 'I do not wish to seem interfering, Miss Hampton, but if I were you, I should not dance with Northaven too often.' His gaze narrowed. 'You know it is strange, but I have the oddest feeling that I have seen you somewhere quite recently.'

'I doubt it, sir.' Susannah's heart caught with fright. What would he think if he realised where he had seen her? One word from a gentleman of his stature and she might be ruined! 'Why do you warn me against Lord Northaven? He seems a perfect gentleman to me, sir.'

'I do not fault his manners or his lineage,' Harry told her. 'I think perhaps he is not a suitable partner for an innocent and very pretty young lady.'

Susannah had received so many compliments that evening that his words made little impression. She had been called beautiful, stunning, a nymph, an angel and many similar endearments. To be called pretty was not remarkable and, besides, she did not like his tone. Anyone would think he was her brother or her uncle! He was arrogant and opinionated—a bore.

'I thank you for your concern, sir,' she replied primly. 'However, I believe I am quite safe here under the eyes of Mama and Miss Royston.'

'Yes, I expect you are, as long as you take care to remain where they can see you,' Harry said and hesitated. 'Forgive me if I seemed to lecture you. It is not my place to do so—but I would never allow a niece of mine to associate with that gentleman.'

'I am not your niece, sir.'

'No, you are not. Forgive me. I have earned your displeasure. I spoke with good intent, but I should not have interfered,' Harry said, then inclined his head to her and walked off.

Susannah stared after him. His back was very straight and she understood that she had offended him. She had thought at first that he was one of the most attractive gentlemen she had met that evening—in her whole life!—but he was a stuffy bore. She did not think he could be much above thirty years, but he behaved as if he were old enough to be her father! He was certainly not the kind of man she was seeking as a husband. Her eyes searched the room for the man that had made the biggest impression on her that evening and found him.

Northaven turned his head and glanced at her. For a moment his blue eyes met hers and her heart jerked, but then he looked at his companion once more and smiled at something he was saying. Almost at once they left the room together. Susannah's gaze followed him, her feelings showing a little too well on her face.

'I could not help overhearing what Harry Pendleton said to you a moment ago,' Amelia said, and Susannah glanced round at her. 'It was not his place to say it, of course, but he is quite right, Susannah. Northaven is a rake and perhaps worse. He is received everywhere, but there has been some talk of late. I should not dream of trying to dictate to you, my dear, for there is nothing so annoying as being told not to do something—but if I were you, I should be careful of Northaven, at least until you know more of him. But please do not think that I mean to interfere, for I most certainly do not. That is something I abhor.'

Susannah caught a look in her eyes that told her she was thinking of the way her own life had been when she was forced to live in her brother's house. Once again she felt indignant that anyone should have made Amelia suffer so. She had been introduced to Amelia's brother earlier that evening, but his stiff manner had not helped to change her opinion, nor the way he had looked at her, as if she were something the cat had brought in! He obviously thought that she was an adventuress, bent on taking what she could from his sister.

'Oh…then, of course, I shall be very careful,' Susannah replied. She did not wish to offend her kind hostess, though she had liked the marquis despite the warning. However, it was Lord Pendleton's advice that rankled. It was just the same as that day he had almost knocked her down. Instead of apologising he had lost his temper—and now he was seeking to lecture her. Did he imagine that she was stupid? He had spoken to her as if she were still in the schoolroom! She had no intention of becoming compromised by any of the gentlemen, several of whom had enquired if she would like to take the air. She was enjoying her success, but she had as yet no thoughts of marrying anyone and must therefore be careful not to do anything that might seem too particular.

Susannah still felt in her heart that the most exciting man she had met that evening was the Marquis of

Northaven, yet it was Lord Pendleton who lingered in her mind long after she had said goodnight to Mama and Amelia and retired to bed. When she dreamed, annoyingly it was of Lord Pendleton, who had somehow acquired a schoolmaster's hat and waved his cane at her, telling her to behave or he would punish her.

How very ridiculous! In the morning her dreams vanished with the sight of the sunshine pouring in at her window and she rose, feeling refreshed and eager for the day to begin. She laughingly dismissed her annoyance of the previous evening. Life was too amusing to be disturbed by such a small thing for long. Lord Pendleton was rich and respected, but he did not fit her idea of a knight on a white horse. Besides, they had so many engagements, so many affairs to attend that she had no time to reflect on that particular gentleman.

She was going shopping again that morning and she wanted to buy a bonnet she had seen in the milliner's window a day or so earlier. Bonnets, pretty gowns and enjoying herself were of far more importance than one gentleman's opinion of her. She did not know why she had let it weigh with her at all!

She would put the disagreeable Lord Pendleton out of her mind and not think of him again.

Harry was undressing that evening when it suddenly came to him. At first he thought that his mind was playing tricks on him. The girl in the country lane and Miss Susannah Hampton were one and the same. In the act of removing his breeches, he swore loudly, causing his valet to turn and look at him.

'Was something the matter, my lord?'

'No, Philips, nothing at all,' Harry said and laughed ruefully. 'I am a damned fool, that's all.'

'I rather doubt it, sir,' the devoted servant said and smiled. 'If there is anything I can do to be of assistance?'

'No, nothing,' Harry replied, realising that the man was brushing the coat he had worn that evening. 'Leave all that now and get off to bed.'

He sat on the edge of the bed as the man went out, then sipped the glass of brandy Philips had thoughtfully put out for him.

'It is a small world…' Harry smiled to himself. He had wondered why the Hampton girl seemed a little prickly, but now he understood perfectly.

She had looked very different in her simple country dress, her hair blown by the wind and roses in her cheeks—but those eyes did not lie. She really did have the most remarkable eyes.

Had he given her an irrevocable dislike of him? She had called him rude and arrogant at their first meeting, and tonight he had committed the unforgivable sin of lecturing her as if she were a schoolgirl. He had no idea why he had done that, for it was certainly not his business to warn young girls he did not know of Northaven's character. Some instinct had made him want to protect her from a man he knew unworthy.

Harry pulled a face, chuckling at his own stupidity. He would have to apologise the next time they met. Or perhaps not? She might find it embarrassing to be reminded of that day in the lane. It might be better to try to mend fences before he confessed that he had remembered the incident.

'What a charming bonnet,' Amelia said as Susannah tried on the white silk tied with pale blue ribbons and trimmed with matching blue bows. 'It would compliment that blue pelisse we ordered for morning wear. Why do you not buy it?'

'I have already bought three hats,' Susannah objected, mindful that it was not her money they were spending. 'Do I really need it?'

'Thankfully, we do not have to consider need, only pleasure,' Amelia said and nodded to the milliner to indicate that they would take the bonnet. 'Now, my love—what do you think of the green bonnet in the window? It is a little older in style and I was thinking of it for myself. Do you think it will become me?'

Susannah went to the window and looked at the bonnet. A gentleman was passing at that precise moment, and by chance he happened to look up and see her. He tipped his hat to her, smiling in a manner that made her heart skip a beat. She gave him a look of disapproval and moved away swiftly. Honestly! Was it impossible to go anywhere in London without seeing Lord Pendleton? He had been present at every affair they had attended this week! It almost seemed as if he were following them. She returned to Amelia, determined to put him from her mind.

'I think the green would suit you very well—' Susannah began and then broke off as the shop door opened and her mama came in, carrying parcels and closely followed by the offending gentleman in person. 'Mama…you are loaded down. I thought you meant only to borrow one book from the library. Had you said you wished for more, I should have come with you to help carry them.'

'There was no need, dearest,' Mrs Hampton said. 'I found so many volumes that I had been wanting and I was carried away. It was all going splendidly until a large dog jumped at me and I dropped them—only two doors away from here. Lord Pendleton saw my predicament and helped me. When I told him I was coming here, he insisted on accompanying me. Was that not kind of him?'

Susannah looked at the books, which had been set down for a moment. 'Very kind, Mama. I am not sure when we shall find time to read all of these, for we are invited out every day, to more affairs than we can easily accommodate.'

'Well, I may not always wish to accompany you on every occasion,' Mrs Hampton said. 'You and Amelia are so full of life…' She smiled at the gentleman standing silently at her side, his dark eyes observing them with a hint of amusement. 'It is such a thing to be young, is it not, sir?'

Lord Pendleton's eyes were centred on Susannah as he answered, 'To be so very young is sometimes as much a trial as a pleasure, ma'am. I think we sometimes forget all the problems being young and insecure may bring.'

'Very true,' Mrs Hampton agreed, giving him a look of approval. 'Especially for a young man fresh upon the town, I dare say. I met your nephew earlier. He was just leaving the lending library. A charming young man, if I may say so.'

'Toby is charming,' Harry said. 'This is his first Season in town, you know. I have been trying to warn him of the pitfalls of deep play. There are some gentlemen who do not scruple to invite young men to play deeper than they ought.'

'Scandalous!' Mrs Hampton said. 'They should know better—it can cause real misery for their families.' Her attention turned to Amelia, who had tried on the green bonnet and was asking for her opinion. 'It looks very well on you, Amelia. I am sure you should take it—it will go well with several of your gowns, and I like you in colours.'

'Yes, I think perhaps I may.'

'Miss Hampton,' Harry said as the two older ladies discussed which gowns the bonnet would compliment, 'do you attend Lady Silverson's dance this evening?'

'Yes, I believe we do,' Susannah replied. 'Shall we see you there, sir?'

'Yes, I think you will,' Harry told her. 'Indeed, yes, I believe I shall come. Tell me, do you intend to return home shortly? I have my carriage near by if you should require help with all your parcels.'

'Oh, no,' Susannah denied. She felt a little warm as she felt his gaze upon her. 'The milliner will deliver our purchases and Mama's books will be easy enough for the three of us.'

'Then I shall continue on my way, for I have an appointment with some friends, though it could easily be postponed if you required my escort,' Harry said. 'Miss Royston, you must definitely buy that bonnet. It becomes you charmingly. The colour might have been made for you. Good day to you, ladies. I shall see you this evening.'

'How odd,' Amelia remarked as Harry went out and the door closed. 'I did not expect an opinion from Lord Pendleton. It is rare that he speaks in such a frivolous fashion these days—though he was more free in his manners when he was young, of course.'

'He is not so old, Amelia, and charming in my opinion,' Mrs Hampton said, her eyes thoughtful. 'Besides, he is right. You should buy the bonnet.'

Susannah was thoughtful as Amelia completed her purchase. Lord Pendleton had enquired if they were to attend the dance that evening before telling her that he was going. Of course he was invited everywhere, but it was a little surprising that everywhere they went he was almost certain to be near by.

'We carried Toby off to play with us last evening.' Max Coleridge grinned when Harry raised his brows as they spoke at their club a little later that morning. 'Northaven was trying to bully him into a game and he was clearly unwilling.'

'I have warned him of it, but you have my thanks,' Harry said and beckoned to the waiter to bring them more wine. 'It would be wrong to try to keep him on a leading string. He would resent it and I won't do it. However, I would be obliged if you could have a word with him. He might take it better from you.'

'Already done,' Max said and grinned. 'You don't want to smother the boy, Harry. He has to learn—and we were all young once. Hard as it may be to remember in your case.'

Since there was only a couple of years between them, this brought a shout of laughter from Harry. 'Take care, Max! I might challenge you to a duel for that!'

'You would undoubtedly have done so once,' Max replied carelessly, a spark of mischief in his grey eyes. His hair was a dark brown, thick and with a tendency to curl at the nape of his neck if he allowed it to grow longer than he liked. 'Getting a bit lazy…grumpy in your old age?'

'Damn it, I'm not that old yet,' Harry said ruefully. 'Though there are times when I feel it.' He eyed his friend thoughtfully. 'Honestly—have I become too serious of late? I feel that I may be stale…set in my ways…'

'Is there a reason for your feeling that, perhaps?'

Harry shook his head. 'Just a notion that I may be coming down a bit hard on Toby. He hasn't said anything to you?'

'Not at all, admires you,' Max assured him, his gaze narrow and thoughtful. 'No other reason?'

Harry saw the laughter hidden just below the surface. 'None at all—what makes you ask?'

'Just wondered. Lady Sinclair told me she thought it was time you set up your nursery. Wondered if you meant to oblige her?'

'Damn her—and you.' Harry scowled. 'I have no intention of it yet, Max. You seem to have a bee in your bonnet—when am I to wish you happy?'

'I have been thinking of it…'

'Really? Who is the young lady?' Harry stared in astonishment.

'There is no one as yet, but I think it is time to start looking.'

'This is sudden, isn't it?'

Max nodded and sipped his wine. 'I think perhaps I ought to consider it or the alternative,' he said and shook his head as Harry arched one eyebrow. 'No, I shall not explain, Harry. It's a small problem I have to work out for myself. Anyway, we kept Toby out of trouble for you the other evening, but Northaven ensnared another young idiot. I didn't know him, but I think perhaps Toby did.'

'There's always one,' Harry agreed. He lapsed into silence, sipping his wine and thinking about what his friend had said about it being time to think of marriage. Max was, after all, two years his junior….

Susannah's heart raced as she saw the marquis turn and look at her. He immediately began to walk towards

her. She had just two dances left on her card that evening
and she wondered if he would ask for them both.

'Miss Hampton,' a voice spoke at her side. Susannah
turned to look, feeling a spurt of annoyance as she saw
that it was Lord Pendleton. He had told her he would be
there that evening, but she had not seen him earlier. Why
did he have to speak to her at just the moment the Marquis of Northaven was about to approach her? Glancing
back, she saw that the marquis had turned away and was
speaking to another young lady, Mary Hamilton, a girl
whom Susannah had come to know as they were often
invited to the same affairs. 'May I hope that you have a
dance for me?'

Susannah blushed, because her thoughts were unworthy. 'Yes, of course, sir. Perhaps you would like the waltz,
which is just about to start? I believe it is my last…' She
was not lying because the supper dance was not a waltz
and all the others had been taken.

'I should be delighted,' Harry said and took her hand.
'May I say that you look delightful this evening, Miss
Hampton? Not every young lady wears white as well as
you.'

'I thank you for the compliment, sir,' Susannah said.
She put her annoyance at his untimely interruption aside,
because however annoying it might be to have missed an
invitation from the marquis—who was infrequently at
these affairs—Lord Pendleton was wonderful at waltz-
ing. 'But I think there are many young ladies here this
evening who look just as pretty.'

'Perhaps. Yes, I agree there are many pretty girls, but
only a handful are beautiful. Miss Royston is beautiful.
You are beautiful—and Miss Hamilton is beautiful. The
others are pretty.'

Susannah frowned at him. 'I suppose you mean to compliment me, sir...'

'No. I mean to be truthful,' Harry told her. 'You will discover that I am usually honest in my observations, Miss Hampton.' He looked at her for a moment, as if considering something he wished to say, but nothing was forthcoming.

'Oh...' Susannah was thoughtful. She hardly knew how to answer him. She had thought he was paying her an exquisite compliment, but now he had made it seem almost a reprimand. He was such an odd man! She was not even sure that he liked her, though of course he was always polite. Lord Pendleton had some of the most exquisite manners, far more so than any gentleman she had met in the country; he was one of the most respected gentlemen in the drawing rooms of London, beloved of the hostesses. However, that did not particularly recommend him in her eyes. He seemed a little severe and she had not forgiven him for scolding her the first time they met. 'Of course I do not know you well, sir.'

'No, we are not well acquainted as yet,' Harry agreed. 'I shall hope that we may become so as the Season goes on, Miss Hampton.'

Susannah smiled at him uncertainly. She was not sure whether he was just being polite or whether he meant it—and even if he did, she was not sure that she truly wished to know him well. He was a little older than most of her admirers, and serious—though he had a habit of lingering in her mind and her dreams.

Their dance ended and Lord Pendleton left her with Amelia, but it was only a matter of some minutes before her next partner claimed her. Swept up in the excitement of the evening, Susannah forgot her disappointment at missing the chance to dance with the Marquis of Northaven. He did not approach her again and left the room long before the supper dance. In the meantime, another gentleman asked for a dance and she was obliged to give her last one to him.

Lord Pendleton did not ask her for another dance that evening, though she saw him dance with several other young ladies, including Mary Hamilton and Amelia.

It was as she was leaving the ballroom to refresh herself before supper that she happened to overhear two young ladies talking. They were whispering and giggling, and she could not help but hear what Mary was saying to her friend.

'Mama says that I should encourage Pendleton if I get the chance, but I heard that he has an expensive mistress. Mama says that gentlemen often have them, but I am not sure I approve.'

Her friend giggled and whispered something. Miss Hamilton laughed harshly. 'Well, I suppose he has fortune enough to pay for both a wife and a mistress if he cared for them, but I shall expect him to buy me more lavish presents than he gives her—if I encourage him, of course. I prefer Northaven, but Mama will not hear of it. She says he is a rogue and…'

Susannah hurried up the stairs, not wanting to hear more of their nonsense. She had been wondering why Lord Pendleton was always to be seen at these affairs, but if he were thinking of making Mary Hamilton an offer, he would naturally make certain of every chance to fix his interest with her.

Susannah could not help feeling disappointed. Not because her feelings were engaged, for they most certainly were not! However, she would not have expected a man like Harry Pendleton to be caught by Mary

Hamilton. He had remarked that she was a beautiful young lady—but did he have any idea how very silly Mary Hamilton was? Susannah did not dislike her, but she would certainly not count her amongst the particular friends she had made since arriving in town.

Shaking her head over what she had learned, Susannah went into the bedchamber put aside for the ladies to use. She wondered if she ought to be shocked at the suggestion that Lord Pendleton had an expensive mistress. If it were true, she must be either very tolerant or very angry, for she could not have seen very much of her protector recently.

It was highly improper of her to think of such things, but she could not help wondering what it was like to be a gentleman's mistress. How did one go on in such a situation? Susannah did not think it could be pleasant, even if there were handsome presents. She would not like to be Lord Pendleton's mistress if he were thinking of marrying Mary Hamilton. Oh, dear, what a wicked thing to have come into her mind. She would not want to be any man's mistress! And particularly not that rather annoying gentleman. She might have been even more annoyed if she had guessed at his thoughts that evening.

Harry was wondering why he had not yet made his apology. He was still hesitating because he thought it might have embarrassed her to know that he had recalled their first meeting.

'Did you enjoy your drive, my love?' Mrs Hampton asked when Susannah returned from an engagement with her new friend Miss Terry and her brother Sir James Terry two days later. 'It was a beautiful morning for a drive in the park.'

'Yes, it was,' Susannah agreed and smiled. It had been a very pleasant morning—they had met so many people, all of whom seemed as if they wanted to stop and talk, particularly to Susannah, if they happened to be gentlemen. 'We met several of our friends, Mama, and I was introduced to some new ones by Lord Northaven.'

'I am not sure that I would wish you to know that gentleman's friends,' her mama said with a frown. 'I know he is a most attractive gentleman and no one could fault his manners—but I have heard a few things that make me feel he may not be quite suitable for you to know, Susannah. You must greet him politely, of course, should he speak to you, but I think it best if you do not go out of your way to encourage him, dearest. I have heard him described as a rake. You must think of your reputation.'

'I should not dream of encouraging the marquis any more than I would encourage the attentions of any gentleman I do not know well. I believe I have more sense than that, Mama.'

'Yes, of course you do, my love,' Mrs Hampton replied fondly. 'At least, if there should be a suitable gentleman you rather liked—someone like Lord Pendleton, say—then you might be permitted to show a little encouragement, though nothing particular, of course. I do not like to see young ladies throwing themselves at the gentlemen, it is most unbecoming. Any advance must always come from the gentleman—though a smile does not go amiss.'

'Oh, Lord Pendleton,' Susannah said dismissively. Lord Pendleton seemed always there when she looked round, his serious eyes seeming to reproach her. She had not spoken to Northaven for some days—until that morning by chance in the park. After the last time, when he had changed his mind about asking her for a dance, she had believed he was indifferent to her, but that morning he had flirted with her outrageously, bringing a blush to her cheeks. Of course she could not tell Mama that! 'Lord Pendleton is all very well, Mama, but a little stern—do you not think so?'

'He seems to me an excellent gentleman in every way,' Mrs Hampton said. 'We see him quite often. Has he given you an indication that he likes you, my dear?'

'Mama! No, of course not,' Susannah replied, a little wrinkle daring to mar the perfection of her smooth brow. 'I believe he admires Miss Hamilton. She certainly believes it, for she expects an offer—and I think he imagines me to be a foolish child, far beneath his notice, I dare say.'

'I am very certain he does not!' Mrs Hampton responded on a laugh. 'What makes you think he may have an interest in Miss Hamilton?'

'He told me he considered her beautiful—and I overheard something she said to a friend. I believe she expects an offer soon. You must not imagine Lord Pendleton comes to these affairs just to see me. He has friends everywhere. I hear him spoken of all the time and I think he must be very popular. He is invited to all the best houses!'

'Why would that be, do you imagine?' Mrs Hampton asked innocently. 'I am surprised he has an interest in Miss Hamilton. I had not noticed it myself.'

'Oh, I suppose he is popular because he is rich, and of course he does have excellent manners,' Susannah said thoughtfully. 'He fetched me a glass of champagne when mine was accidentally knocked over last evening and I did not even have to ask, though he was not sitting with me.'

'Quite an observant gentleman, as well as thoughtful,' her mother said. 'He served in the army with Wellington for a few years, you know, and was commended for his bravery; then he came home to take over the estate when his father fell ill and subsequently died. They say he has improved things considerably. He is very modern in his thinking when it comes to the land and agriculture.'

'You clearly approve of the gentleman,' Susannah said. Her mama obviously thought him a good catch! 'Since you have been talking to him a great deal.'

'Oh, not so very much,' Mrs Hampton said airily. 'One hears things, you know. I have not heard his name linked with any lady in particular.'

'He has a mistress…' Susannah blurted out and then blushed as her mama stared at her. 'Forgive me. I should not have spoken of it, Mama. I know it was not proper, but I heard someone say that she was expensive.'

'Such unfortunate ladies are to be pitied,' Mrs Hampton said. 'If Lord Pendleton does have an arrangement of the kind—which is not unusual—I dare say he will end it at the proper time. I do not think he would do anything improper. I imagine if he thought of marriage, he would end any such arrangement, Susannah.'

'No, I am sure he would not do anything improper,' Susannah said and could not think why she felt disappointment. 'It would be nice if Lord Pendleton proved to be less than perfect. It is very hard to live up to someone who is so particular.'

'Oh, I dare say he has his faults,' Mrs Hampton said with a smile. 'Do not let the idea of a mistress worry you, my love. Whoever was speaking of it in your hearing was wrong to do so.'

'Yes. I thought her a very silly girl.' Susannah looked at her with interest. 'You do not condemn him for it?'

'No, I do not. Nor, if you are sensible, should you.'

'I do not,' Susannah said. In fact, she had decided that it made him seem less dull than she had first thought him. 'And now, Mama—I have seen a picture of a gown I should like to have made for the dance Amelia is to give for me, if I may...'

Susannah frowned as she saw that Lord Pendleton was already at Lady Hamilton's musical evening when they arrived. He was talking to a very pretty young lady, but he had noticed them and smiled, nodding in their direction. Susannah inclined her head. She accepted a glass of lemonade from one of the footmen circulating and wandered over to look at some particularly fine plants that her hostess had caused to be arranged by the deep bow windows. The view was over a particularly pleasant garden, and Susannah was admiring it when she became aware of someone at her shoulder. She turned, not in the least surprised to see the gentleman standing just behind her, for he usually sought her out at some time in the evening.

'Good evening, Lord Pendleton,' she said. He was looking extremely handsome that evening dressed in a fine blue coat with pearl-grey breeches that fitted him superbly. 'I did not know you were coming this evening.'

'I was not sure of it myself,' Harry told her. 'It is odd that we seem to meet almost everywhere, Miss Hampton—but delightful. Your presence enlivens many a dull affair.'

'You flatter me, sir. I am a very ordinary girl.'

'I would not call you that,' Harry replied. 'Indeed, I

would say that you are far from ordinary, Miss Hampton. Are you looking forward to this entertainment? The tenor has an exceptional voice.'

'I have heard that he is excellent,' Susannah replied. 'Do you enjoy music, sir? I like to play the pianoforte, though I am not an accomplished musician. I enjoy good singing, though I have little voice myself.'

'Music is one of life's true pleasures,' Harry agreed. 'Reading, poetry and good works of fiction are also very agreeable—do you not think so?'

'Yes. Yes, I do,' Susannah replied. They had not often spoken at such length and she warmed to him, for he was an intelligent man and seemed to think much as she did about such things. 'I love to ride when I have a horse available and to walk in the country...' A flush touched her cheeks—she had realised that she ought to be honest with him. 'I believe I should tell you something, sir. When we met in company, it was not for the first time.'

'Did you know me at once?' Harry asked. 'I did not place you until my return home later that evening. I must apologise for my behaviour that day, Miss Hampton. I was so shocked by the knowledge that I might have killed you that I lost my temper. It was abominably rude of me.'

'I think I was as much at fault,' Susannah said, a flush in her cheeks. 'I did hear something before I dashed across the road, but I thought I had time and I was not truly thinking—I had my head in the clouds, as Mama would say.'

'You are a remarkable young lady,' Harry told her. 'However, you must allow me to bear the fault, for it was my damnable temper. I try to control it, but sometimes when I am much moved it escapes me.'

Susannah laughed, her eyes alight with amusement. 'You speak of your temper as though it is a wild beast, sir.'

'Exactly so,' Harry replied, amused by her perception. She was refreshingly honest and utterly charming, and he was becoming more and more addicted to her company. 'Perhaps we should take our places? I believe they are about to begin....'

He offered her his arm and they walked to an unoccupied sofa, sitting down next to her as the musicians began to play.

'What do you think of the latest "rage"?' Toby asked when he met his uncle outside White's the following afternoon. Harry was leaving the gentleman's club, Toby just arriving, having spent the previous night at a gaming hell where he had drunk a little too much, sleeping heavily that morning as a consequence. He grinned at his cousin. 'Have you heard the rumour that you are in the petticoat line at last? At the moment they cannot decide between Miss Hamilton and Miss Hampton, though the delightful Susannah is thought to be slightly in the lead.'

Harry grimaced. 'If you waste your time listening to gossip, you will never acquire the skills you need to join the Four-in-Hand. Had you forgotten our appointment this morning? I thought you wanted to drive my team to Richmond?'

'Good grief!' Toby smote his forehead with the palm of his hand. 'It went right out of my head, Harry. I went to a gambling hell last night and drank a little too much and slept late this morning. I'm dashed sorry!'

'So you should be,' Harry told him with a severe look. 'I dare say your pockets are to let this morning?'

'It isn't quite that bad,' Toby said with a wry grimace. 'Northaven did try to involve me in a high-rolling card game again last night, but I stuck to the dice with my friends and lost about five hundred to Jackson. It was a sum I could afford to lose, particularly as I won a thousand from Ravenshead the other evening.'

'I am relieved to hear it,' Harry said. 'I do not wish to carp, Toby, but it can be very expensive in town if you play too deep. You will end up owing your tailor and everyone else bills you cannot pay if you are not careful. If the worst happens, you may apply to me, of course—but I should warn you that I shall take a dim view.'

'I dare say I should be in trouble had I let myself be cajoled into playing with Northaven,' Toby said. 'I saw young Harlow sit down with them a few nights ago. He lost a fortune. I am not sure of the amount, but I know it was a great deal, for a crowd gathered about them at the last. When Harlow rose from the table he could not pay the whole immediately and his face was as white as a sheet.'

'I imagine he will have to apply to his father for funds, and I do not know how General Harlow will pay,' Harry said, looking thoughtful. 'I know he has had some trouble himself with his investments. If the play was too deep, he may have to sell land to pay his son's debts.'

General Harlow had served with Harry at one time on the Peninsula. Toby knew that his uncle liked and respected his neighbour.

'Would you buy?' he asked. 'If he is forced to sell?'

'If he truly wishes to sell,' Harry replied. 'I think I should post down to the country and have a word. It might be possible to arrange a loan to tide him over. I would not pay the young idiot's gambling debt—that would encourage him to play deep again—but I may help his father. What passes between them regarding this is their own affair.'

Harry was a good friend in an emergency, as Toby knew well. He had told him the tale of Harlow's downfall, knowing that he might wish to offer assistance to his neighbour. Although it was not generally known, Harry was one of the wealthiest men in England. His investments were always kept private, but Toby believed he had a finger in several pies and was not above being involved in trade if it would turn a profit. Naturally, he was too much the gentleman to discuss these things, but Toby had learned to read between the lines. He had not enquired into his uncle's business, for it wasn't done, but one day, after he'd had his fun, sown a few wild oats, he intended to ask Harry for a few pointers.

However, for the moment, he had something closer to his heart on his mind. 'Have you spoken to Ravenshead about my becoming a member of the Four-in-Hand?' he asked. He had held back from doing so himself, because he was relying on his uncle to do the business for him.

'If you remember, that was the point of our drive this morning,' Harry replied. 'I am not able to make another arrangement for the time being, Toby, for I shall leave town this afternoon and may be away for a couple of days or so. However, we shall drive together when I get back. I believe Ravenshead means to stay in town for a while. He was undecided at the start and refused all invitations, but he told me that he thought he would attend a ball next week. If you prove yourself worthy, I may speak to him for you.'

Susannah paused outside the parlour door. She had returned home earlier from an expedition than expected

and was about to join Amelia for tea when she heard
voices and hesitated, uncertain whether or not to go
in.

'I am glad to see you, John,' Amelia was saying.
'Shall I ring for wine or tea? I am alone, as you see. My
friends went out…'

'Father was put out when you invited them to stay
with you,' John Royston answered in a frank tone that
carried easily to Susannah's ears even as she lifted her
hand to knock. She hesitated as he continued, 'I must
tell you that I think Miss Hampton charming. If she had
fifty thousand, I should join the queue of hopefuls, but
I do not think she could afford me.'

'Susannah has too much sense to marry a man who
cares only for her fortune, though she has something,'
Amelia told him. 'Are you in trouble again, John?'

Susannah hesitated, knowing she ought to leave, but
her feet refused to move and she continued to listen.

'Lord, no,' he said. 'I won a thousand from Carstairs
last night, which will tide me over until next quarter if
I am careful—which I shan't be, of course. I wondered
if you would speak to Father for me, Amelia?'

'I have little influence with my brother,' Amelia
replied. 'If you aren't in debt, what is the matter?'

'I have asked Father to buy me a pair of colours,' John
said. 'He says I should settle down and take an interest
in the estate, but he would hate it if I did. If I offered
advice, he would soon tell me to take my nose out of
his affairs. But he says he can't afford to support me as
an officer.'

'Yes, he would,' Amelia agreed. 'Are you sure the
army is for you?'

'Father will live for years yet,' John told her. 'I have
nothing but my allowance, which is barely enough to

support the life I lead in town. I must either look for an heiress or take myself off for a few years. Of the two, I think I prefer life in the army.'

'If I bought you the colours, and gave you an income of, say, two thousand a year, could you live within your means? Even in the army it is not cheap for an officer.'

At this point, Susannah decided that she had heard too much already and must either knock or move away. Just as she was deciding what to do, her mother called to her from the top of the stairs.

'Are you waiting for me, my dear? Go in, Susannah. Amelia will send for tea and I am ready for mine.'

Susannah raised her hand, knocked and entered, feeling awkward. She was in time to see John Royston kiss his aunt's cheek. He tucked something into his breast pocket, managing to look as if nothing unusual had happened.

'Miss Hampton,' he said and came to her, bowing elegantly. He took the hand she offered and kissed it. 'I was just saying to Amelia that you are the toast of the town. I would offer my suit, but I have no fortune to recommend me.'

'I would not accept a gentleman just for his fortune,' Susannah replied, a little reserved. She was embarrassed at having heard something that ought to have remained private, feeling herself at fault for having listened. It was the second time she had done so and something she must correct! 'I shall give my hand and heart only when I find love.'

'Quite right too,' he said, eyes twinkling. He was a handsome young man and Susannah thought him charming enough. However, it seemed that he had visited to ask for money, and she could not help thinking that Amelia was not well used by her family. Her nephew had been pleasant in his manner to his aunt, but there was sadness in Amelia's eyes. Susannah felt her heart go out to her, for she sensed that she was hiding some deep hurt. She glanced at the young man as he continued, 'Well, I shall go and leave you ladies to enjoy a good gossip about me....'

'Do not flatter yourself, John,' Amelia said drily. 'I assure you that we have far more of interest than your escapades.'

He grinned and went out, leaving them together. Susannah glanced at Amelia.

'I realised that you had company and did not wish to intrude...'

'Thank you, Susannah. My nephew came to me for help, which I gave freely. John is a charmer—as unlike his father as it is possible to be. I have promised to buy him a pair of colours. I think he will do well in the army. It could be the making of him.'

'What a fine thing to do for him,' Mrs Hampton said approvingly as she came in, in time to hear Amelia's remark. 'It could well be the making of him, as you say, Amelia. I knew you were considering what would be best for him, for you have said as much to me. If he truly wishes for an army life it will suit him, and life in town is the ruin of many a young man.'

'Yes, I think it will suit John, which is why I was happy to oblige him,' Amelia agreed and smiled at Susannah. 'You are back a little earlier from your walk than I expected.'

'It came on to rain and we thought we might as well come back for tea.'

'I am happy that you did, because I am feeling a

little low.' Amelia glanced at Susannah. 'Nothing to do with my nephew's visit—another matter entirely. Something happened when I visited the library...' She paused and that odd sadness was in her eyes. 'I thought I saw someone—a ghost from the past—and it brought back memories.'

'I am sorry if it made you sad,' Susannah said. 'I do not like to think of anyone hurting you. You are such a lovely person...' She blushed, afraid she had said too much, but Amelia laughed and shook her head.

'You are a sweet girl, Susannah. I love both you and Margaret dearly, and so I shall tell you that I once thought to marry, but the marriage was not permitted and he went away. I caught a brief glimpse of someone I thought might be the gentleman I once wished to marry, but it was probably not he. Besides, it was some years ago and I have put it all behind me.' Her eyes rested on Susannah. 'I did not wish you to imagine it was John who upset me, for I was happy to see him.'

Susannah blushed, her eyes dropping as Amelia turned away to ring for tea. She thought that Amelia was gently reprimanding her for eavesdropping again, and indeed it was very bad of her. She must not do it again, but it was so very tempting when one heard one's own name.

'Well, my dear,' Mrs Hampton said, 'you are much admired, you know, Amelia. I am perfectly certain you could marry if you wished. After all, you may please yourself now.'

'Like Susannah, I would marry only if I could both love and respect the gentleman,' Amelia said, but there was such a wistful look in her eyes that Susannah suspected she was still in love with the gentleman she had been denied—even if she would not admit it to herself.

* * *

Harry was thoughtful as he left town that afternoon. He would not have expected the gossips to latch on to his interest in Miss Hampton that quickly. He thought that he had been careful to show no particular interest in her in public, though he had spent much of the previous evening at her side. It must have been remarked, which was a nuisance—he had not meant to draw the attention of the gossipmongers just yet. He had been watching Susannah as she settled into her niche as the latest rage. Her vivacity was what set her apart from the crowd. She was clearly a girl of spirit and took to any new suggestions eagerly, showing her appreciation. He thought perhaps she might be a little reckless at times, but she would surely grow out of it—and he did find her charming company.

However, as yet Harry had not truly thought of marriage, even though Anne had been urging it on him for the past couple of years. If he were to consider the idea, Susannah Hampton might be the kind of girl he would wish to make his wife; she was certainly suitable and he liked her. For the moment he had no such intention and must be scrupulous—he would not wish to cause gossip that would affect her good name. He was therefore pleased with an excuse to leave town for a day or two. It would give him a chance for some quiet reflection, and he wanted to speak to General Harlow.

His neighbour was a proud gentleman and Harry would need to think of a scheme whereby he could help him without appearing to offer charity.

Chapter Three

Susannah glanced round the ballroom. Most of the dances she had attended so far had been modest affairs. This was the first large ball she had been invited to and it was a glittering event. Magnificent chandeliers shed their light on the assembled company, picking up the sparkle of jewels around the throats of the ladies and in the gentlemen's cravats. The wealthiest members of society had gathered at the Duke and Duchess of Morland's grand affair, their laughter and chatter making such a noise that it was difficult to hear one another speak. From a room further on, Susannah could hear the faint strains of music, but the receptions rooms were so crowded that it was almost impossible to progress, especially as people kept stopping them.

It must have been at least twenty minutes later that they finally arrived at the ballroom itself, which was so magnificent that it took Susannah's breath away. The floor had been polished so hard that it looked smooth and glossy, great glittering chandeliers of glass lit by hundreds of candles overhead as the dancers moved gracefully to the music. Banks of flowers had been arranged at the foot of the dais and the scent of the blooms was so heavy that it was almost stifling.

Susannah fanned herself. The rooms were overpoweringly hot, even though long windows opened out on to terraces that led to large gardens. However, she had been in the ballroom only a moment or two when the gentlemen began asking her for dances. She offered her card and the spaces were quickly taken, all save the one before supper, which she had reserved. Susannah was not sure why she had reserved it or for whom, but she had thought it prudent to hold one dance open just in case. Swept away to the dance floor by one partner after the other, she hardly had time to breathe, let alone think, and it was not until it was almost time for supper that she realised she had not seen Lord Pendleton.

That was a little strange, for this was one of the most important affairs of the Season and Lord Pendleton would certainly have been invited. When she thought about it, she realised that she had not seen him for two days, which was most unusual. Susannah was given no time to dwell on the small puzzle, however, for as the supper dance approached and she realised she would be left standing alone, a gentleman walked towards her and her heart caught.

'Miss Hampton—' Northaven's deep tones sent little shivers down her spine '—dare I hope that you have a dance for me? Pray excuse my tardy appearance. I had hoped to come sooner, but was delayed.'

Susannah's breath caught in her throat. She suspected that she must have been hoping for this when she saved the dance, but had not allowed herself to think of it. He was, after all, the most romantic gentleman of her acquaintance; that hint of danger about him was fascinating and caused little chills up and down her spine. She remembered her mama's warning, but almost immediately dismissed it. He might have a slightly tarnished reputation, but he was still received, so he could not be so very bad, surely?

She smiled at him, a little challenge in her eyes. 'You do not deserve it, my lord, but as it happens I kept the dance before supper free.'

'I am blessed by your good sense.' Northaven gave her a look that made her pulses race. He really was a very exciting gentleman! 'I hope you will grant me the dance—and also allow me to take you into supper?'

'I am not sure…' Susannah teased and then laughed at his expression, which was half-frustration, half-disappointment. 'Yes, of course. I should be delighted, my lord.'

'I am honoured,' Northaven said and held out his hand to her.

Susannah felt a little shiver at the base of her spine as his strong fingers closed about hers. She was not sure why, but his touch made her tremble. She had dreamed of this moment, but, now it was here, something did not feel quite right.

As they began to dance Susannah relaxed, letting him guide her about the floor, giving herself up to the music. She loved to dance so much and there was no need to feel nervous. Northaven might be a little dangerous, but he was a gentleman after all. Besides, they were in a crowded ballroom so she was quite safe. After a moment or two the slight apprehension left her and she found herself laughing at his teasing.

'You are an enchantress,' Northaven told her, giving her a burning look that sent tingles down her spine. 'I did not realise how exciting a creature you were at first,

Miss Hampton. I see that I must pay more attention to you in future.'

Susannah laughed. She had lost her shyness and was behaving exactly as she did with all the friends she trusted, natural and innocent, but with a little boldness in her eyes.

After their dance, Northaven gave her his arm, escorting her through the crush to the large room that had been set aside for supper. Several tables were set about the room, some of them already occupied. At one end there was a table laden with a magnificent buffet. Northaven guided her to a table near one of the open French windows and indicated that she should sit.

'I shall fetch you a glass of champagne and something to eat,' he told her. 'What will you have?'

'Just a syllabub, if it is no trouble,' Susannah said and smiled when he replied that it was no trouble at all.

As he went off to fetch their supper, she glanced around the room. Seeing a gentleman enter, her heart did a funny little skip. It surprised her, because until this moment she had not realised that she had missed seeing him these past couple of days. Lord Pendleton had arrived late, it seemed, because the duchess went up to him and seemed to berate him, tapping him with her fan and then nodding her approval at something he said. He glanced towards Susannah, appeared to frown and turned back to his hostess. He would in the past have smiled or inclined his head to her and the neglect was oddly hurtful. Susannah looked away, but he did not seem to notice, for he was deeply engaged in conversation.

Northaven had returned with her syllabub when Lord Pendleton glanced her way again. Susannah saw the disapproval in his eyes as the marquis handed her a glass of champagne and set a little tray on the table. Remembering his warning and those of her mother and Amelia once more, she felt uneasy. It might have been wiser not to allow the marquis to escort her to supper, but there could be no real harm in it.

'You do not eat?' Susannah asked, for he had brought only her syllabub and a bottle of champagne.

'I seldom eat much at these affairs,' Northaven told her. 'Try your champagne, Miss Hampton. I managed to find a bottle—one glass is never enough, is it?' He sipped his own glass, nodding in approval as Susannah drank hers. 'I see you like champagne,' he said and refilled her glass. 'You have excellent taste, for it is the Queen of the grape.'

'I used to giggle when the bubbles went up my nose,' Susannah confessed and laughed. 'But I am used to it now, and, yes, I do like it.' She seldom drank more than one glass, but it was making her feel warm and pleasant and she did not demur when he refilled her glass once more. However, by the time she had drunk a few sips of that, she had begun to feel too warm and fanned herself. 'It is so hot in here this evening, do you not think so?'

'Indeed, you are right,' Northaven said. 'Would you care for a stroll on the terrace, Miss Hampton? You will not wish to be too warm when the dancing begins again.'

'Yes, thank you,' Susannah said. She did feel as if she needed a little air and had quite forgot the apprehension she had felt when he took her hand earlier. Her head was a little fuzzy and she could not think clearly. She stood up and went out of the French door, feeling that she needed some air, hardly noticing whether he was following her. Her head was spinning and she felt odd, though she did not know why. She walked along the terrace, and then down the three steps that led to the lawns. She had expected the air to make her feel better, but instead she had begun to experience some sickness in her stomach and her instinct drove her towards the shrubbery where she could vomit, if need be.

Feeling oddly light-headed, she did not even remember the marquis until she felt a hand on her shoulder. Turning, she stared at him in a daze, hardly knowing or understanding what was going on. She was beginning to feel decidedly unwell. Surely two glasses of champagne should not have affected her so badly?

She tried to focus as the marquis came towards her, but his face was a blur. She blinked, because she felt that she might faint at any moment.

'My beautiful darling...' Northaven's voice sounded peculiar, perhaps because her head was whirling '...how clever of you to find somewhere we can be alone. I have been wanting to do this ever since I saw you.'

Susannah made a murmur of protest as he reached for her. The last thing she wanted was to be kissed at this moment! She held up her hands as if to ward him off, but her head was swimming.

'No! No, you should not...' she cried as his face loomed large in front of her and she knew what he intended. She put up a struggle, but it was ineffectual because she hardly had the strength to stand up, let alone defend herself. 'Please, do not—'

Her protest was in vain, for Northaven's greedy mouth fastened over hers, his tongue probing at hers in an attempt to make her open to him. She became aware of his hands at her breasts, moving beneath the satin and lace of her expensive gown, touching her flesh.

Suddenly, she was aware of danger and, gathering all her strength, pushed him away and screamed.

'Be quiet, you little fool,' he muttered, holding her arms, his fingers bruising her tender flesh.

Susannah's head was whirling as she struggled to break free of Northaven, but she was feeling so ill and dizzy that she knew she could not fight him. All at once she felt him move sharply away from her, as if he had been jerked back. She stared hazily at the little scene played out before her eyes, hardly knowing what was happening because she felt so sick and dizzy.

'Take your hands from her, Northaven! She is not some country cit's daughter you can ruin. Miss Hampton is a lady and innocent, and you are taking foul advantage!'

'You mistake the matter,' Northaven drawled. 'I assure you the little innocent brought me here with no prompting. She was willing at the start, even if she did take fright.'

'Damn you! You insult an honourable lady!' Harry Pendleton said angrily. 'Take your hands from her this instant or you will answer to me.'

'I am prepared to—' Northaven began, but at that moment Susannah made a gurgling sound and then lurched towards him, the vomit bursting out of her mouth and spraying in his direction. 'Good grief!' He jerked back in disgust, a look of horror in his eyes as some of the vile-smelling liquid splashed on his shoes. 'She is ill. Take care of her, Pendleton. I swear, I had no idea…'

As Northaven beat a hasty retreat towards the house, Harry took hold of Susannah's arm. 'You are unwell,' he said gently. 'You had best come and sit down.'

'I am sorry,' Susannah wailed and jerked away from

him to be sick behind a bush once more. Harry waited until she had finished and then handed her a large white kerchief. He watched as she wiped her mouth. She was about to hand the kerchief to him, then looked at it and crumpled the fine lawn in her hand. She felt like weeping, and his shoulder looked so broad and dependable. She found herself laying her head against it, her tears soaking into his pristine coat. After a moment, her distress subsided and she drew away from his supporting arm. 'I am so sorry. I will have the kerchief washed.'

'Do not trouble yourself,' Harry said. 'Keep it until you feel better and then give it to me. I shall dispose of it. Sit here on this bench for a few moments until you recover.'

Susannah's head was beginning to clear. She looked at him uncertainly, feeling a little unwell and ashamed. 'I do not know what happened,' she said. 'I drank two glasses of champagne, but...would they have made me ill?'

'I do not think it,' he said. 'Something may have been slipped into your glass. I did try to warn you, Miss Hampton. Northaven is known for his misdeeds. You would not be the first young woman he has seduced and led astray, though the first gentlewoman to my knowledge. He normally chooses country wenches or the daughters of merchants, I believe. I cannot say for certain that he drugged your drink, for I did not see him do it, but I think it may be so. I would never be surprised at anything that rogue did!'

'Oh...' Susannah gave a cry of distress. Her cheeks stung with humiliation as she realised what might have happened to her. 'You think me so foolish. I have been foolish, but he was...exciting. I enjoyed the idea of... an adventure.' A tear slipped from the corner of her eye and slid down her cheek. 'Is that so very silly of me? I have always dreamed of a knight who would sweep me off and ride away to his castle—' She stopped in dismay as she realised what she had said. 'Now you will think me very stupid. I should have put away such childish dreams, should I not? It is all very well for children to dream, but the real world is not like that, of course. You are so very sensible—you must despise my foolishness.'

'Dreams are pleasant at times. We all have them when we are younger,' Harry said, a little smile on his mouth. 'But men like Northaven are not to be trusted. He is a ruthless rogue and would use you for his pleasure. You would be unwise to trust men of his ilk.'

'Yes, I know,' Susannah said in a small voice. She felt so ashamed! 'I must thank you for coming to my rescue, sir.'

'Do not look so ashamed,' Harry told her gently. 'Northaven was at fault, not you. You would not have behaved so recklessly had he not given you that champagne—and perhaps some kind of a drug. I shall not scold you, Miss Hampton. I think you have learned your lesson.'

'The schoolmaster…' Susannah said and laughed. She blushed as he looked at her, for she could never tell him of her dream. 'I beg your pardon. I do not quite know what I am saying.'

'I think I should fetch your mama,' Harry said. 'Unless you feel well enough to go back to the ballroom?'

'I should like to go upstairs and wash my face,' Susannah told him. She was feeling better, but not yet ready to return to the dancing. 'Would you tell Mama that I am unwell, please? I think I should like to go home.'

'Yes, of course, that may be for the best,' Harry said.

'We will allow everyone to think you were simply taken ill—there need be no scandal.'

'You are very good, sir.' He was being so kind and she felt so embarrassed, so foolish.

'Not a bit of it,' Harry said. 'Let us return now. You must go to the room provided for your comfort, and I shall speak to your mama.'

Susannah got to her feet. She was still feeling a little shaky and felt glad of his arm. When they reached the house, she entered by one of the French doors and slipped quietly away to the bedchambers. It was not until she reached the one provided for the ladies to tidy themselves that she realised she still had Lord Pendleton's kerchief. It was stained and smelly, but she slipped it inside her reticule. She would have it washed before she returned it to him.

She was feeling a little better, having washed her face and tidied her gown, by the time her mother arrived. Mrs Hampton looked at her anxiously.

'Lord Pendleton told me that you were unwell in the garden, my love?'

'Yes, I was sick—twice, in fact,' Susannah said. 'I do not know what made me feel so ill, Mama. I am beginning to feel better, but I think I should like to go home, if you will take me?'

'Yes, of course, dearest,' Mrs Hampton said. 'I do hope you are not sickening for something, Susannah. You were doing so well, enjoying yourself…'

'I am sure it will pass,' Susannah said. She could not tell Mama what had happened, for it would distress her! 'Perhaps it is something I ate.' She had actually eaten hardly anything all day. She wondered if that might be the reason the champagne had gone to her head like that—unless the Marquis of Northaven had deliberately tried to drug her so that he could seduce her. 'We need not disturb Amelia, if you will take me home, Mama.'

'Amelia has already ordered the carriage,' her mother assured her. 'She was concerned as soon as Lord Pendleton came to tell us you were not well.'

'I am sorry to have spoiled the evening for you both,' Susannah said, feeling guilty. It was her foolishness in trusting a man she had been warned against that had led her astray. She should have listened to her mama and would make certain that she did not repeat her mistake! Instinctively, she knew that her ordeal could have been much worse had Lord Pendleton not come to her rescue.

'Nonsense, my love. We shall go home and hope that you are better by the morning.'

'Thank you,' Susannah replied and followed her mother downstairs. Lord Pendleton was talking to Amelia and looked at her with concern. Susannah could not meet his gaze, for she knew he must think her so foolish. He had come to her rescue so gallantly! Indeed, he had been more like the knight of her dreams than the marquis, who had used her so shamefully.

Her mind was confused and she was in some distress as she sought her bed. Lord Pendleton would have lost all respect for her—and she had come to realise that she liked him far more than she had imagined. However, he would think her foolish beyond anything and she would do best to avoid both him and the marquis if she could....

Harry frowned as he sat in the library at his town house later that evening, brandy glass in hand, staring at nothing in particular as he thought about the incident with Northaven. The man was a menace and deserved to be taught a lesson. Had Susannah not been so ill, he would have challenged the insolent marquis to a duel or simply thrashed him in the garden. He would be well within his rights to take a horsewhip to the rogue! No gentleman would behave so badly towards a well-bred young lady.

Harry had tackled Northaven about it before he left the Morlands' home that evening, but the marquis had insisted that Susannah had drunk two and a half glasses of champagne and that he had done nothing except follow her to the shrubbery.

'Damn it all, Pendleton. If I intended her harm, I'd hardly choose the ball of the year. It would be easy enough to run off with her, I dare say.'

'Are you implying that she is of easy virtue?' Harry bristled at the suggestion.

'Dash it, no! Don't be a fool. If we fight over her, she will lose her reputation. The kiss was an impulse. I had no idea she was feeling ill. I thought she meant me to make love to her.' Something had flickered in Northaven's eyes. Harry Pendleton was acknowledged as the best shot in London and a man would have to have a death wish to enter a duel with him! 'As you said, she is a lady of quality, though unfortunately little fortune.'

'Some would consider her dowry adequate. A gentleman would offer marriage after the way you behaved, Northaven!'

'I might consider it—but I need a substantial heiress or a run of luck at the tables. I have overdone it of late and must recoup my losses.'

'Then you should not have embarrassed her. If I hear a word of this spoken in the clubs, I shall thrash you!'

'I dare say you would try—but you have my word that it remains our secret. I apologise for my behaviour. I did not realise I was treading on your toes, Pendleton. If I'd known you were interested, I would not have taken her into the garden.'

Harry had accepted his explanation, because to call him out over the incident would cause a scandal and that might damage Susannah. To bring her harm was the last thing Harry wanted. He was developing an interest in Susannah—she was just so unlike any woman he'd ever met. The few days he had spent in the country had resolved nothing, except his neighbour's problems. Harry had cleverly managed to buy a worthless piece of land for a large amount of money, because it adjoined his park and he had told General Harlow that he wanted to build a lake. The general had probably not been fooled for one instant, but the face-saving gesture had been much appreciated.

Returning to town as swiftly as he could, Harry had put in a belated appearance at the Duchess of Morland's ball in the hope of seeing Susannah. He had seen her leave the supper room with Northaven, and, feeling that she might find herself in trouble, had followed them out. When he heard her scream he went to her rescue at once, no thought of anything but her safety in his mind. Seeing her ill and wretched aroused his desire to protect her—he hated to see anyone in trouble, and, as spirited and independent as Susannah appeared, she was still innocent to the ways of London society.

She had been subdued, of course, but she had spoken of wanting excitement—an adventure. He supposed Northaven must seem a dashing fellow to young ladies.

Clearly Susannah did not find him exciting! Though

he had no plans to settle down as yet, he'd like to think a beautiful woman like Susannah might at least show a spark of interest in him. Harry nursed his brandy ruefully. He knew that his manner might seem serious, even forbidding sometimes. He had not begun well by warning her about the marquis, and she would probably resent the fact that his warning had been necessary. Susannah had felt foolish and guilty, a look of shame in her eyes as they talked afterwards. He had tried to reassure her, for he had not meant to scold, only to reassure.

Was he really as stern and forbidding as all that? There had been a time when he'd cut enough larks, behaved as wildly as any young man, and had attracted the attentions of many attractive and available young ladies, but that was before he joined the army and learned the nature of war. Watching your friends die in agony was a sobering experience, and when his elder brother died suddenly of a fever and his father was taken ill, Harry had come home to try to save the family estate. Before Harry's brother Alan had died, he had managed to gamble away a large portion of the family wealth. It had taken some years of hard work to restore the estate to its former substance and amass the fortune he now possessed. A fortune that grew steadily as the months passed.

Harry had become respected, popular, especially amongst the sporting community, because of his prowess at fencing, shooting, driving and riding. However, most of his friends were his own age, sensible men who had known the horrors of war and, like him, were intent on making their estates secure. They would find no fault in his manner, but he was afraid that he had become dull, his time given too much to building the business that had brought him his fortune. The fact that he was prepared to indulge in trade was something that he had managed to hide from all but a few, for it would be frowned on by many. However, he now owned a flourishing import business, dealing in fine wines.

He would have to ask Toby his opinion. Harry was in the habit of offering his nephew advice, but the lad had never appeared to resent it. Indeed, Toby strove to gain his good opinion and was bent on following in his footsteps. Harry had never been given cause to imagine that he had become staid or boring, and it had shocked him. How could he expect a lively young lady like Miss Hampton to feel anything for him? He was several years older, and, while that in itself was not a barrier, if his manner had given her a dislike for him…

Sighing, Harry put down his glass and went upstairs to his bedchamber, though he did not feel inclined to sleep. What had happened to him? Once upon a time he had known how to laugh and tease. If he wanted to catch Miss Hampton's attention, he would have to change his ways. Did he want her enough to change? That evening had made him aware that his feelings for her were stronger than he had previously thought, so perhaps he should make an effort to know her better.

Harry was frowning as he picked up the book he had chosen for bedtime reading. It was a solemn treatise on the works of an eminent Russian writer. He opened it, looked at the first page and then cursed, throwing it across the room in sudden disgust. He could hardly introduce that as a topic of conversation to a spirited young lady!

Harry grinned suddenly, seeing the funny side of his situation. Here he was, courted on all sides by hopeful mamas, sighed over by at least a dozen simpering young ladies, and he was floundering like a green youth in the first throes of love!

His reading matter could be changed immediately. He would subscribe to Byron's latest and a few other popular novels that were circulating, but that would get him only so far. He enjoyed music and he rather thought Susannah did too. He knew she loved to dance and he would be certain to arrive earlier at all the best affairs in future, but he needed something more to arouse her interest. However, at this moment he had no idea what that might be.

Sighing, he retired to bed, still searching his imagination for something that would delight Susannah and make her smile for him, as she did for others. He smiled as his eyelids flickered, on the brink of falling asleep…a white knight to take her up on his charger and ride off into the sunset with her.

Didn't the foolish girl know what had probably happened to most of the young wenches who were abducted by knights? They surely suffered a fate that was very far from the happy ever after that Susannah had in mind. Unless, of course, the knight was in love with the lady…

Chuckling at an outrageous thought that popped into his head, Harry at last drifted into sleep.

Susannah entered the parlour in a rush of excitement, stopping abruptly as she saw that Amelia had a visitor—and one she knew to be Amelia's brother, Sir Michael Royston. He gave her a look of dislike, which made her blush and feel uncomfortable.

'Do forgive me for bursting in, Amelia,' she apologised. 'I had some news and I did not realise that you had a visitor….'

'You should learn to knock, young lady, especially when you are a guest in another's house.' Sir Michael glared at her and then turned to his sister. 'Well, Amelia, you know my feelings, but I shall say no more on the subject—on your own head be it.' He nodded curtly and then strode from the room, leaving a silence behind him.

'I must apologise for my brother's rudeness,' Amelia said. She was hiding her distress, but Susannah knew that she was very upset. She wondered what Sir Michael had said to her and thought that she disliked him very much. He was a horrid man to treat his sister so badly! 'He had no right to speak to you that way, dearest.'

'He was right,' Susannah replied. 'It was thoughtless of me to come rushing in here the way I did—but I was excited.'

'I am glad you had a lovely time today,' Amelia said. 'You are enjoying your visit, aren't you? You have been quiet for a few days. I wondered if you were still unwell?'

'No, I am much better and having a wonderful time,' Susannah told her. 'The Roberts twins were there this afternoon, Amelia, and the talk was all of a race. It was between Lord Coleridge and—who do you think his challenger was?' Susannah clapped her hands as Amelia shook her head. 'I am not surprised you cannot guess, for I should never have thought it. Lord Pendleton beat him, but they say it was a close-run thing.'

'Yes, I imagine it must have been,' Amelia said and laughed softly. 'They are both Corinthians and known for their driving and other sports—did you not know that?'

'Well, I had heard something. But a curricle race

in town! I had not imagined Lord Pendleton would do something like that.'

'It does not surprise me. When he was younger, I believe he indulged in the occasional prank. Max Coleridge, Pendleton, Northaven and one other—' She stopped speaking abruptly.

'The Marquis of Northaven? Lord Pendleton does not approve of him…' Susannah looked puzzled. 'I did not think they were friends.'

'They were friends when they were first on the town, I recall; I was quite young then and did not know them well—but a friend of mine did and she told me…' Amelia hesitated, then, 'But Northaven has become more ruthless and the others have…grown up. In most respects, though it seems they are still mad enough to race through town.' She arched her brows. 'It is rather amusing, though perhaps unwise.'

'Yes, a little dangerous, perhaps,' Susannah replied. 'I would not have suspected it of Lord Pendleton—but it must have been exciting. I wish I might have seen it. I should like to take part in a race, if it were possible, which it is not, of course.'

'Yes,' Amelia agreed. 'I would like to have been there. Gentlemen have all the fun, do they not? It seems a little unfair, but there are compensations in being a lady—do you not agree?'

Susannah realised that she was being teased and smiled shyly. 'Yes, of course. I know I am foolish to long for adventures. I suspect I should not like them if they truly happened.'

'Nor should I,' Amelia agreed. 'I think to be settled and happy with someone one cares for is perhaps the best of all…'

Seeing her look so wistful, Susannah spoke without

thinking. 'I believe Sir Michael must be thoughtless to cause you so much distress, Amelia. I wish he would not visit you if he only means to quarrel with you—' Realising what she had said, Susannah clapped her hand to her mouth. 'Oh, forgive me! How very forward and rude of me! I ought not to have said it, but…'

'You were thinking it,' Amelia supplied as Susannah stared at her wide-eyed and anxious. 'Come and sit down, dearest. I am going to tell you something so that perhaps you will understand and cease to be anxious about me, for I know that you have been—have you not?'

Susannah nodded and sat down in a chair near the window. 'You do not have to tell me, Amelia. I really should not have passed an opinion…'

'Why—because you are younger and a guest?' Amelia shook her head. 'The difference is not so very great and I think of you as a friend. I shall tell you, because I think you will treat my confidence with respect.'

'I promise,' Susannah vowed fervently and Amelia smiled.

'I told you that I loved someone, but the match was denied me?' Susannah nodded. 'Well, it caused a rift between Michael and myself, a rift that has never quite healed—and there was my aunt's fortune. I stayed with her for more than two years before she died. She loved me and I loved her and she left almost everything to me. My brother resented the fact that he did not receive a share. He has tried to…persuade me to give him a substantial share, but it does not stop there. He wishes to rule my life. It was for precisely this reason that my aunt made me independent. Michael cannot touch my money, nor can I give him what he asks for, because it is tied up in property and trust funds. I should not even if I could—but I cannot give away large amounts of capital. However, my income is many times larger than I require and I am able to give smaller sums now and then. I am in no danger from my brother, for I am strong enough to resist…his arguments. It is sometimes unpleasant, but there is nothing more to cause you concern.'

'I see…' Susannah looked at her. 'Thank you for telling me, Amelia. I am honoured by your trust. I have known that your brother is unkind to you and I know how generous you are…have been to me…'

'I give what I wish to give. Both my nephews have had small incomes from me, which I can easily afford, but I shall do nothing for my brother, because he does not deserve it. Unfortunately, he believes he is entitled to control my fortune and that will cause friction at times.'

'I wish you had someone to protect you,' Susannah said. 'If you were married, you would have a husband to care for you and look after your fortune.'

'Yes, I should, but I have good friends. I have not asked them for help, because as yet I do not need it—but they are there if I should need them.'

'I am so glad,' Susannah said. 'Forgive me if I am impertinent to ask—but is there no one you like enough to marry?'

'Perhaps there may be one day,' Amelia told her and smiled. 'I hope your mind is at rest now, my love?'

'Yes, it is,' Susannah said. She stood up and went to kiss Amelia's cheek. 'It was good of you to tell me, for I know it was not easy for you.'

'No, it is never easy to speak of these things, but I wanted to set your mind at rest, Susannah—and now we shall forget it. Tell me, is there a gentleman you feel you like more than the others?'

'There might be,' Susannah confessed. 'I was not sure that I liked him, but of late I have begun to change my mind.'

'I think I might guess,' Amelia said. 'But I shall not guess for you have not yet made up your mind and I do not wish to influence you—and now we really must ring for tea. Your mother should be home at any moment— she went to fetch something I needed…' She smiled as the door opened and Mrs Hampton entered, as if to order. 'We were just about to have tea. Susannah has some interesting news…' She got up to ring the bell for tea.

'You look so lovely this evening,' Harry Pendleton said, taking Susannah's hand and lifting it to his lips to kiss it when they met at a soirée that evening.

Susannah blushed faintly but did not remove her hand from his grasp immediately. She had tried to avoid him when they met for the first time after that disastrous affair at the Duchess of Morland's ball. However, he had made a point of seeking her out and was so charm- ing that she had overcome her feeling of awkwardness. Since then they had met everywhere. He had formed a habit of seeking her out, and Susannah could not doubt that he liked her. She had believed he must have a dis- gust of her for her foolish behaviour, but it was not so. No one seemed any the wiser about the incident with the marquis and she suspected that she had Lord Pendleton to thank for it. The Marquis of Northaven had not been present at any of the affairs she had attended with her mother and Amelia, and someone had told her that he was out of town. Susannah could feel nothing but relief. She would be quite happy if she never saw him again!

The knowledge that she might well have lost more

than her reputation if Lord Pendleton had not come to her rescue that night was sobering. However, Susannah was an incurable romantic and she still had her dreams of a white knight on a charger. His face was indistinct, and she had begun to accept in her heart that her romantic ideas were nonsense. The Marquis of Northaven had frightened her and opened her eyes to the nature of certain types of men. She understood better now why both Amelia and her mother had warned her against being intimate with some of the gentlemen.

'I was wondering how much longer you plan to stay in town,' Lord Pendleton was saying to her. 'And what you will do when you leave?'

'Oh…' Susannah's thoughts had wandered a little, but she gave him all her attention. 'I believe we are to stay for at least another two or three weeks. I have no idea what we shall do afterwards. I suppose we shall go home.'

Susannah frowned at the idea. If she returned home in three weeks without having secured an offer, it would be the end of her dreams. She knew her mother had hoped that she would make a fortunate match, but as yet she did not think she wished to marry any of the gentlemen she knew. At least, there was only one she might feel able to accept, but she did not imagine he would ask her, for, despite his unfailing kindness, he must think her a foolish girl. A little sigh left her lips. She had hoped for so much and it might all come to nothing.

'Does something trouble you, Miss Hampton? Or are you bored?'

'Oh…' Susannah blushed as Lord Pendleton looked at her in concern. 'No, of course I am not bored, sir. Forgive me if I gave that impression. It is just that…' She shook her head because it was impossible to explain.

She did not even know herself what was making her feel restless and hastily turned the subject. 'I heard of your race, sir. It must have been exciting.'

'Yes, perhaps,' Harry said, with what she thought a boyish grin on his lips. 'It was quite mad, but we suggested it as a joke and people started to bet on the outcome and then we had to go through with the nonsense.'

'I thought it was thrilling. I wish I had been there to see it.'

'It would not have been suitable. I believe we attracted quite a rough crowd.'

'Oh, then perhaps—' She bit back her words of protest. 'I like horses and I should enjoy watching them race—at a suitable venue, of course.'

'Perhaps one day I could take you to the races, if your mama would make up one of the party.'

'Yes, that would be interesting. I attended a balloon race with Amelia and some friends, you know. I found that great fun. We followed in the carriage and it was a great spectacle.'

'Yes, I believe it is. You enjoy music and reading, I know,' Harry said. 'Tell me, what other pursuits please you?'

'I love to walk with my dogs,' Susannah told him, realising with a shock that she missed the freedom of the countryside here in town. 'One can be so free in the country, do you not think so, sir? I am often scolded for traipsing all over the place like a hoyden but the air is so fresh...'

'You enjoy the country.' Harry smiled. 'I like it myself. The pleasures of town are well enough for a few weeks, but home is best, I believe. Do you ride or drive yourself in the country, Miss Hampton?'

'I used to ride before Papa died,' Susannah said. 'I have never driven myself, but it is something I should like to learn. Perhaps I shall one day.' She was unconscious of the wistful look in her eyes.

'I dare say your husband will teach you when you marry, Miss Hampton.'

'Perhaps...' Susannah's cheeks coloured. She dared not look at him and searched for a new topic of conversation. Her eyes lit on a gentleman who had just that minute entered the room. She did not know him and it gave her the excuse she had been looking for to avoid answering. 'I do not believe I know that gentleman....'

Harry looked across the room and smiled. 'That is the Earl of Ravenshead,' he told her. 'He is newly come into the title, for his father died a few months ago; I think he has been busy sorting out the estate. He returned from France, I think, where he had been staying for the past year or so. He came to town some days ago, but has not accepted many invitations, for at first he intended to return home almost at once.'

'I did not think I had seen him before. He looks... nice.'

Harry smiled. 'Gerard is a year or so older than myself, but a great friend. I must go and greet him, because it was I who persuaded him to come this evening. Will you forgive me if I leave you, Miss Hampton? I shall see you later this evening—perhaps at supper, if not before?'

Susannah nodded, watching as he left her to greet his friend. The warmth of their greeting left no doubt in her mind that they held each other in high esteem and, intent on observing them together, she was not immediately aware that Amelia had come up to her.

'Are you enjoying yourself, Susannah?' Amelia asked.

Susannah turned to her at once. 'Yes, of course. It is a very pleasant evening.'

'I thought you looked happy.' Amelia glanced across the room. As her gaze fell on two gentlemen talking, she seemed to stiffen for a moment and her cheeks paled. 'Oh…'

'Is something the matter?' Susannah asked. Amelia seemed distracted and did not answer. Susannah looked at her and saw that she had turned pale. 'Are you unwell? Should you like to go home?'

Amelia blinked, looked at her and smiled. 'No, nothing is the matter, my dear. I have just seen someone I once knew, but it is not important.'

Susannah followed her gaze and saw that Lord Pendleton and the Earl of Ravenshead were still talking. It must be the earl who had caused Amelia to look startled and turn pale. He was the only newcomer that evening. Her gaze narrowed in thought as she remembered Amelia's confidences.

'Do you mean the Earl of Ravenshead?'

'Oh…yes, though he was simply the earl's son when I knew him,' Amelia replied. The colour had returned to her cheeks now and she had recovered from her slight shock. 'I had heard that his father had died.'

Susannah knew immediately who the earl must be. For Amelia to have received such a shock, the gentleman must have been important to her. He was the man she had wished to marry—the love that had been denied her. From the stricken look in her eyes at the moment she saw him, it was clear that she still cared!

'He and Lord Pendleton are good friends, I think?'

'Yes, I believe they always were, despite the difference in age. I believe Ravenshead is slightly older.'

Susannah wrinkled her brow. 'Do you think age difference is important in marriage?'

Amelia gave Susannah her full attention. 'I think the gentleman should be a few years older,' she said. 'Though I do not believe in marrying very young girls off to men old enough to be their grandfathers! That is a disgusting practice in my opinion! But age is not important if there is love and mutual respect. Without it, life would be intolerable, I think.'

'I do agree with you,' Susannah said. She had the feeling that Amelia was talking for the sake of it, as though she were trying to calm herself. 'I believe they are about to begin the music once more. Shall we take our places?'

'Yes, certainly,' Amelia said. She turned away at the same instant as the Earl of Ravenshead became aware of her. Susannah was watching both him and Lord Pendleton and saw the way his expression changed. He seemed stunned and then concerned, and he spoke urgently to Lord Pendleton.

Susannah was thoughtful as she followed her friend to a small couch near where her mother was already seated. The music was just beginning as they sat down, so she could not mention the earl's reaction to Amelia, and by the time they rose to go into supper she had forgotten it.

However, she recalled it later that evening when she happened to catch sight of the earl in conversation with Amelia. His manner was everything that was correct, as was Amelia's. No one could tell from their manner whether they were old friends or new acquaintances—they were being polite, but no more.

Remembering Amelia's shock, and the gentleman's violent reaction when he saw her, Susannah was certain that she was right. The earl was the gentleman Amelia had spoken of on two occasions. She had loved him once and she was not indifferent to him now, though she was trying to give that impression.

What a wonderful thing it would be if they could find each other again now that Amelia was independent of her overbearing brother! Was the earl married? She must ask Lord Pendleton, for he was sure to know. However, this evening was not the place or the time, because she must be discreet. Careless talk might lead to hurt for Amelia and she would not wish that for the world....

Chapter Four

Susannah did not need to wait long to put her questions to Lord Pendleton—they met when she was walking with some friends in the park the next morning. He tipped his hat, asked if he might join them, and after a few minutes she found that they were side by side and somehow a little behind the others.

'Would you mind if I asked you something?' she said impulsively. There was a sparkle in her eyes that had sometimes been missing for a few days, and her smile was compelling.

'You may ask me anything you wish,' Harry said, responding with a twinkle in his own eyes. 'I assure you that any confidence you place in me will be strictly kept.'

'Well…it is not actually my confidence,' Susannah said. 'Do you know—have you any idea if there has ever been anything between your friend the Earl of Ravenshead and Miss Royston?'

'What makes you ask?' Harry said, hesitating. 'Have you noticed something?'

'Yes, I did actually. Miss Royston was startled to see him last evening, and for a few moments it quite overset her. And I think he was equally perturbed when he saw her, for I was watching him at that moment.'

'Ah…' Harry considered; he would not wish to betray his friend's confidence, but there could be little harm in admitting what she had already observed. 'I believe they may once have known each other quite well. Something occurred and nothing came of the friendship. However, I can tell you no more, for I am not certain of the details.'

'Or you are not at liberty to tell me,' Susannah replied astutely. 'I should not want you to betray a friend's confidence, sir, but you have told me enough. Amelia had already mentioned that she once knew him and I too know things that I am not at liberty to tell anyone…' She paused, a look of conspiracy on her face. 'You must know that I should not have been given a Season in town if it were not for Amelia's generosity, sir. I am very grateful for it and should like to do something for her…' She hesitated, then, 'He isn't married—is he?'

Harry frowned. 'Not to my knowledge. No, I think not…why do you ask?'

Harry was wary as he looked at her. Susannah had completely recovered from her loss of spirits after the incident with Northaven, and her eyes were bright with mischief.

'I just wished to be sure,' she replied airily.

'What are you suggesting, Miss Hampton?'

'Do you have to call me Miss Hampton all the time? Could you not call me Susannah in private? I believe we know each other well enough now, sir.'

'Only if you will reciprocate by calling me Harry.'

'Oh…I am not certain I should do that, but I could

call you Pendleton,' Susannah said, looking so adorable that he gave her a broad grin. 'Anyway, I was talking about Amelia and the earl—do you think we could sort of encourage them to get together in some way? I should so like to see Amelia happy. Nothing obvious, just making sure they are at the same affairs and that kind of thing.'

'I do not think we should meddle in things that do not concern us,' Harry said, a little doubtful. He imagined his friend had been too busy getting his estate into order to think of mixing in society much, but something had made him decide to stay on in town. 'Surely—' Harry stopped as she frowned at him. He was doing it again! He must try for lightness. She wanted a white knight on a charger and he had to become what she needed or risk losing her. 'It is true that I have always believed he cared for her, but something went wrong for them.'

'Oh, I knew I was right about him!' Susannah cried. 'It was a tragic love story. Someone prevented their happiness…but now they have a second chance. How romantic it would be if they could be together again!'

'It might be the very thing,' Harry agreed, not wanting to hurt her feelings. 'But I really think we should not interfere, Susannah. If they still like each other enough, it will happen without any interference from us.'

'All I meant was to mention her name now and then— and I will mention how handsome he is to her.'

'Gerard is very handsome, I suppose,' Harry said doubtfully. 'And Miss Royston is an attractive lady. I have wondered why she has not married before this. However, I must strongly urge caution. It would not be right to push them together. It can do no good and might do great harm.'

'Do you think it wrong?' Susannah's face fell. 'You

must think me such a foolish creature. It was merely that I so wished to do something for her. She often looks… sad…' she finished on a sigh.

'Yes, I have remarked it myself,' Harry told her. 'I will make certain that Gerard attends various functions and parties, for it is time he mixed more in company, but I will do no more, and I think you should exercise caution—you would not like to make your friend angry, I think? She would perhaps feel annoyed if she thought you were meddling in her affairs.'

'No, I should not do so,' Susannah agreed. 'Very well, I shall not go out of my way to praise him, though if the occasion arises…' She gave him a look that was a mixture of defiance and appeal. 'Surely you cannot censure that?'

'I am relieved. I had thought you would beg me to arrange an elopement!'

Susannah saw that he was teasing and shook her head. 'I should not dream of suggesting it for Amelia! I know she would dislike it of all things. It might be romantic with the right man, of course—but I do not think Amelia would care for such a thing at all.'

'I am very sure Gerard would never agree. He is very much the gentleman, you know. It would not suit his notions of propriety.'

'Is an elopement so very bad?' Susannah asked, meaning to tease him now. 'It would be an adventure—if one cared for such things….'

'Perhaps, though it might be uncomfortable, unless the lady was very sure of the gentleman's affections, of course.'

'Yes, I suppose so,' Susannah agreed. 'She would have to love him to distraction, and then she would care nothing for discomfort.'

Her inhibitions concerning Lord Pendleton had quite disappeared. She had accepted Harry as her confidant and chattered away happily, as she discussed how they could bring the star-crossed lovers together, without interfering in their lives.

Listening to Susannah's laughter and watching the changing expressions on her lovely face, Harry understood that he was fairly caught. He was not sure how it had happened, for he had had his reservations at the start. However, they had somehow melted away the night he found Northaven trying to seduce her.

Susannah held his future happiness in the palm of her soft hand. Being drawn into this enchanting intimacy was such a pleasant experience for a man who had, he admitted to himself, been very much inclined to hold his feelings in check. Harry was certain his feelings were more than the natural lust any man might feel for a beautiful girl. Yes, he wanted to kiss her until she melted against him, wanted to feel the softness of her yielding body beneath him as he taught her the pleasures of desire, but even more pressing than those very strong instincts was the need to protect her.

He smiled inwardly as she offered him a smile that was both innocent and provocative at the same time. She was enchanting! Indeed, he felt himself under her spell. He was not at all certain that she felt more than liking for him, though that in itself was an advance. He was certain that two weeks previously she would not have shared her thoughts concerning Miss Royston with him.

She had spoken of an elopement and for a moment he toyed with the idea of gratifying her wish, but he was fairly certain that she would in her heart enjoy a society wedding far more. It was merely a matter of convincing her that he was the man she ought to marry.

'We must plan your dance,' Amelia said when they had tea together that afternoon. 'I had thought we would hold it a few days before we go home and we should begin to think of what to do once we leave London...' Her gaze met Susannah's. 'Your mama and I have settled it that we shall go from here to Bath, my love. I wish to purchase a house there and I have asked my agent to find me a suitable property that I may rent and then purchase if I like it. I hope to spend quite a bit of time residing in the town in future. You are both welcome to live with me until you have other plans.'

Susannah understood that Amelia was speaking of her marriage. She could offer very little on the subject; although she liked Harry Pendleton very well and thought perhaps she might feel more, she was not certain—nor had he spoken to her.

'I told Amelia that we shall certainly stay with her until she finds herself a companion,' Mrs Hampton said. 'However, we have another two weeks at least in town. Who knows what may happen?'

'Plenty of time,' Amelia said and smiled at Susannah. 'We must draw up a guest list. We shall invite everyone who has invited us to their affairs, which is all of our close friends—but is there anyone special you would like, Susannah?'

Susannah was silent for a moment. 'I should like the Earl of Ravenshead if that is acceptable to you, Amelia? He is a close friend of Lord Pendleton and I think him a pleasant gentleman.'

'Yes, they are close friends,' Amelia said, looking

pensive. 'I suppose it would seem odd if he were not invited. I shall add his name to the list. Anyone else?'

'Mr Sinclair—but I dare say he is on the list, for he is at most of the functions we attend and he is Lord Pendleton's nephew.'

'Yes. Toby Sinclair is a pleasant young man,' Amelia agreed. 'I like him very much myself.' She smiled as she said it and Susannah wondered. Could she have made a mistake in thinking that Amelia was interested in the earl? Toby was younger than Amelia, but that would not matter if they were in love.

She must not speculate! It was not her affair. Harry Pendleton had been right to reprimand her in the park. Amelia's affairs were her own. However, she was pleased that the Earl of Ravenshead was to be invited to the dance.

The next week was the height of the Season so far, and Susannah was too busy to indulge herself with flights of fancy or even to think about her own feelings very much. They never seemed to have a free evening. Often, they attended more than one event in an evening, going first to a musical soirée and then on to a card party or something of that nature. There was a ball held on four separate occasions that week, which meant that Susannah was forced to buy another pair of dancing slippers, for hers were quite worn out.

However, she could not refrain from mentioning that she had arranged for the earl to be asked to her dance when she met Harry at a particular function.

'I think she was a little affected by my request, but you do not censure me for making it, I hope?'

'How could I? There is no harm in such an invitation. I hope you have not been doing anything worse?'

She blushed. 'You are right to scold me. I should not meddle—but I still think she likes him. I should like to see her married and safe, because I care for her. She is not so very old, you know, though I dare say some may think she is past the age of marrying.'

'I do not think it at all,' Harry replied. 'I am older than Miss Royston by some seven years, I believe.'

'Well, it is different for a man, is it not?' Susannah asked innocently. 'Do you not think it would be a fine thing—if they were to decide to marry?'

Harry hesitated. He knew that Gerard had suffered a disappointment of some kind. He was fairly certain that the young lady in question had been Amelia Royston, but he did not know what had happened. Gerard had been a changed man when they next met, slightly bitter at first, though he had changed again later. Having his life saved had seemed to instigate a new reason to live in Gerard, and then something else had happened. Harry wasn't sure what it was, because he had never asked. Gerard was a man who kept his secrets. If he wished someone to know, he would tell them. They were good friends, but they did not intrude on each other's lives.

'If they decided it for themselves—I would think it a very fine idea,' he conceded. 'However, I do not think it right that we should make a push to help bring such a marriage about, though I confess I should like to see him settled in England.'

Susannah bestowed a look of glowing approval on him. 'You are such a good friend,' she told him with a confiding air. 'I think you must be my very best friend.'

Harry hesitated. He was tempted to tell her that he would like to be much more than a friend, but she was clearly enjoying his friendship and he did not wish to

startle her by declaring himself too soon. She was many
years his junior and he wasn't sure that it would be fair
to ask her to be his wife. She would find her life much
changed—as the chatelaine of his various estates, she
would have many duties.

'I should always wish to please you,' he said. 'I think
you must know that, Susannah?'

'Yes, I do…' she replied and glanced away, suddenly
shy.

He was on the point of pressing further when they
were interrupted by the arrival of some friends, who took
Susannah's attention. Harry was asked to make up a four
at whist and departed. His eyes strayed across the room
to where Susannah was playing a game of jackstraws
with some of the younger members of the company. Her
laughter was music to his ears and he felt his heart jolt
when their eyes happened to meet for a moment and she
lowered her eyelid, giving him a saucy wink.

Harry knew that by naming him as her very best
friend she had paid him the highest honour she could
accord, but it was still not quite what he wanted from
her. She had learned to trust and like him, but that was
not the wild passion he wanted her to feel—the passion
he thought necessary in a marriage. He was certain there
was passion in Susannah. He just needed to awaken it.

He had been thinking for some days of things that
might make him seem a hero or a little bit exciting in
her eyes. His mind kept coming back to an idea that
had been growing for a while now. It was completely
mad, a wild flight of fancy that he would not normally
consider—but it might just work. If it did he would gain
so much, but he could also lose everything on the toss
of the dice.

Harry had nerves of steel at the gambling table or

in the face of the enemy, but when it came to losing Susannah, he knew himself a total coward. To have her turn away from him now might be a blow from which he could never recover. No other woman had come close to having this effect on him, and he had begun to understand what might have made Gerard lose the will to live during those hellish months in Spain.

Harry's plan was risky. He was weighing the consequences, gradually gaining more confidence in the outcome. If he managed to pull it off, he would win the best prize of his life!

It was not to be thought of until Susannah's own dance was over, of course. He knew that she was looking forward to her special evening and he would do nothing that might interfere with her pleasure. However, he might just put his risky plan into place a day or so after. Her visit to town would be nearing its end, and if it did not work…but Harry dared not allow himself to think of failure, for that would be terrible.

He would wait until after the dance, but if Susannah still seemed to think of him as simply a friend, he would do it!

Susannah retired happily to bed that night. She had noticed Amelia looking pensive a few times during the evening, which surely meant that she had been missing the earl. He had not been invited to the dinner or the card evening they attended, for it was a small affair consisting of about twenty-five guests.

'I happen to know Gerard has other things on his mind at the moment,' Harry had told her. 'Some problem with his estate, I understand. I believe he has actually left town for a few days.'

'He will be here for my dance?'

'Oh, yes, I am certain of it, for we have a meeting of the Four-in-Hand club,' he told her with a smile. 'I have proposed my sister's boy as a new member and we shall be taking a vote.'

'Oh, yes, Mr Sinclair is very keen to join, I believe,' Susannah said and laughed. 'He wants to be just like you, Pendleton! He is for ever telling me how much he admires you. I had no idea of what an excellent sportsman you are until he told me that you are held to be top of the trees by the Corinthians. He never ceases to sing your praises.'

'Indeed?' Harry looked thoughtful. 'How very kind of him. I wonder what he is after now.'

'That is unkind!' Susannah cried, scolding him, but with a gleam of mischief in her eyes. 'I am quite sure his affection for you is genuine.'

'Yes, I know it is,' Harry replied and smiled oddly. 'Toby likes to kick up a few larks, but he is actually a very sensible young man. I am thinking of taking him into a new venture I am setting up—but you will please not mention that to him. I want to give him a chance to…enjoy himself before he knuckles down.'

'Oh…' Susannah stared at him. Lord Pendleton never ceased to surprise her. Every time they spoke she discovered something new about him, and she was beginning to like him more and more. She knew that he attended every function where he might expect to see her, and he had offered to take her driving in the park whenever she wished. As yet she had not accepted that particular invitation, because she had a feeling that once she did their relationship might become more serious. She was not yet sure that she wished Harry to make her an offer. He was the most generous, easiest gentleman of her acquaintance, but she still could not help feeling that she would like something exciting to happen.

Climbing into bed, Susannah dismissed her small doubts. She had another eight days or so before they were due to leave for Bath and in three days it would be her dance. She did not know why, but she felt something exciting might happen then....

Susannah emerged from the lending library the next morning. She had been to return some books for her mother and collected two others that she hoped she might have a chance to read before they left town, though she was not at all certain she would even attempt them. Her maid was carrying a small parcel they had collected for Amelia and Susannah carried the books. She had turned aside to glance in the window of a milliner's shop when she became aware that more than one person had stopped behind her to look at the bonnets displayed there.

'When is your engagement to be announced?' a feminine voice asked behind her. Susannah stiffened as she recognised the voice and the one that answered.

'Oh, I think it must be quite soon,' Mary Hamilton said and giggled. 'He has been most particular in his attentions recently. Mama is certain he will come up to scratch before the week is out.'

Susannah stiffened her resolve and then turned to look at the two young ladies, who were giggling and clutching at each other. 'Good morning, Jane—Mary...'

'Oh, I thought it was you,' Mary said. 'Are you thinking of buying a new bonnet? I shall be making several purchases soon...' She looked coy. 'I cannot name the gentleman yet, though you may guess—but it is not official, you know.'

'I see. I must wish you happy,' Susannah said. 'Excuse me, I must go home. I am expected…'

She walked away, head high, trying not to show that she was feeling agitated. She could only imagine that Mary Hamilton was speaking of Lord Pendleton, for it was he she had been thinking of when Susannah had overheard her at a dance a couple of weeks earlier.

Susannah's heart was heavy as she walked home, accompanied by her maid. It was foolish of her to feel like this, because, kind as he was, Harry Pendleton had said nothing to her. He had never suggested in any way that he found her more enchanting than any other lady of his acquaintance. It was quite ridiculous of her to feel disappointed or let down. Indeed, she was not. Truly she was not…but it did hurt just a little that the gentleman she thought of as her particular friend should have been intending to make Mary Hamilton an offer all the time.

Susannah decided that she must put a brave face on it. She knew that she would meet both Lord Pendleton and Mary at the dance that evening. She would not let them or anyone else see that she was suffering from a heavy disappointment.

She happened to be wearing white again that evening. It was not a new gown, but one she had worn several times before. Glancing at herself in the mirror as she left Amelia's house, she knew that she looked very well. However, when Mary arrived, she looked stunning in a gown that took Susannah's breath. It was obviously very expensive, the silk sewn with diamonds across the bodice and trimmed with Brussels lace at the hem, and the necklace of rubies and diamonds she was wearing was worth a small fortune; she also wore a stunning ring on the finger of her left hand. It was hardly any wonder that she had a look of triumph in her eyes! Susannah's heart sank as she heard the news circulating. Mary Hamilton had been right to anticipate a proposal and, when it was made, she had accepted.

Susannah had not seen the party come in, but she caught sight of Harry moments before she saw the triumph on Mary Hamilton's face. It was little wonder that she should look so proud—she had claimed for herself one of the best matches of the season!

Susannah would not let herself listen to the gossip. Instead, she threw herself into the evening, flirting with her partners and laughing at their jests. Her heart was aching, for only now had she realised how much Harry meant to her—but it was too late. He had made his choice and it was not her.

It was not until more than an hour had passed that Harry came to her. She thought how handsome he looked, dressed immaculately in the style made fashionable by Mr Brummell, once the Regent's favourite, his coat and breeches black, his shirt pristine white and his cravat a masterpiece set off by a diamond stick pin that sparkled in the light of the candles. His simple elegance made him stand out from many of the other gentlemen, who appeared overdressed by comparison. He smiled ruefully. 'I am late,' he apologised. 'I suppose it is too much to hope that you saved a dance for your best friend.'

'I fear that it is,' Susannah said in a reserved manner. 'I did not think you would wish it now—and so I gave them all away.'

'What do you mean?' Harry was puzzled, but before she had time to answer, her next partner was there asking

her to dance. He watched as she was whisked away and
stood frowning as she laughed up at the young man.
Devonshire was the heir to a duke, but it was unlikely
he would look at Susannah, for he needed an heiress to
support his expensive tastes.

Harry took up a position next to the French windows,
watching Susannah as she went from partner to partner.
He could not understand what had happened to her. She
was always a lively girl, but this evening she seemed
almost reckless. Yet he would swear that her laughter
was not her usual carefree mirth. She was upset about
something and she blamed him—but for the life of him
he could not think what he had done to distress her.

Could it be that he had been deceived in her? He had
thought he was gaining ground, but now it seemed they
had gone back to the start. Harry shrugged. He did not
care to stay and watch. He would go to his club or perhaps visit the lady who had been his mistress until a few
weeks previously. He had finished his affair with Elaine,
for it no longer pleased either of them, but he could talk
to her—and he was in need of some female advice at this
moment. Advice that he would never dream of asking
from his mother or his sister.

Susannah did not see him leave, but she became
aware that he was missing just before supper. Glancing
round the supper room, she thought he might be found
there, but he had disappeared. However, she saw Mary
Hamilton, Lady Hamilton and a gentleman of about
fifty years she recognised as the Marquis of Stavely.
He was wearing a puce coat, tight breeches that showed
off his rather large stomach and a black wig that was
really rather odd. As if aware of her interest, he lifted a

gold lorgnette to his eye and looked her way. Susannah blushed and hastily averted her gaze.

She had turned her attention to the food and was deciding what to eat when Mrs Hampton came up to her. 'It is good news concerning Miss Hamilton, is it not, Susannah? Have you taken the opportunity to wish her happy?'

'No, Mama—I met her this morning. She told me she expected a proposal, but I did not expect it this evening…' Her voice quavered a little and her mother gave her an odd look. Her look of distress was plain and Mrs Hampton frowned. 'He said nothing of her to me even this evening…'

'Are you thinking…?' Mrs Hampton smiled all at once. 'Susannah, my dear—Miss Hamilton is engaged to the Marquis of Stavely.'

'The marquis…' Susannah stared in dismay. 'But I thought…I knew she had thoughts of…another gentleman.' How could Miss Hamilton have accepted an offer from a man nearly old enough to be her grandfather?

'I imagine that is the reason for your behaviour this evening.' Mrs Hampton looked a little disapproving. 'I knew there was something. I told you once I did not think Pendleton was interested in Miss Hamilton. I believe you should go and congratulate her, Susannah. It may look as if you are jealous of her good fortune if you do not.'

'Yes, Mama, of course,' Susannah said. She went at once and said everything that was proper, ignoring the smirk on Mary's face. It was clear that the young lady was very pleased with her bargain—indeed, the marquis was wealthy and titled—but Susannah did not envy her one little bit. She would rather remain a spinster than marry the man Mary Hamilton had accepted.

After congratulating her, Susannah went back to the ballroom. She looked for Lord Pendleton, but could not see him. She ventured to the open door of the card room and glanced in, but he was not there. Obviously he had left at some time earlier and she had not seen him go. What must he think of her?

'If you are looking for Pendleton, he is visiting his mistress,' a harsh voice said behind her. She swung round to find herself looking at the Marquis of Northaven. 'I heard him give the address to a cab driver as I got down from one myself.' Northaven sneered. 'I know the lady well. She is not particular in the company she keeps.'

Susannah bit her lip. She would not trust herself to answer such a remark, for it was said spitefully and not worthy of notice. 'Excuse me, I must find my mama.'

She walked away from him, her heart racing. It was not her affair if Lord Pendleton had gone to visit his mistress. She regretted refusing him a dance when she might have given him a choice of two had she wished, but it would not have made any difference if he wished to spend the evening in the arms of his mistress. Susannah felt close to tears, because she had been foolish. She should have made sure of her facts before sending Harry Pendleton away. He must have thought her most rude, as she had been, a fact she now bitterly regretted.

Susannah did not see Harry the following day. He called while she was out walking with some friends and left her a posy of flowers. He renewed his promise to see her at her dance, but nothing more. She knew that she could not expect more. Indeed, she had not expected as much after her behaviour the previous evening. He must think her a flighty creature who changed her mind at the slightest whim.

She had, after some thought, decided to forget what the marquis had told her. She had no way of knowing that it was true—and even if it had been, Harry was a single man and entitled to visit any lady he chose.

Susannah knew that she cared for him more than was proper. He had not declared himself and she had no reason to expect it. However, if he should propose, she would make it clear that she would not wish him to visit other ladies if they married.

But she was foolish to consider it. Harry might not even be thinking of taking a wife. It was quite improper of her even to think such things! Yet she had begun to think of him as hers, and she could not help feeling jealous of the woman who had taken him from the ball.

It was a glorious day for her special dance. Susannah was allowed to sleep a little later than normal before Iris brought in her breakfast tray and a pile of notes and small gifts.

'What are all these?' Susannah asked, staring at them in surprise. 'It isn't my birthday for ages yet. I knew I might receive some flowers, but I didn't expect anything more.'

'Why don't you open them?' Iris asked. 'See what you've got.'

Susannah picked up the first parcel and looked at the card. 'This is from Mama—what can it be?' She tore off the pretty wrapping and found a small velvet-covered box. Opening it, she discovered a pretty pearl-and-diamond clip for her hair. 'Oh, that is lovely. It must have cost Mama some guineas to buy it for me.'

'Well, it is a special day, miss,' Iris said, smiling at her. 'Go on, open the other two.'

Susannah knew her maid was excited and curious,

so to oblige her she picked up the second parcel, which
was from Amelia. Inside that she found a pair of pearl-
and-diamond drop earrings, which she held up for Iris
to admire. Picking up the third box, she looked for a
card, but found none.

'How odd,' she remarked. 'There is no card with this
one. I cannot think who sent it.'

'Perhaps it fell off,' Iris suggested. 'I'll look for it
when I go down, miss. Open it and see what's inside.'

Susannah removed the wrappings and discovered a
beautiful posy holder. It was fashioned of basketwork
gold filigree, very delicate and pretty, and it had a large
diamond set into the rim.

'Oh, how charming,' she said. 'Do you see how it
works, Iris? You can insert a small posy into this and
wear it pinned to your gown if you wish.'

'It is lovely,' Iris said. 'It isn't just a trinket, miss;
that's a real diamond and a nice one. I expect your mama
bought it for your dance.'

'Yes, perhaps,' Susannah agreed.

However, when she went to her mother's room later
to thank her for the clip and show her the other gifts,
Mrs Hampton immediately asked who had sent the posy
holder.

'I thought it might have been you,' Susannah said and
looked thoughtful as she tried to imagine who else might
have sent it. 'There was no card. Iris thought it might
have fallen off and she means to look for it. Amelia gave
me the earrings. I do not think she would also have given
me the posy holder, do you?'

'I am very sure she did not, for we discussed what
we should give you,' Mrs Hampton replied with a
little frown. 'The trinket may have come from a secret

admirer, Susannah. If there is no card, he may not have wished you to know he had sent it.'

'Oh…' Susannah felt a thrill of excitement as she looked at the posy holder. A secret admirer! 'Do you think so, Mama? What should I do? I had thought I might use it to pin flowers at the waist of my gown, but now I am not certain….'

'Well, I should do so if I were you,' Mrs Hampton said. 'It is a little difficult to be sure, for you would wish to thank whoever sent it—but if there is no card you cannot.'

'Perhaps whoever sent it will mention it,' Susannah replied. 'Besides, I cannot return it if I do not know who sent it, can I?'

'I imagine you may receive other gifts as the day goes on,' Mrs Hampton said. 'You will almost certainly have lots of flowers, though that holder is rather valuable and I would usually tell you to think carefully about accepting such a valuable thing.'

Susannah nodded—she knew that it was not usual for gentlemen to send such an item unless there was an understanding. She could not think of anyone who would send her such a thing secretly. Had a card accompanied it from—say, Lord Pendleton, she would have taken it as an indication of his intentions to speak. It really was such a pity that there was no card, though if Iris were right… A little shiver went down her spine. She had put the incident in the garden with the Marquis of Northaven from her mind, and he had not been invited to her dance. He would surely not have sent it? No, of course not!

She smiled as she pondered on the identity of her secret admirer, but after a moment or two an odd thought occurred to her. There really was no one other than

Harry Pendleton that she wished to send her something like this beautiful trinket.

Now that was very strange, wasn't it? Susannah wondered why he had become so firmly fixed in her thoughts as the only gentleman she really wanted to admire her. She wasn't at all sure of his feelings. At times, she felt sure he would make her an offer before her Season was over, but at other times she thought that they were just very good friends. The uncertainty made her a little cautious, and yet she believed that if she were to encourage Lord Pendleton he might speak. She was beginning to think it might be pleasant to be married to a man she could really trust and like.

If Susannah were in doubt of the identity of the giver of the posy holder, Mrs Hampton was not. She felt quite sure that only one gentleman would have sent the holder and therefore she had no qualms about allowing Susannah to keep it. If it was discovered that it had come from a different source, it could be returned at a later date with a polite note explaining that the card had been missing.

Flowers and tributes poured in during the day. Susannah received several small gifts of sweetmeats in beautiful boxes, flowers and cards wishing her a lovely evening, but nothing that compared to her posy holder. These gifts were the acceptable trifles commonly sent on such an occasion, and she noted with pleasure that Lord Pendleton had sent both chocolates and a wonderful little posy of roses, which would fit very well into her holder.

She deliberated over what she ought to do as she dressed, but eventually decided that she would use the delicate trinket to hold the flowers Harry Pendleton had sent her. Wearing a gentleman's flowers was often an indication of the lady's preferences, and Susannah would not wish to give any of her other admirers the wrong impression. She knew that one or two of them might have spoken had she given them reason to think she would be pleased with an offer, but none of them had touched her heart. Only Lord Pendleton had become a true friend, one she would wish to know better than as a casual acquaintance. Therefore she would wear his flowers—and if the giver of the holder hinted at his gift she would thank him and explain that the card had gone missing.

It was very odd, for Iris had searched everywhere for the card and questioned the other servants, but no one had seen it. The only explanation was that it had become detached on the way to their house, and that was a nuisance. Unless of course it *was* from a secret admirer?

While it was exciting to think that she might have a secret admirer, Susannah had begun to understand that such a thing would only be pleasant if that admirer turned out to be someone she truly liked. The idea that a gentleman of the same nature to Northaven might admire her from afar was chilling and she almost changed her mind about wearing it. However, she decided that it must have come from a friend, because it was so perfect for her.

It might just have come from Lord Pendleton.

Harry looked for Susannah as he entered the ballroom that evening. She was wearing white, as she had been the first time he had seen her. Her gown was cut so that it wrapped about her body in swathes of silk and lace—

and at her waist was pinned the posy of pink roses he had sent.

He had not been sure that she would wear white, but hoped it might be so. His first choice was for red roses, but he had thought it might be too blatant a statement of his feelings. The last thing he wanted was to make Susannah anxious. Now he saw the pink was a good choice. She was also wearing the posy holder he had sent. He smiled as he thought of the message he had written on the card.

Wear this for me if you have forgiven me for whatever I did. I hope to be your best friend again. Harry.

She was wearing it, but he could not tell from her smile whether she had forgiven him. He was not sure what he had done to displease her, but it had made him change his plans. He had thought of declaring himself and suggesting an elopement, but he no longer considered it a good idea. He had thought Susannah might see it as an adventure, but he wasn't sure that she liked him enough to consider marriage to him exciting. He would continue to offer friendship for the moment and see what happened. In the meantime, he would begin by asking her to dance—he would ask for three dances, but she might only give him one.

Susannah danced three times with Harry Pendleton that evening. She had hoped he might take her into supper so that they could talk for a while, because she would have liked to ask him to forgive her for her behaviour the last time they met, but she found herself as part of a group of young ladies and gentlemen bent on having fun. It would have seemed rude had she refused their request to join them, for it was her dance and she was part hostess of the affair.

However, the disappointment was small, for Harry asked her if he might take her driving in the park. He suggested that she might be too tired the following morning, and arranged to fetch her the day after at nine-thirty. Susannah had decided that she would accept the next time he asked, and felt a warm glow inside when she saw his smile as she assured him she would be delighted.

He really was the most generous, considerate gentleman of her acquaintance. Indeed, when he spent some time talking to another young lady, who was reputed to be an heiress, Susannah knew a moment of jealousy. It was ridiculous, of course, but she could not help herself. However, he came to her before taking his leave, and his smile reassured her once more.

'You will not forget our appointment?' he asked, his eyes intent on her face.

Susannah felt a delicious little shiver down her spine. When he looked at her that way she was almost sure she was in love with him—and that he cared for her.

'I shall not forget,' she told him, her eyes brighter than she knew. 'I shall look forward to it.'

Susannah went to bed feeling tired, but very happy. She smiled to herself as she remembered that she had begun by disliking Lord Pendleton, but now she liked him very well indeed.

As she was brushing her hair free of tangles she thought about something else she had seen that made her smile. Amelia had danced not once, but twice with the Earl of Ravenshead! She had seemed to enjoy herself very well and she had looked happier than Susannah recalled seeing her before. There was a smile of content on Susannah's face as she got into bed and blew out her candle.

* * *

Susannah slept soundly. It had been a long day and she had danced all night. She did not wake until after twelve in the morning, and felt grateful that her mother had decided on a quiet day at home following the dance.

Several notes were delivered to her during the day, and a spray of red roses arrived. They were from Harry, reminding her of their appointment to go driving. Susannah took them up to her room, placing them in a tiny vase. Lord Pendleton had made such a point of the drive in the park that she felt he must be ready to speak. She thought that she might say yes, though at the back of her mind she was still searching for that elusive excitement. Shaking her head, Susannah laughed at herself. If she wished to be comfortable and happy in the future, she could do no better than to marry Lord Pendleton. It was time to put aside her foolish dreams of being carried off by a white knight. Having thought about it more sensibly of late, she had decided that such an occurrence would perhaps be more frightening than exciting.

She was feeling relaxed and happy as she went downstairs. She was about to enter the parlour when she heard voices coming from inside. They were raised and she could not help hearing what Sir Michael was saying. She turned away at once, for she had made up her mind she would not listen to private conversations, but the voices were so loud that she could still hear them quite clearly as she started up the stairs.

'I hope you are not thinking of becoming involved with that scoundrel again? I shall tell you now, Amelia. I will not stand for it! I sent the impudent rascal on his way once and I would not hesitate to do it again if need be.'

'You may not tell me what I shall or shall not choose

to do with my life, Michael. I am not prepared to be dictated to in this or any other manner.' Amelia was angry and her voice carried through the open door.

'You will listen to nothing I say. You were always too stubborn for your own good. Do not look to me for help when all your money has gone, Amelia. I dare say Ravenshead is sniffing around again because he has learned that you have come into a fortune.'

Susannah was halfway up the stairs by the time Sir Michael stormed out of the room. She had tried not to listen, but even as she retreated she could not avoid it for he had been shouting. What a brute he was to his sister! He did not glance Susannah's way, but stormed straight out, slamming the heavy door behind him.

Immediately, Susannah ran back down the stairs and entered the parlour. Amelia was sitting in an elbow chair, her face hidden in her hands. Her shoulders were shaking and Susannah knew that she was crying.

'Do not,' she cried. 'Oh, do not, dearest. He is an awful brute and you must not let him hurt you.'

Amelia looked up and the look of grief in her eyes tore at Susannah's eyes. 'I do not cry because of what Michael said—but because it may be partly true. All those years ago, Gerard went away without trying to see me, Susannah. Had he asked me then, I would have run away with him even though my brother forbade me—but he went without seeing me. I know that Gerard has had difficulty with his estate. It may be that he is interested now because I have a fortune. I am not sure that he cares for me at all…'

'Oh, but he does,' Susannah declared impetuously. 'I have seen the longing in his face when he looks at you—' She broke off in case she had said too much. 'Forgive me for my presumption, dearest Amelia, but I have seen the way he looks at you sometimes. I am sure that he loves you.'

'He has given me no sign,' Amelia said. She took the kerchief Susannah offered and wiped her face. 'This is foolish! It was all such a long time ago. I should not care for such foolishness now.'

'It is not foolish to wish to be loved,' Susannah said. 'Especially if the other person loves you.'

'No—not if the other person loves you,' Amelia said, returning her kerchief. 'How ridiculous of me to weep like this. I seldom do so, I assure you. It was just that we danced and I thought… But no matter. He has not spoken and I dare say he will not.'

'You cannot know that,' Susannah said and pressed her hand. 'You must not give up hope—and you must not listen to Sir Michael.'

'Well, I shall not listen to my brother, because I know that he intended to hurt and humiliate me, as he has so often,' Amelia said and kissed Susannah's cheek. 'How fortunate for me that I have such friends. I shall miss you when you marry, dearest Susannah. I have felt able to tell you things I could say to no one else, dearest.'

'I am not sure when that will be,' Susannah told her ruefully. 'Harry has not spoken, either. I do not know if he ever will. What a pair we are!'

'Yes, indeed! Gentlemen are so trying! We shall forget them and visit the milliner. A new bonnet will banish the blues as nothing else.' Amelia stood up. 'I shall tidy myself and then we shall go out.'

Chapter Five

Harry had been fencing with his regular sparring partner when he saw Northaven walk into the club. He frowned—he had not been aware that the man was a member here.

'That is enough for today, Monsieur Ferdinand,' he said and accepted a towel from one of the attendants. 'I am not sure when I shall find time to train with you again, but I have enjoyed today's session.'

'We look forward to your visits. It is seldom that I have the pleasure of sparring with so complete a swordsman. Even the Earl of Ravenshead is not as accomplished, my lord.'

'Thank you. I take that as a true compliment.' Harry inclined his head and turned away. He might have stayed for another hour, but he did not care to have Northaven watch him. 'Until we meet again.'

He frowned as he walked away. He might have to change his fencing master if Northaven and his clique were permitted here. It would be a pity, for Ferdinand was a specialist, but he did not want to find himself facing the marquis in a practice bout. He might be tempted to run him through!

'Leaving so soon?' Northaven asked, a sneer on his mouth. 'I came especially to watch you, Pendleton. They tell me you are almost as fine a swordsman as you are a shot.'

'I believe I am an adequate match for most,' Harry said. 'However, fencing for sport is one thing, fighting for your life on the battlefield is quite another.'

Their eyes met and held for a moment and Northaven looked away first. 'If you imagine I had anything to do with what happened to you and Coleridge in Spain, you are mistaken. Why should I betray my own countrymen?'

'I have no idea,' Harry said. 'Believe me, had I been able to find proof I should have had you court-martialled.'

'I am no traitor,' Northaven snarled. His eyes glittered with fury. 'I may not be as much of a gentleman as you, Pendleton——but I wouldn't have told the French of your intentions. In that you have maligned me and I resent it.'

'I heard that you were drunk, shooting off your mouth about it being a risky mission,' Harry told him, his expression hard, unforgiving. 'Surely you must have been aware that we were surrounded by spies? Even if you did not betray us intentionally, it was because of your loose talk that so many died that day....'

'Anyone can have too much to drink,' Northaven told him. 'If I did what you say, then challenge me to a duel. Let's fight it out and get this quarrel over. It has festered between us long enough.'

'Is that why you decided to take fencing lessons?'

Harry asked. 'I shouldn't bother if I were you. I have no desire to fight you, and if I did I should choose pistols.'

'You think I'm too much of a coward to face you with pistols, don't you?'

'I really could not care less,' Harry said. 'You are wasting your time trying to provoke me. I shall not challenge you to a duel—and you would do well to forget the idea. If I wanted to kill you, I had my chance when you insulted Miss Hampton. I did not think you worth the effort then and I do not now.'

'Damn you! You insult me. If I wanted you dead, a bullet in the back would do it,' Northaven retorted. 'Since you think me a coward and a scoundrel, why shouldn't I just hire someone to kill you?'

'Because you might die at the end of a rope,' Harry said. 'The best thing for all of us would be if you took yourself off abroad, Northaven. Go to Paris or Rome and fight your brawls there. Your welcome grows thin in London, believe me.' He walked away, leaving Northaven to stare after him, resentment and anger in his eyes.

One of these days Harry Pendleton was going to get what he deserved. Northaven had no idea whether or not his careless words when drunk had led to the ambush on Harry and his men, but he knew that all three of them blamed him for the death of the ten men killed that day.

Before that day he had been one of them. Since then they had treated him like a pariah—and he hated them all, Harry Pendleton more than the others. He would wait his chance for revenge! If it took him a lifetime, he would bring them down one by one. There was more than one way of skinning a cat...

He would find something—a weak spot—and then he would strike!

* * *

Susannah wore a new gown of green silk with a pelisse of pale yellow; her bonnet was green with a trim of yellow daises at the brim; her reticule was fashioned of yellow silk and trimmed with beads. She had York tan gloves and half-boots of kid, her hair peeping out from beneath her bonnet in a most fetching manner.

Harry's heart caught as he saw her. She looked so young and innocent, the very essence of spring, and he was a little sorry he had changed his mind about eloping with her. However, it was not the behaviour of a gentleman and he would never have even thought of it, had Susannah not told him that she craved adventure. He was pleased that his plans now were simply to drive her to the park and back. He might even speak to her during their excursion. He thought she liked him well enough, but in his heart he wanted her to love him wildly, passionately—the until-death-do-us-part kind of love that his saner side knew belonged only in romances. Yet if he married her without believing that she loved him, he knew that he might find it unbearable.

'You look beautiful, as always,' he told her as he handed her into his high perch phaeton. 'Are you quite comfortable, Susannah?'

'Yes, thank you,' she said, settling on the seat beside him. 'I have heard of your fabulous blacks, Harry. I understand that you have an extensive stable?'

'Yes, I have,' he replied and grinned at her. 'I cannot offer to let you drive the blacks—they would be too strong for you. However, I should feel privileged if you would allow me to teach you to drive something suitable. One day in the future, perhaps?'

'Oh…' Susannah's heart fluttered as she waited, wondering if he might go on to propose. However, as he said nothing more she went on, 'I should enjoy that very much if it could be arranged, though I am not sure how.' She rather thought it would not do to begin in a public park, though she would have considered it an adventure.

'It is my habit to invite friends to my estate in the summer,' Harry told her, though his gaze did not waver from the road. She glanced at him and saw a little nerve throbbing at his temple. 'My mother stirs herself to come down and play hostess. If Mrs Hampton would consent to the visit, you might both stay for a week or two....'

Susannah's heart raced. It was not a proposal, but it might be the first step, for it would help them to know each other better. They would be able to spend more time together at his estate. He would not have asked if he did not like her.

'I know Mama has been making plans, but, if you were to ask her, sir, I am sure she would consider it an honour to visit your home. She told me that she has heard of your modern innovations with the land.'

'Did she, indeed?' Harry gave her an odd look that brought a blush to her cheeks. 'It is true that I am thought to be forward thinking, for I have made it my business to experiment with new ideas, but few know of it.'

'I believe Mr Sinclair is an eloquent advocate for your good stewardship, sir.' Susannah smiled, a dreamy look in her eyes. 'Toby is such a charming companion. He sent me flowers yesterday, because he said that everyone sends them on the day of a ball and he thought I should have some the next day.'

'You find him good company?' Harry glanced at her, but she was smiling, looking about her.

'Oh, yes!' Susannah's eyes glowed as she turned to him. 'Toby is great fun, sir. We met him out walking yesterday and took a turn in the park together. Nothing would do but for him to join some children in their play. They had a ball and a dog and it was a noisy affair.'

'Yes, I can imagine it might have been.' His eyes narrowed as he looked at her. Toby was only twenty, perhaps a more suitable age. 'I dare say the children enjoyed it?'

'Yes, indeed. It was most amusing.'

'I imagine so…'

'I believe everyone enjoyed the dance,' Susannah remarked and smiled at him. 'It was a successful evening. Everyone has sent cards and letters to thank us.'

'Yes, I am sure they did,' Harry said, a little nerve flicking at his temple. He hastily changed the subject for fear of giving himself away. 'Did you notice that the earl danced with Miss Royston?'

'Yes, I did,' Susannah replied. The sparkle died out of her face as she recalled Amelia's brief lapse into despair after her brother's visit the previous day. 'I have decided that I will not try to promote their friendship further. You were right to scold me, sir—it is not my affair.'

Harry studied her profile. She looked serious, a little sad and he wondered at it. He would have liked to speak to her further and enquire whether her sadness was for herself or her friend, but they were entering the park at that moment and there was a press of carriages and people on foot. It seemed that quite a few of London's fashionable ladies and gentlemen had decided to take the air on such a lovely day. No sooner had they managed to get through the crush at the gates than they were forced to draw up to speak to a crowd of young gentlemen who wished to pay their respects.

Harry smiled wryly as the young bucks vied to catch Susannah's attention. She was even more popular than he had imagined and the wonder of it was that she had not received at least half a dozen proposals before now. He could not know it, for Susannah would never have boasted of her conquests, but she had already received three requests for her hand, which she had turned down with a smile, and would have had more if she had encouraged her suitors.

It was obvious that a visit to the park was not the occasion to make a proposal of marriage. Harry decided that he must be patient a little longer. He would write to his mother on his return home and ask her to invite the Hamptons and Miss Royston to stay at his home. If they consented, it would at least give him a chance of some private conversation.

On her return home, Susannah did not know whether to be disappointed that Lord Pendleton had not proposed or pleased that he had spoken of an invitation from his mother.

Mrs Hampton was of the opinion that she should take it as a sign that his intentions were serious. 'I do not see why he would invite us if it were not so,' Mrs Hampton told her and smiled. 'Did you give him to understand that you would welcome the invitation?'

'He had been saying that he would teach me to drive one day if it would please me,' Susannah told her a little uncertainly. 'I said that I would enjoy it of all things if it could be arranged—and then he mentioned a house party.'

'Yes, well, it sounds promising to me,' Mrs Hampton said. 'He does know that we leave for Bath in a few days?'

'Yes, Mama,' Susannah said. 'He said that he might post down himself soon and would have an invitation from his mother. I think the visit is intended for next month.'

'Which will give us time to see Amelia settled in her new house,' Mrs Hampton said and looked pleased.

When consulted, Amelia said that she thought the situation looked promising. 'At the very least, Pendleton must be thinking that he wishes to know you better, dearest.' Amelia lifted her brow in enquiry. 'Have you made up your mind what you will say if he asks you?'

'I believe I should have said yes if he asked me today,' Susannah said. 'As you know, I was not certain at first that I liked him, but he is such a pleasant gentleman....'

'Then I shall accept the invitation when it is given,' Mrs Hampton said. 'Shall you come with us, Amelia? I am certain you will be invited for it would seem odd if you were not, and Pendleton would never give offence.'

'It will depend on my situation in Bath,' Amelia told her. 'I shall accompany you and Susannah if I am able, for I have heard that Pendleton is very fine, but I have never seen it—though I believe parts of it are opened to the public occasionally.'

'There is so much excitement going on,' Mrs Hampton said. 'I think all this must be enough for even you, Susannah?' She threw her daughter a teasing challenge. 'I do hope Pendleton will not let you drive those wicked great brutes of his.'

'He says the blacks are too strong for me, but I dare say he may have others more suitable.' Susannah was smiling to herself as she went up to change for the afternoon. She had regretted that Harry had not spoken to her that morning, but if both Mama and Amelia believed

Harry to be on the verge of making her a proposal, then perhaps he would. She could only hope so—her dreams had all become centred on becoming his wife.

At the start she had been foolish, thinking him a stuffy bore and arrogant, but now she knew it was not so. She had dreamed for so long of a knight who would sweep her up on his white charger and ride off with her into the sunset, but that was all nonsense. Now she had a clear picture of a charming house where they would live in complete contentment with roses growing up rose-pink walls and two pretty children playing on a swing….

Susannah might not have been quite as happy had she seen the face of her prospective fiancé some twenty minutes later. He was scowling over a letter he had received from a friend, his own mood changing from one of pleasant anticipation to something rather different.

I hesitate to ask for help, the letter began. *Indeed, I would not do so, but I am at my wits' end, Harry. I am in such trouble! I became involved with some gentlemen—they were born to the name, but do not deserve it!—and now I am ill. I have debts I cannot pay—but that is not the worst of it. I beg you to come to me in haste, not for my own sake—I doubt that I shall last more than the week—but for the sake of another…my poor sister, who has no one but me and will now be alone. Your one-time friend, Hazledeane*

Harry crumpled the paper in his hand, tempted to throw it away. Frederick Hazledeane had been a friend in the years he had spent at Oxford, before Harry went into the army. He had always been on the wild side and

it seemed that his bad ways had led him into the kind
of trouble that might have been expected.

It was a dashed nuisance! Harry would have normally
been only too willing to help a friend, even one he had
not been particularly close to. However, to leave London
now on such an errand was not what Harry needed or
wanted. He was at a delicate stage of his courtship of
Susannah and he did not wish her to think he had abandoned her.

He must go, of course! Hazledeane must be in desperate straits and his sister was younger. If she truly
had no one, Harry was duty bound to help her as best
he could. He sighed because this was a duty he could
well have done without, but there was nothing for it. He
sat down at his desk and began to write a note to Mrs
Hampton, telling her that he was called away on business
and would hope to see her in Bath in no more than two
weeks from now. That would surely give him enough
time to complete his business in Cambridgeshire!

Susannah had felt some misgiving when her mother
read the short letter to her. It had sounded abrupt, as if
Harry had been in a hurry, and it caused a cold shiver
to run down her spine. She did not know why it should
have made her feel so apprehensive—after all, it would
only be a matter of a few days longer before he came
to Bath. Besides, they had been so taken up with saying
goodbye to their friends, returning books to the library
and picking up packages that had been ordered from
various shops that the time had flown.

The day for their departure to Bath arrived and they
set out on the journey in good spirits. Susannah could

not help looking forward to Harry's visit and the letter that might spell the beginning of her happiness.

However, she had determined that she would carry on as usual, and it was a pleasant surprise when Toby Sinclair came to call the day after they arrived in Bath.

'How nice to see you, sir,' Mrs Hampton said when he was shown into the parlour where they sat together. 'We did not know that you intended to come down, Mr Sinclair.'

'Oh…I posted down to visit some friends,' Toby said airily, but his eyes were on Susannah. 'Mama asked me to call on her, which I shall, but I think I shall spend a few days in Bath first. My visit to Mama is not urgent. I wondered whether Miss Susannah would care to drive out to see some of the sights—ma'am—Miss Royston? I have another seat in my curricle if you wish?'

'I think we may trust her to your care, sir,' Mrs Hampton said. He was a pleasant young man and his attentions to Susannah had become more particular of late. Nothing was settled with Lord Pendleton yet and there was no certainty of anything. 'I trust you have your groom with you?'

'Yes, ma'am,' Toby said, his eyes never moving from Susannah. 'Would you care for a drive, Miss Hampton? It is pleasant out today.'

'If you will give me a moment to collect my parasol and pelisse,' Susannah told him, 'I shall be happy to drive with you, sir.'

She was pleased to be on such good terms with Harry's nephew. If she had not liked Harry Pendleton so very much, she might have thought Toby a very good sort of husband.

'Lord Pendleton has offered to teach me to drive when

we visit his estate,' she told Toby when he handed her into his curricle. 'I am looking forward to it so much.'

'Harry is one of the best whips I know,' Toby said. 'However, I shall be happy to give you a few lessons myself. It would be too difficult for you on the road, but I shall be visiting with Lady Pendleton and Harry next month, and it will please me to give you a few pointers.'

'Show me how to hold the reins as we drive,' Susannah said, giving him such a brilliant smile that a passer-by grinned to himself and thought he had seen a pair of young lovers. 'I should be pleased to know a little before Harry takes me driving.'

'Well, you hold them in one hand like this,' Toby said. 'That gives you a free hand for the whip. Not that you need it often with well-trained cattle. I only use it if I have to get somewhere in a hurry, but you will drive at a sedate pace. It wouldn't be fitting for a young lady to race, of course. Not done at all.'

'Oh…' Susannah looked at him wistfully. 'Would it not, sir? I am disappointed. I should have liked to race—when I am able to drive well enough, and on a private estate, of course.'

'Dashed if you ain't a girl of spirit,' Toby said and chuckled. 'We might manage it some time—once you are safe behind a pair. You would have to keep it to yourself, of course. People talk so much, you know.'

'Do you really mean it?' Susannah's eyes lit with excitement.

'Yes…' Toby knew a moment of disquiet, for he had spoken on impulse. 'It would have to be our secret, of course. I do not think Harry would approve and your mama certainly would not.'

'No, she wouldn't,' Susannah agreed. 'However,

neither of them need know. We cannot do it until the moment is right, but I should so like to do something exciting—an adventure. It could not harm anyone and if it were in private it would not be scandalous at all, would it?'

'Lord, no,' Toby assured her airily and then wondered if he had been wise to encourage her. It did not seem that way to him, but he could not vouch for his uncle's opinion. Harry could be stern at times. However, he did not want to take the glow from Susannah's lovely face and it might never happen. It was probably just a piece of nonsense and she would forget all about it.

'Lord Pendleton should return soon,' Susannah said. 'We are being spoiled! A visit to London, now Bath and then Pendleton—I do wish it might go on for ever.'

'Well, perhaps it may,' Toby told her and grinned. 'I tell you what—we're coming to a quiet spot now. Would you like to hold the reins for a bit?'

Susannah's smile was all the reward he needed. She was a beauty and a good sport too. Toby wasn't sure if his uncle meant to offer for her or not, but she was certainly a dashed pretty girl!

Harry watched as the sick man signed what amounted to his last will and testament, making Harry his sole executor and the temporary guardian of Hazledeane's sister Jenny. The innkeeper and the scribe added their names and the innkeeper departed, clutching the small purse of gold that paid his debt in full. Harry looked at the solicitor's clerk.

'Tell your master that I will call tomorrow and discuss Mr Hazledeane's estate.'

'Yes, sir,' the clerk said and accepted the guinea

Harry offered for his pains in answering the summons. 'Mr Humberston will expect you in the morning.'

Harry turned back to the dying man. Hazledeane's breathing was growing more laboured. Time was short now. 'You understand that I shall hand the care of Miss Hazledeane over to Lady Pendleton? I am not the right person to care for your sister, Hazledeane. I shall rescue what I can from this mess, though by the sound of it the sale of your estate will scarcely pay your debts. What possessed you to play so deep when you knew you had mortgages on the land? You must have known it meant ruin?'

'They draw you in, Harry. You have no idea what kind of men they are,' Hazledeane said. 'I've known for some months that my chest was weak, that I had consumption. It was desperation, I suppose—' He broke off as a fit of coughing overtook him, the cloth stained with bright crimson. Harry gave him water and after a moment he fell back, exhausted. 'Nothing matters but Jenny. He wanted her, Harry. He said he would pay my debts if I gave Jenny to him, but he would use her and desert her. She deserves better even if I have let her down.'

'Save your breath,' Harry told him. 'You speak of these men—and of one in particular—but you have not named them.'

'It was him…Northaven…' the dying man gasped. 'I swear he cheated me in the hope of getting her, but I wouldn't…' His body arched, a bubble of blood issuing from his mouth as he twisted in pain for some minutes, then he fell back.

'You must rest and then tell me all of it—all their names,' Harry said, but as he bent over the man he saw that it was too late. Hazledeane had spoken his last, and he had named Northaven as the architect of his downfall.

Harry closed his eyelids and placed copper coins over the lids, then made the sign of the cross over the dead man. 'God rest your soul. May He pity you and give you peace.'

Glancing around the room, Harry picked up the few things of value Hazledeane had possessed and pocketed them, together with the deed of Hazledeane's will. He would make arrangements with the landlord for the vicar to be fetched and return for the funeral as soon as it could be arranged. For the moment he must make a journey of some fifteen miles to Hazledeane's estate, where he hoped to find Miss Jenny Hazledeane. She might wish to be present at her brother's funeral. Hazledeane had refused to have her fetched to his sickbed, saying that he did not deserve her forgiveness. Harry had respected his wishes, but he was not sure how Miss Hazledeane would feel about the prospect of being under his guardianship.

He sighed as he realised his business would take him a little longer than he had imagined, for he could not travel with Miss Hazledeane unchaperoned. If she had a suitable maid it might be accomplished, but otherwise he must find her one. The sooner he could deliver her to his mother, the better—and he was not sure she would thank him for it! However, he knew her well enough to believe that she would not refuse him. He prayed she would accept the burden, otherwise he would have to find either a school or a companion for Hazledeane's sister.

All he wanted was to drive to Bath to renew his relationship with Susannah, but he had been unable to refuse a dying man's request to care for his sister. He must do what he could for her and hope that his mother would take responsibility for her quite soon.

* * *

'Lord Pendleton sends his apologies,' Mrs Hampton said as she finished reading her letter that morning in the elegant parlour of Amelia's house in the Crescent. 'He will not be able to come for another day or so and...' she turned the page '...Lady Elizabeth Pendleton is to accompany them.' She looked puzzled. 'I did not know that Lord Pendleton had a ward called Miss Jenny Hazledeane, did you, Susannah?'

'No. He has never mentioned her to me,' Susannah said. She had been poring over a copy of the *Ladies' Monthly Journal*, but she laid it aside. 'But I see no reason why he should...do you?'

'No, I suppose not,' Mrs Hampton frowned. 'He says they will spend a few days here in Bath and then his mother and Miss Hazledeane will go ahead to prepare for guests. He says he shall visit us as soon as he arrives.'

'Oh, that will be nice,' Susannah said and smiled. 'I am sorry that he is not to come tomorrow as he thought, but it will not be so very long...' She turned her head as she heard the rattle of wheels on cobbles outside the house. 'Ah, I think that must be Toby Sinclair. He has come to take me driving.'

'Again?' Mrs Hampton lifted her brows. 'That is the third time this week, Susannah. He is paying you a great deal of attention, dearest.'

'Oh, it is nothing—mere friendship,' Susannah replied. She did not wish her mother to know that Mr Sinclair was teaching her the first stages of driving a curricle and pair, because she might not approve. They had, after all, been driving in public places, though Toby was careful to choose very quiet spots, and he kept a strict eye on the horses. He was a patient teacher and she had formed a strong bond with him these past few days. 'Excuse me, Mama. I must not keep the horses standing for it is very warm.'

'Run along then, dearest,' her mother told her. 'Do not forget we dine with friends at six this evening.'

'No, Mama, I shall not forget,' Susannah said. 'I promise to be home on time.' She went hurriedly to meet Toby, for she was looking forward to a little longer lesson today. He had promised that they would drive out of town and she might take the reins as soon as they reached a quiet road.

It was an hour later when the accident occurred. Susannah had been driving at a steady pace in a quiet country lane for some minutes. Toby was praising her skill with the ribbons when they heard three shots in rapid succession just to the right of the road. They had come from within the woods, and were probably someone hunting for game, but the horses took exception and bolted for their lives. Susannah was jerked forward and quite unable to hold the terrified creatures. Toby made a grab for the reins, but it was some minutes before even he began to get them under control—and it was at that point that a farm cart came out suddenly from a concealed entrance, causing him to swerve to avoid the collision. As it happened, the wheels of the cart scraped the side of the curricle, causing it to sway violently. In that moment, Susannah was thrown to the ground and everything went black.

It was a while before her senses cleared enough to discover that Toby was bending over her, his face ashen. He was patting her face and begging her not to die, which struck Susannah as rather amusing, for she was clearly not dead.

'Toby, pray do not look so worried,' she begged and sat up. Her head went round and round for a moment and then cleared. 'I am not so very much hurt. I think I can stand if you would help me.'

'Of course.' He gently pulled her to her feet, putting an arm about her waist. Susannah swayed for a moment, but he held her steady and she leaned against him until the faintness passed again. 'Forgive me, Susannah. You might have been killed and it was all my fault....'

'Nonsense,' Susannah told him. 'You could not have known the horses would bolt. Besides, we should have been all right if that cart had not come out so suddenly.'

'I should have taken more care of you,' Toby said, looking rueful. 'Please forgive me. Had you been badly hurt, I should never have forgiven myself.'

Susannah took a step forwards and winced. 'I think I may have sprained my ankle. It hurts a little.'

'I shall carry you,' Toby said solicitously. 'If you will permit me?'

'No, no I can manage to hobble to the carriage. What of your horses and curricle?' Susannah said. 'Are they much hurt?'

'The curricle has sustained some slight damage, the horses are merely blown, which they must have been after that mad flight. However, we shall go slowly to the nearest hostelry and I shall hire a pair to get you home. I think it best if we wait for your mama to call a doctor—unless you are in such pain that you cannot go on?'

'I should be a poor dab of a thing if I let such an accident upset me,' Susannah said. 'If you could help

me to the curricle and take me to the nearest hostelry. I
am a little shaken—a glass of wine, perhaps, while they
change the horses?'

'Anything you wish,' Toby said fervently. 'I am much
at fault, Miss Hampton. I cannot bear to think what might
have happened…'

Susannah touched her fingers to his lips and smiled.
'No more foolishness. Please help me to the curricle and
we shall forget this, for I am as much to blame as you,
sir. I teased you to let me drive.'

It was perfectly true, but Toby knew himself at fault.
Had anything happened to her, he could hardly have
faced her mama and friends—and he did not dare to
think what Harry might say to him!

Susannah's ankle was so much better by the time
they stopped that she was able to get down with Toby's
assistance and hobble to an outside seat while he fetched
her a glass of wine and had the horses changed. It was as
she was sitting sipping her wine that a large, important-
looking carriage swept into the yard and two ladies got
down, making their way towards the inn. A gentleman
followed them on horseback. He dismounted, spoke to
the groom and then turned to go into the inn, stopping in
astonishment as he saw Susannah sitting on the wooden
bench, sipping her wine.

'Miss Hampton,' Harry said and frowned disapprov-
ingly. 'What are you doing here?'

Susannah smiled up at him. 'We have had a little
adventure, sir. Toby is finding us some horses, for the
others are blown.'

'An adventure! What nonsense is this?' he demanded,
for it was most improper for Susannah to be alone drink-

ing wine in the sunshine at the inn. 'Has Toby got you into some trouble, Susannah?'

'It wasn't his fault, truly,' Susannah told him. 'The horses were startled by a gun firing three times close by and they bolted—and then, just as he had them just under control, a farm cart came out and—' She broke off as she saw the flash of anger in his eyes. 'It was not so very terrible and Toby says—'

'The young idiot may tell me himself!' Harry said as Toby came towards them, looking awkward. 'Miss Hampton tells me you let your cattle bolt? And you wish to be a member of the Four-in-Hand? It seems you cannot control a pair, sir! What have you to say for yourself?'

'Nothing that helps,' Toby said, looking guilty. 'However, Miss Hampton was not much hurt and—'

'Hurt? Susannah was hurt?' He swung round, staring at her accusingly. 'You did not tell me that you were hurt.'

'I—I fell when the cart struck us and banged my head,' Susannah said. 'Everything went black for a moment, but I have recovered well enough now.'

'You must go home at once and you should not be drinking wine in this heat, especially after a knock on the head.' Harry glared at Toby. 'What were you thinking of to bring her here?'

'I had no choice. We had to change the horses and Miss Hampton wished for a drink.'

'Then you should have given her water or a cordial,' Harry said. 'I shall take her home instantly in your curricle. You will take my horse and escort my mother and Miss Hazledeane. You will explain why I have left them to your care. Please see if you can escort them the short distance to Bath without causing more harm!'

Toby stared at him, his face red with embarrassment. Susannah threw him a look of sympathy and touched his arm as she followed Harry to the curricle. She tried not to limp, even though her ankle hurt, because she did not wish to bring another torrent of abuse down on Toby. Harry's outburst had shocked her. Poor Toby did not deserve it and she was not pleased with Harry's behaviour at all; he was arrogant, unfair and shockingly rude. It made her wonder if she really knew him at all. She had considered him the gentlest, kindest man of her acquaintance and it really was too bad of him to treat Toby so!

Because she was upset, she ignored Harry's hand and accepted help from Toby's groom, who was observing the shocking scene in silence. Susannah took her lead from him and kept a dignified silence as Harry climbed into the curricle with her and the groom jumped up at the back. She noticed the way Harry took the reins, how strong and powerful his hands were as he gave the order for the horses to walk on. It was odd that she had not noticed it in particular before. Perhaps it was because she had been spending so much time in Toby's company that she now understood the difference between the charming young man and his uncle.

Lost in her thoughts and feeling subdued, she did not speak once during the short drive back to Bath. She risked a glance at Harry's face once, but he still seemed angry and she discovered that she did not wish to talk to him. He had scolded her for drinking wine and he had unfairly abused Toby. She hunched her shoulder

towards him, deliberately keeping a distance between
them. He was too bad! To stay away so long and then
return just when he was not wanted, earlier than promised. If he had not come until the day after tomorrow,
as his letter said, he would have known nothing of their
adventure.

Outside the house in the crescent, Harry brought
the horses to a standstill, tossed the reins to the groom
and offered Susannah his hand, giving her no chance
to ignore him. To have done so would have been the
height of rudeness, and, even though she was still a little
bruised by the unfairness of his attack, she would not go
to such lengths to show displeasure. She allowed him to
help her down, thanking him in a small, polite voice.

'Forgive me if I have offended you,' Harry told her. 'I
was perhaps a little abrupt, but I was shocked and anxious. Had anyone else drawn up and seen you…some-
one may have seen you in passing. It is not as bad as it
might have been, for it was the middle of the day—but
you might have found yourself severely censured. To
sit outside an inn alone with only my nephew as your
escort—'

'And his groom!'

'A groom!' Harry dismissed the man. 'It could have
meant a loss of reputation, Miss Hampton.'

'It was my suggestion. We needed to change the
horses and…you were unfair to Toby, sir. It was not
his fault, truly it wasn't.'

'You are on intimate terms with my nephew. Am I to
take it there is an understanding between you?' Harry
glared at her.

'No! Of course not. How could there…?' Susannah
turned away abruptly as the tears threatened. How could

he even ask such a thing? He must know...he must know she would never do anything improper. The groom had rapped at the door; as it opened, Susannah went inside, managing not to hobble until she had pushed the door to after her. She went slowly upstairs, hoping that her mother and Amelia had taken their walk to the Pump Room, as they had talked of doing. She did not want to have to explain why Harry had brought her back—or perhaps she ought to think of him as Lord Pendleton, for she doubted he would make her an offer now. In his eyes she had disgraced herself!

Susannah went into her room, throwing herself down to weep until the tears were finished. When her maid came, she asked if she could put a cold compress on her ankle and the girl obliged. She wanted to summon a doctor, but Susannah refused. Quite enough fuss had been made already over a sprained ankle!

She felt hurt that Harry could accuse her of behaving badly—and to ask if she had an understanding when he must know she cared for him was the limit. She was so angry with him she almost wished that she had fallen in love with Toby just to spite him. She dashed her angry tears away as temper gave way to distress.

How could Harry think that she would wish to marry anyone but him?

In the morning Susannah's ankle was still sore. She explained it to her mama by saying that she had twisted it when getting down to walk for a little at a beauty spot and made nothing of it. She claimed that she was pleased to have a day sitting quietly at home.

'I have an appointment for tea this afternoon,' Amelia told her. 'Should I cancel it, my love? I shall sit with you if you are lonely, for your mama also has an appointment and I think hers is more important than mine. She has been asked to go driving with Lady Elizabeth this afternoon.'

'I shall do very well with a book,' Susannah said. 'Please, you must both keep your engagements. I have none until this evening when we attend the theatre and I shall be glad to rest my ankle.'

'If it is no better, I shall have the doctor brought in when I return,' Mrs Hampton said. 'Unless you would like him now, dearest?'

Susannah insisted that her ankle would be better after a day of rest and that she would be able to accompany them to the theatre that evening. Amelia and Mrs Hampton were reluctant to leave her alone, but after more objections they went and Susannah settled down to her book. She had read no more than a chapter when she decided that she was far too restless to concentrate. Oh, why had Harry been so horrible to her the previous day? She had longed for him to come so much and now it was all spoiled!

Susannah frowned and put her book aside. She got up and went out into the garden at the rear. It was not a large garden, but it was pretty and she knew Amelia had plans for the borders, which would mature the following spring. She felt wistful, as if she had lost something without knowing what it was. She found a bench in the garden and sat down, watching some birds squabbling over a piece of bread they had found.

'I trust you are feeling better, Miss Hampton?'

Susannah jumped and turned, startled by Harry's voice. 'Who let you in? I did not know you had been admitted.' Her voice was harsher than she knew and he frowned.

'Would you have forbidden me if you had?' Harry

asked. 'Forgive me. I wished to speak with you alone—but if you would rather I went...'

'No, do not go...' She blushed as she saw his look. 'I dare say Amelia and Mama will be back soon.'

'Your maid told me to go through into the parlour and I saw you out here. I think we are permitted the garden, for we may be seen from every window in the house. However, I shall not stay long. I came only to enquire if you had seen a doctor. Toby told me that you were unconscious for a short time.'

'Barely a minute,' Susannah told him. 'I did not wish to alarm Mama, and I am perfectly well. She does not know that I fell—only that I twisted my ankle a little.'

'I see—do you think that wise?'

'I wish to save her anxiety. I am perfectly recovered.'

'And yet your ankle is still a little sore.' His expression was serious, even severe. 'I came here to apologise for my outburst yesterday, Susannah. I was shocked to see you sitting there, apparently alone, and I fear that I was too harsh.'

'I do not think I deserved such censure.'

'No, you did not—but you must admit that you were careless of your reputation.'

'Perhaps...' Susannah glanced away, her cheeks pink. 'Your mother sent a note, inviting Mama to drive out with her this afternoon. They know each other a little...' She hesitated, then, 'I hope you still mean to invite me to stay at Pendleton, sir?'

'I do not withdraw my invitations or my friendship lightly, though others may,' Harry said. She glanced at him, but his friendly smile was missing. 'I shall see you tomorrow. I am glad you have recovered from your fright.'

'I was not frightened at all, even when the horses bolted,' Susannah told him, lifting her head high. 'It was an adventure and I enjoyed it—even if you do not approve of my behaviour.'

'I see…' Harry inclined his head curtly. 'I see that I have made you angry. Please excuse me, Miss Hampton.'

Susannah sat on long after he had gone, the tears trickling down her cheeks. She had quarrelled with him again and she did not know why. She wanted him to like her—to love her—just as she did him! She had not meant to do anything improper, but she was very much afraid that she had lost Lord Pendleton's good opinion. He had stood by her when the Marquis of Northaven attacked her, but this time he seemed very angry indeed.

Harry *was* angry as he walked away from the house, though he could not have been certain why he felt so very aggrieved. His business had proved more complicated than he could have expected, for Miss Hazledeane was not quite the meek child he had imagined. She was twenty, beautiful with dark brown hair and greenish brown eyes that some called hazel. She had thanked him for his care of her brother, but seemed reluctant to accept him as her guardian. However, when he told her that they were to go to Bath for a few days before going on to his mother's estate she had accepted with a good grace.

'I hope I shall not need your help for long, sir,' she had told him with a flash of her remarkable eyes. 'When I am one and twenty I shall have a small bequest that was left to me by my maternal grandmother. It is enough so that I can live independently. In the meantime, I would be glad to set up my own household—if you could arrange for me to have whatever Frederick left me.'

Harry had explained that she would be lucky to have a hundred pounds, and after that she had been more amenable to his plans, but it was clear that she was a lady with a mind of her own.

He shrugged—he had not asked to be her guardian and would have preferred to hand her over to a relation. However, he had given his word to keep her safe and he would do so—at least until two months' time when she gained her independence.

Miss Hazledeane was a mere inconvenience, but the matter of Susannah was more difficult. Before they all left London he had been on the verge of making a proposal and it had been in his mind to do so as soon as he saw her again. Now he was not sure how he felt. Indeed, she seemed to have abandoned her feelings for him. She had been seeing a lot of Toby and he was beginning to wonder if the pair were not better suited.

Once again, Harry was thrown into confusion. He was certain of his own feelings, but there was a reluctance to be married simply for the sake of wealth and position. He might have married long ago if all he required in a wife was compliance. He had this foolish notion that his wife should love him, at least as much as he loved her—and he knew that he would die for Susannah if it were necessary. While he would not expect such heroics from her, he did want her to feel that she could not happily live without him.

Perhaps he expected too much. After all, she was beautiful, charming and much admired. Most men would be satisfied with that. He knew that he must be a perverse creature, but he wanted so much more.

Chapter Six

Susannah was able to visit the theatre with her mother and Amelia that evening, but she did not enjoy it as much as usual, because as the seats were filling up she saw Harry Pendleton come in with two ladies. Her mother identified them as Lady Elizabeth and her ward Miss Jenny Hazledeane, whom she had met briefly that afternoon.

'Miss Hazledeane is very beautiful,' Susannah said and sighed. There was something about the other girl that made her feel an instant antipathy, though she knew it was unfair, for they had never met. She would not allow herself to dislike the other girl just because she was holding Harry's arm as if she were on intimate terms with him! She would instead make an effort to be friendly when they were introduced. 'Do you not think so?'

'Yes, she is,' Mrs Hampton agreed, looking reflective. 'I thought her a little cold, even reserved, but perhaps I do not know her well enough to judge. We only spoke for a moment. No, I was wrong to say it. She is in mourning for her brother, who died recently. His death left her alone in the world and that is why she has come to stay with Lady Elizabeth. It is hardly to be remarked if she had nothing to say for herself.'

'Has she no one at all?'

'No one. Her brother was once a great friend of Lord Pendleton. He was ill and Lord Pendleton is in charge of his estate.'

'Oh…' Susannah was thoughtful. 'Do you imagine she is an heiress, Mama?'

'I have no idea,' her mother said and glanced at her. 'You may be certain that the gossips will find it out if it is so—but it cannot matter. Lord Pendleton is not in need of a fortune. Besides, Lady Elizabeth was most kind to me, Susannah. She said that she would be pleased to have me visit her often in the future.'

Susannah frowned as she saw the satisfied look in her mother's eyes. Undoubtedly the two mothers had settled it all between them. Susannah was torn between a pleased feeling that an announcement was expected and annoyance that Harry should have taken her for granted. Before she left London she had been on fire for a proposal, but now she was uncertain. His anger at the inn—and when he called on her the next day—had made her feel that he must have a shocking temper. It was grossly unfair to give Toby such a set-down! He had also been very sharp with her! Surely she had not done anything so very terrible?

She tried to put their quarrel out of her mind, but she dreaded the interval, for she suspected that Harry would visit their box. Her heart sank when he did just that, accompanied by his mother and the beautiful Miss Hazledeane. The introductions were made and Susannah received a warm kiss on the cheek from Lady Elizabeth.

'I am very pleased to meet you, Susannah. I may call you Susannah, I hope? My son has told me many nice things about you, my dear.'

'Oh…thank you,' Susannah said and a faint blush warmed her cheeks as she looked at Harry. His expression was unreadable, though she did not think he was angry. However, he did not give her the warm, intimate smile she was used to receiving from him and she missed it. Had she lost his good opinion completely? 'You are very kind, ma'am.'

'You must have tea with me soon, privately, so that we may have a comfortable gossip; it will be best when we are at home,' Lady Elizabeth said and turned to the other lady, bringing her forward. 'I think you have not met Miss Hazledeane? Jenny is going to make her home with me for the time being. She recently lost her brother, as you may have been told, but we have decided she shall not go into official mourning since her brother expressly forbade it. So you must not think the less of her for wearing colours.'

'Miss Hazledeane—' Susannah dipped a small curtsy '—I am truly sorry for your loss. I have no brother, but should be sad to lose him if I had. You must be very distressed.'

'Indeed.' Jenny raised her brows. 'You are kind to say so, Miss Hampton, but you know nothing of me or my brother.'

Susannah blushed hotly, feeling that she had been slapped down. She had been sincere and had not meant to offer meaningless sympathy, but it was clear that Miss Hazledeane thought she had done so. She was too embarrassed to offer anything further and listened to the general talk, while she watched the crowd begin to move back to their seats.

'Jenny did not mean to be rude,' a voice said at her ear and she swung round to look at Harry. 'Her circumstances are awkward and she is upset.'

'Of course,' Susannah agreed, though she was certain the rudeness had been intentional. 'It does not matter. In her place I should not feel like talking much to people I did not know.'

Harry gave her a look of approval. 'It is like you to say so. I hope you will find her more amenable when you are staying with us. Jenny could do with a friend nearer her own age.'

'Yes, I expect she may,' Susannah replied. 'I am sure that is not impossible, sir. I am willing if she wishes it.'

'Thank you.' Harry hesitated and then frowned as the bell rang. 'We must return to our seats. I am engaged to take Mama and Jenny to the Pump Room tomorrow morning. I wondered if I might take you driving in the afternoon?'

'Yes, please,' Susannah said and gazed at him earnestly. 'I do not wish to fall out with you, sir. If I was rude when you called on me, I apologise.'

'I believe I made you angry,' Harry said. 'I think we should agree to put the incident behind us.'

'If you are willing to forget, then so shall I.'

Harry nodded. 'It would be a pity to spoil a friendship, Susannah. I shall call on you at two in the afternoon—and now I must go, for Mama is anxious to return to her seat.'

'I shall expect you, thank you. You must go…'

Susannah took her seat as the Pendleton party left and made their way hastily to their own box just as the curtain went up. Watching the play unfold, Susannah reviewed the brief interlude in her mind. Miss Hazledeane had clearly taken her in dislike—why? Did she want Lord Pendleton for herself?

Since she had no engagements the following morning, Susannah decided to return some books to the lending library. Her mother had agreed to go driving with friends and Amelia had arranged to pay a morning visit to Lady Jamieson. Promising to return in plenty of time, Susannah set off to the library. She returned the books, resisted the temptation to borrow more and crossed the road to the small tea shop where they sold the most delicious peppermint creams.

Amelia was very partial to peppermint creams, especially those covered in chocolate. Susannah went inside, making her way to the counter that displayed them. She had her back turned to the door when some people came in, but, hearing a voice she recognised, she turned her head to look. A lady dressed in dark blue with a rather fetching hat set on the back of her head at a jaunty angle, and a tall, distinguished gentleman, had seated themselves at a table in the far corner where they were almost, but not completely, hidden from view. A little start of surprise went through Susannah as she saw Miss Hazledeane and recognised the gentleman with her.

The Marquis of Northaven! Susannah felt cold all over as she observed the way Miss Hazledeane seemed to have come to life. At the theatre she had seemed to be cold and distant, but now her lovely face was alight with excitement, her eyes glowing. She looked like a woman in love!

Susannah looked away swiftly as Miss Hazledeane glanced her way, deliberately keeping her head averted as she bought and paid for her bonbons. She left the shop at once and walked quickly home, vaguely disturbed by the scene she had just witnessed. It was not her affair who Miss Hazledeane met, and it was certainly not her place to question the look of happiness on her face—but she could not help recalling Harry's severe warnings to her concerning the marquis. What would he think if he knew that his mother's ward had been having tea with a man he thought of as untrustworthy? She was certain he would not be pleased. He might find it necessary to scold or censure Miss Hazledeane.

Susannah could not tell him! It would be a dreadful thing to do, because she must not meddle in the affairs of a woman she did not know. To go behind her back with tales would be unkind and might be thought spiteful. If Miss Hazledeane chose to meet Northaven, it was entirely her business. Yet if anything happened to her, Lord Pendleton would think himself responsible and if he knew that Susannah had witnessed a meeting between his mother's ward and the marquis, he would be angry.

Susannah was uncomfortable with having to conceal it from him. Even so, she must say nothing. It truly was not her business to tell tales. Susannah thrust the scene from her mind as she went into the house. Amelia was just coming downstairs, having changed for nuncheon.

'I bought you some peppermint creams,' Susannah told her and handed her the little box. 'Lord Pendleton will be here soon. I must not keep him waiting.'

She ran upstairs, Amelia's exclamation of pleasure following her as she hurried to get ready for her appointment. Susannah had decided that it was quite impossible to say anything to anyone about seeing Miss Hazledeane with the Marquis of Northaven. She was not a gossip and she had no wish to bring censure on Miss Hazledeane—even though she could not truly like her.

'You look lovely, as always,' Harry said as Susannah came downstairs dressed in a dark green carriage gown. 'I am sure all the gentlemen tell you how beautiful you are, Susannah.'

'Several have done so,' she admitted with a shy look. 'However, it is all foolishness—besides, I do not think beauty is everything, do you?'

'No, though many find it so,' Harry said, giving her a thoughtful look as they went outside to where his groom was holding the horses. He handed Susannah up and told his groom to stand back as the tiger jumped up on the back behind. 'I shall not need you this afternoon, Jed. The lad is sufficient for my needs.' He smiled at Susannah. 'I think character and a good heart more important myself.'

Susannah digested that in silence. She was not sure what he thought of her character. She was a spirited girl and did not hesitate to say what she felt. Would he consider that an asset or a fault in her character?

'Good humour and kindness are important too.'

'I think I agree,' Harry told her. 'Tell me, Susannah, are you still looking forward to your visit to Pendleton?'

'Yes, of course. Your nephew has told me that the grounds are very beautiful, and you know that I love to walk and collect wildflowers—' She broke off, her cheeks hot as he glanced at her. 'It was unfortunate that your carriage came so quickly round the corner that day—but we have both apologised for that.'

'And then I shouted at you again after the accident just recently. You must think me a brute and a bear.'

Susannah blushed and looked down at her gloved hands. 'I dare say it was improper of me to sit on a bench outside the inn drinking wine, but it was such a lovely day and I felt a little shaken....'

'My concern was for your safety,' Harry said and frowned. 'Toby was an idiot to leave you there alone, but had I known of the accident I should not have condemned you.'

'I thought that I must have lost your respect.'

'My damnable temper. I was anxious and at such times I am liable to say things I perhaps ought not.'

'It is all forgotten. We decided to put it behind us.'

'Yes, we did,' Harry said. They had left the town behind now and were driving through some pretty countryside. Seeing a place where the road widened, Harry drew the horses to a sedate halt, threw the reins to his tiger and then offered his hand to Susannah. 'Walk with me for a moment, if you will.'

'Yes, of course,' she said, giving him her hand. 'It is such a pleasant afternoon, is it not?'

'The sun is certainly warm,' Harry said as Susannah put up her parasol. He offered his arm and she took it. 'I wanted to speak to you alone. I have something to say to you. Indeed, I meant to speak yesterday when I called, but we got off on the wrong foot, as it were.'

Susannah's heart missed a beat. Her cheeks felt warm and she wished for a fan so that she might cool herself.

Harry had stopped walking. He turned her to face him, looking down at her so seriously that her heart slammed against her chest and she felt breathless.

'You must know that I have a high regard for you, Susannah?'

She lowered her gaze, feeling unsure. 'I did think that you liked me when we were in London…'

'My regard is much warmer than liking.' Harry reached out, tipping her chin with his hand so that she looked up at him. 'I had hoped that you might feel something similar for me?'

'Oh…I do,' Susannah said. 'Not at first, but then…I came to like you very well, sir. Very well…' She did not know why she felt so shy all of a sudden. It would be more truthful if she told him that she loved him, but she was afraid to confess her passion, for his words had been restrained, cautious rather than passionate.

'What of this friendship with my nephew?' Harry's brows arched.

'It is mere friendship,' Susannah assured him. 'You must know that…I could not like anyone else…as much…' Once again she floundered to a halt, for she was unsure of how to behave. If he had swept her into his arms and kissed her until she could scarcely breathe, she could have shown him her feelings by her response, but this polite proposal made her shy of revealing the passion within her. Perhaps for him it was a marriage of convenience with a young lady he thought suitable to give him an heir.

'Then would you do me the honour of becoming my wife?' Harry asked, gazing down at her. At that moment his eyes seemed to smoulder with something much stronger than mere liking and her heart jerked. Surely he must love her?

Susannah swallowed hard, looking up at him, her cheeks still a little pink. 'Yes, sir, I shall.'

'I am very happy,' Harry said and bent down to kiss her softly on the lips. His kiss was tender and sweet, making Susannah long to melt into his body. Her hands were against his chest, but even as she began to slide them up over his shoulders, he moved back, releasing her. 'I think we should continue this another time, in a more private place.' Harry smiled. 'In the meantime, we must tell your mama—at least I must ask her permission.'

'Yes, of course,' Susannah agreed. She was aware of a slight disappointment, for she would have liked him to kiss her again…to show in some way that he felt all those strange and wonderful feelings that his kiss had aroused in her. 'I am sure Mama will be pleased that we are to marry.'

'I told my mother that I intended to ask you this afternoon. She knew what was in my mind and this morning was pleased to tell me that she approved my choice. When we go to Pendleton you will meet others of my family. It will be a chance for us to spend more time together, Susannah. Meeting in society is all very well, but we have seldom been alone. My estate is large enough for us to escape at times.'

'I shall look forward to it,' Susannah replied, her heart racing. It was foolish of her to feel a little disappointed and uneasy. She had dreamed of this happening so many times. She had been living in a dream world of her own, Susannah realised. She must understand that this was real and not just a dream. Harry was not the white knight of her dreams but a real man, with all the faults and passions that entailed.

'Mama and I leave for Pendleton in the morning,' Harry said. 'Miss Hazledeane too, of course. Mama needs to prepare for our visitors, and it is only fair that Jenny should have a chance to settle in before everyone arrives.'

'Yes, of course…'

Susannah felt a little guilty as she wondered whether she ought to tell him of the meeting between his mother's ward and the Marquis of Northaven. Jenny had behaved like a woman in love, but Susannah could not think that it was her place to report what she had seen. Perhaps at Pendleton she might have a chance to warn Miss Hazledeane that the marquis was a rake and not to be trusted.

'Are you looking forward to this visit?' Mrs Hampton asked as her daughter came downstairs two days later. Susannah was wearing her travelling gown of dark green cloth, and carried a lighter green parasol to match the ribbons on her straw bonnet.

'Yes, Mama, of course,' Susannah told her. 'Why do you ask? I am engaged to Lord Pendleton and it will be a chance to get to know him better.'

'Yes, naturally. I just wondered if you knew what to expect. Lord Pendleton has a very large estate, you know.'

'He told me it was quite big,' Susannah replied, looking at her in a puzzled way. 'Is something wrong, Mama?'

'Oh, no, nothing. You have been very fortunate, my dear. It is just that you will find the life very different…' Mrs Hampton nodded. 'Mr Sinclair is outside in his curricle. Will you drive with him or Amelia and I?'

'Would you mind if I were to drive with him, at least for a part of the way?'

'I should not mind at all,' Mrs Hampton said and looked thoughtful. 'It was kind of him to offer his escort, was it not?'

'Lord Pendleton suggested it,' Susannah said, 'to

make sure that Amelia's coachman did not lose his way. We have a beautiful day for the journey, Mama.'

'Yes, we do indeed,' her mother agreed. 'Ah, here is Amelia. Now we are ready.'

Susannah went outside to the waiting carriages. Her mother and Amelia were to travel in Amelia's smart coach, but she was glad that she would be in the open air, for the sun was warm. Toby smiled as he saw her, coming to hand her into his curricle.

'You look lovely, Susannah,' he told her with a smile. 'Green becomes you very well. Please make yourselves comfortable.'

'Thank you,' Susannah replied and took his hand. 'I think I must ride with Mama some of the time, sir— perhaps you will take Amelia up next time?'

'I should be delighted,' Toby said. 'I am yours to command, Miss Hampton.'

Susannah giggled as he swept her an elegant bow. He looked very handsome in his superfine coat of dark blue and buff breeches, his top boots polished to a high gloss. His cravat was tied in a new way, which she believed was a style favoured by the members of the Four-in-Hand. Toby had clearly decided that he needed to improve his image if he wanted to become one of that elite set. 'I am so glad we are friends,' she said. 'I would ask you if I could drive a part of the way—but somehow I do not think Mama would approve.'

'I am very certain she would not,' Toby said and gave her a rueful look. 'You must not ask, Susannah. I should hate to refuse you anything, but you must be patient and wait until we are at the estate. I dare not think what Harry would say if it came out, especially after he has forbidden it.'

'Yes, I shall wait. I was merely teasing you,' she said.

She threw him a look of mischief as he climbed up beside her and his groom jumped on the back.

As they set off through the crescent, she saw a gentleman walking towards them. He pulled off his hat as they drew nearer, giving her a sweeping bow, his gaze intent as he brought it back to Susannah's face.

'I wish you a safe journey, Miss Hampton,' the Marquis of Northaven said, a mocking smile on his lips and what she thought was a challenge in his eyes. 'We must pray that no unfortunate accidents occur.'

Susannah felt a chill run down her spine. There was something menacing in his look, but she could not tell what he meant by it. It was clear that he had never forgiven her for that incident in the garden, when Harry Pendleton had given him a tongue-lashing.

'What the devil was that about?' Toby asked and frowned. 'The damned cheek of the rogue!'

'Do you suppose he heard about the accident we had?'

'I do not see how he could—unless someone told him. Harry wouldn't and no one else knew.'

'No…' Susannah recalled the meeting in the teashop in Bath. It was quite possible that Miss Hazledeane had overheard something about the unfortunate accident. She might have passed it on to Northaven. Susannah would not like gossip to circulate—but there was nothing very terrible about what had happened, so it did not matter. 'Let us forget him, Toby. I think the marquis is not a very nice man.'

'The devil he isn't!' Toby agreed forcefully. 'He has tried to get me to sit down to cards with him on several occasions. It did not please him that I refused.'

'No, I suppose it would not,' Susannah agreed. She pondered over the incident for a moment and then forgot it in the pleasure of driving on such a pleasant morning. Toby's curricle was well sprung and they went at a spanking pace.

They made good time and it was scarce noon when they all stopped to partake of light refreshments at an inn. After their repast, Toby was as good as his word, taking Amelia up with him for the remainder of the journey, so Susannah was in the carriage when they reached the Pendleton estate.

They drove through impressive iron gates, which had the word Pendleton worked into the arch above them and were opened by the gatehouse keeper. However, it was half an hour later before the house was first sighted through the trees. The estate of Pendleton consisted of two farms, besides several other good properties and substantial woods, also a village of some twenty cottages, a blacksmith and a sawmill. Far larger than anything Susannah could have imagined.

She craned to see out of the window as they approached the house. It was extremely large, built in the classical style of pale buff stone with a main building and a wing at either end; the windows were long, square paned and many, and a colonnade of white pillars ran the entire length of the front. Four steps led up to the imposing front door.

Grooms came running as soon as the carriages stopped, steps were let down and the ladies assisted to alight. The front door stood open, several footmen already on hand and a housekeeper dressed in black came down the steps to meet them.

'Welcome, ladies,' she said. 'I am Mrs Saunders. His lordship is out walking with a few of the gentlemen, but Lady Elizabeth awaits you in the front parlour with some

of her other guests. You are not the first to arrive—we
have had carriages from eleven o'clock this morning!'

'Good afternoon—or perhaps it is almost evening,'
Mrs Hampton said. 'I am Mrs Hampton—this is Miss
Royston and my daughter, Miss Hampton.'

'We are expecting you, ma'am,' the housekeeper said.
'Would you like to go straight up? I shall take you up
myself, and send one of the footmen to let her ladyship
know you are here.'

Mrs Hampton thanked her and they followed her into
the house and up the stairs. They were conducted to the
end of the first landing and then up some stairs to a further floor. Here they were taken through double doors
into what was obviously a suite of rooms.

'This is the green suite, ma'am,' Mrs Saunders told
them with a satisfied look about her. 'Royalty has stayed
here in the past and the Duke of Marlborough. His lordship wanted you to be comfortable. You have two private sitting rooms and three bedrooms. When we have a
party of guests it is nice to put them together—especially
unmarried ladies.'

Susannah wandered round the sitting room while her
mother and Amelia explored the other rooms and settled
which would suit them and her. She trailed her hand over
the shining surface of highly polished mahogany furniture, thinking that she had never seen anything quite
so fine. The soft furnishings were a dark green-striped
satin, the hangings a paler shade of the same material.
There was a handsome bookcase, a desk and chair, as
well as a display cabinet containing *objets d'art*. Something she found particularly pleasing was a collection of
Meissen porcelain, little figures of monkeys dressed as
French courtiers from the previous century and playing

musical instruments. She took one of the figures out, examining it with pleasure until her mama returned.

'Come and see the bedchamber we thought you might like,' Mrs Hampton said. 'It has a beautiful view of the park and you can just see a lake in the distance. Pendleton is a large estate, Susannah.'

'Yes, Mama.' Susannah glanced at the fine paintings on the wall as she followed dutifully through the small hall into the bedroom her mother indicated. It was less formal than the sitting room, furnished in paler shades that she preferred, but still with that majestic mahogany furniture—making her very aware that she had never stayed in a house such as this one. Amelia's house was large and comfortable, but this… A little shiver ran down her spine. Could she ever be mistress of a house like Pendleton? Surely she was not worthy of the honour? There was so much she did not know. So many tasks that she feared might be beyond her. She had not realised until this moment just how wealthy and important Lord Pendleton really was. It struck her forcibly that her life would change completely once they were married. She had been living in a dream world, but this was reality! When Susannah had dreamed up her prince on a white horse, she had never thought beyond the moment when the prince took her into his arms and told her that he loved her.

As yet, Harry had merely told her that he had a warm regard for her. What did that mean exactly? Had he proposed because he could not live without her—or because she was suitable to be the mother of his children? Susannah felt a hollow sensation inside. Was she suitable to be any man's wife or a mother? And to be the chatelaine of such a house would be such a responsibility!

'Would you like this room?'

'Yes, of course, Mama,' Susannah said, becoming aware of her mother's odd look. 'I am quite content— unless you would like it?'

'I have chosen mine. Amelia and I thought you would like this one.'

'It will do very well.'

Susannah glanced out of the window. The view was magnificent and she could see the lake sparkling in the distance. Two people were walking towards the house. She could see them clearly, Lord Pendleton and Miss Hazledeane. Mrs Saunders had told them he was out with some gentlemen, but he had returned with his mother's ward. She had linked her arm through his and they seemed intent, engrossed in their conversation. Miss Hazledeane had a presence and seemed very sure of herself, as if she felt at home here.

Susannah could not help feeling a pang of what she suspected might be jealousy. It was very wrong of her, because Harry would naturally be on good terms with his mother's ward.

She drew away from the window and looked around the bedroom again. It was very grand, but she supposed she would get used to living in these surroundings after a while. She must if she were ever to live here as Harry's wife. She had thought only of love and romance, but now a few doubts had begun to creep in. Was she the right bride for Lord Pendleton? Could she do what was expected of her?

'Yes, Mama, it is a beautiful room,' she said, making an effort to smother her doubts. She took off her pelisse and laid it on the bed with her bonnet and gloves. 'It will seem more homely once I have some of my own things unpacked.'

'Yes, Susannah, it will,' Mrs Hampton agreed. She

moved to take Susannah's hand, holding it tightly. 'Are you feeling a little overcome, dearest?'

'I do not think I had imagined the house would be quite this large—or this grand, Mama. I am not sure I belong in a house like this....'

'But of course you feel strange at first,' Mrs Hampton said. 'We have never stayed in a house as grand as this one, I know. Papa's house was modest, and Amelia's— well, she makes one feel so very comfortable when one stays with her. This is a formal house, but I dare say parts of it are more like a home. These are the best guest chambers. We have been given them because we are honoured guests.'

'Yes, of course,' Susannah agreed. She took a deep breath. Her doubts were a mere irritation of nerves. No doubt she was not the first young woman to feel this way when confronted with her husband's home and family. She had yet to meet the family! She must hope that they found her suitable. 'I shall be comfortable here once I am settled, Mama. Please do not worry about me.'

Mrs Hampton pressed her hand. 'You are a sensible girl, Susannah. You know that you can always talk to me about anything that bothers you, do you not?'

'Yes, Mama, of course,' Susannah replied and smiled. 'Do you suppose we should go down?'

Even as she spoke, they heard a voice in the sitting room. Mrs Hampton smiled. 'I believe that is Lady Elizabeth come to welcome us.'

'Yes...'

Susannah followed her mother into the sitting room. Lady Elizabeth was greeting Amelia, but she turned with a smile as they entered, her eyes finding Susannah.

'Forgive me for not greeting you the moment you arrived,' she said, coming towards Susannah, hands out-

stretched. 'Mrs Hampton—Susannah. I hope you like
your apartments?' She kissed Susannah on the cheek.
'They are a little formal, I know, but it meant you could
all be together and I thought that might be more comfortable for Susannah. We shall be quite a large party
once everyone gets here—quite a few single gentlemen—so it is nice for the single ladies to have their
rooms together.'

'You are very thoughtful, ma'am,' Susannah said and
smiled. It was impossible to feel awkward in the face of
Lady Elizabeth's warmth. 'Thank you for arranging it
so....'

Lady Elizabeth's eyes were knowing, filled with
understanding. 'This is such a large house. When I first
visited as a girl I was situated in the east wing and I was
for ever losing my way. I once ended up in the gentlemen's wing, which might have been embarrassing. I did
not wish it to happen to you. Now, Susannah, take my
arm. We shall go down together. I was sorry that we did
not see more of each other in Bath, but it was a short
visit, because I needed to make sure everything was in
order here. Now, my dear, take my arm, I want you to
meet my friends. They are all eager to meet you.'

Susannah did as she was bid, laying her hand on Lady
Elizabeth's arm and listening to her hostess talk as they
went along the landing and back down the stairs to the
first floor. Lady Elizabeth was still a very attractive
lady with a smile much like her son's and Susannah
was feeling more comfortable when they entered the
large salon together. It was elegantly furnished, as was
the rest of the house, but the atmosphere was softer here
and the way the sofas and tables were arranged in small
groups gave it a more intimate feeling. The colours were
crimson, gold and cream, the furniture heavily gilded,

as were the magnificent mirrors and pictures adorning the walls. There were some fifteen or more people in the room, some of them known to Susannah, others not. She saw the Earl of Ravenshead and Lady Manners, Miss Terry and her brother and several gentlemen she did not know.

'My cousin, the Earl of Elsham—Lord Marsham and Sir Henry Booker,' Lady Elizabeth said. 'Lady Elsham and Lady Booker…Lord Coleridge and the Earl of Ravenshead. You must know that Max and Gerard are particular friends of Harry's.'

'I have met them both, though Lord Coleridge only once,' Susannah said, offering her hand to the rather large and magnificent gentleman.

'It is a pleasure to meet you again,' Max Coleridge said, bold eyes twinkling. 'Harry tells me you mean to learn to drive, Miss Hampton. I should be delighted to tool you around the park whenever you wish.'

Susannah smiled and thanked him, desperately trying to remember the names as her hostess introduced her to more ladies. Several of them were older, relatives who had not been in London during the Season, but were obviously welcome guests here. Lady Ethel Booker was in her later years and slightly deaf. She used a lorgnette to good effect, training it on anyone she wished to inspect, and for the moment that appeared to be Susannah.

'Not a bad figure,' she remarked to her husband in a voice that carried a little too far. 'Better than I expected from a country nobody.'

'Be quiet, Ethel,' her husband said. 'You are speaking too loudly again.' He directed an apologetic smile towards Susannah, who could hardly meet his gaze, let alone return the smile.

It was obvious to Susannah that Harry's family were watching her, to see if she would do, and she was much afraid that she would be found lacking. How could she—an ordinary girl—be the right wife for Lord Pendleton when he lived in such splendour?

When Miss Terry and her brother addressed her she answered softly without her usual sparkle, feeling crushed by the weight of expectation all round. When she saw Miss Hazledeane enter the room looking relaxed, self-assured, her cheeks refreshed from a walk in the air, she felt as if she would have liked to run away. However, pride would not let her give in to such an unworthy urge and a moment later Toby came to her rescue.

'Ah, there you are,' he said and smiled at her. 'My mother isn't here yet, but she shouldn't be long in arriving. My sister Anne will be with her. At least there are a couple of ladies of your age, Susannah. Most of the old *crusties* are here, but you mustn't mind them. Their collective bark is worse than their bite. Here comes Harry….'

Even as he spoke Harry saw them and came towards them, a smile of welcome on his lips. 'I am glad you arrived safely, Susannah. I was not sure when to expect you—I thought later this evening—but Toby tells me you made very good time.'

'Yes, we did, sir,' Susannah said and gave him a shy smile. 'I am very glad to be here. You have a beautiful home.'

'Pendleton is a show place,' Harry told her. 'I am not sure I would call it home. I have other houses that are more comfortable I may show you one day, but the family likes to gather here for a few weeks in summer. It is large enough to hold them all should they wish to visit, and I believe most of them are coming this year.'

A smile of unholy amusement touched his lips. 'I am sure I have no idea why. Mama assures me that she did no more than issue the usual invitation.'

'I imagine an invitation to Pendleton must always be accepted.'

'Good lord, no! There are a couple here that haven't bothered for the past five years,' Harry said. 'I dare say they have their reasons for coming this time.' His eyes twinkled at her. 'They have come to inspect the new bride—which reminds me, you do not yet have your ring, my love. I shall give it to you later.'

'Yes…' Susannah glanced down at the points of her white satin shoes. 'You have extensive grounds. I should very much like to explore them one day.' She longed for him to say that they could go for a walk immediately, but he did not.

'You may walk where you wish, of course,' Harry told her. 'However, I shall take you driving tomorrow morning and you will get an idea of where everything is. I would not wish you to get lost and come to harm, Miss Pendleton.' He looked at Toby. 'I visited the stables earlier. You have done well. I heard there was a suitable pair and I am pleased with your choice. You have a good eye.'

'Thank you, Harry.' Toby looked pleased. 'I would have suggested a walk to the lake, Susannah, but Aunt Elizabeth is determined to show you off to everyone,' he said as Lady Elizabeth came towards them with an elderly lady in tow. 'I can't take too much of this! I am off. I shall see you at dinner, Susannah.'

Harry looked amused as his nephew made a beeline for the door. 'I would emulate Toby and escape with you, but I am afraid you will have to smile and bear it,

Susannah. By tomorrow they will all have satisfied their curiosity and you may escape with me to explore.'

Susannah met so many people before she was allowed to go and change for dinner that her head was whirling and she was afraid she would not recall all the names. She had not been sure what sort of a reception she would receive, but everyone seemed friendly enough. Most of them greeted her with a polite smile and she did not hear remarks about her person from anyone but Lady Booker, who had a habit of speaking loudly because she was deaf. However, from the smiles and nods she received during and after dinner, Susannah thought that she must have been generally approved—for the moment at least.

Susannah could not help wishing that they might have had a little time together before all his relatives arrived. She was trying to accustom herself to the idea that she was engaged to a man she loved—a man she was not sure felt quite the same about her. She knew that Harry felt something for her, but most marriages were arranged for reasons other than love, and she could not yet be certain that she was loved, as she would wish to be—to distraction.

Susannah would have felt her situation a little awkward even had she been sure that Harry was in love with her; only a girl of spirit could have coped with being thrust into a family gathering of this nature, and Susannah refused to be crushed by the weight of expectation. She would make every effort to enjoy this visit and she could hardly wait for the next morning so that she could escape for a while to go driving. Perhaps by the time they returned she would have more idea of how things stood.

* * *

She was relieved when she was alone in her room. Her maid helped her to undress, brushed her hair and wished her goodnight and Susannah got into bed. The mattress was harder than she was used to and, despite her efforts to settle, she tossed and turned for some minutes before getting up with a sigh of despair. She would fetch a book from the sitting room and read for a while.

The moon was shining full in the front windows of the sitting room. Susannah found herself drawn to them. She stood looking out for some minutes, and then she saw the man and the woman emerge from the shrubbery. They paused, embraced fervently, and then the man turned and walked away. Despite the moonlight, Susannah was unable to see their faces, though she suspected that the woman was Miss Hazledeane.

Who had she been meeting? Could it be the Marquis of Northaven—had he followed her here from Bath? Susannah frowned. Harry would be angry if that were the case. However, she could not be certain. It might have been Harry himself, for he had seemed quite happy in Miss Hazledeane's company when Susannah had seen them together earlier that day. No, no, that was a terrible thought! Completely disloyal and unworthy. Susannah did not know whether Harry truly loved her or not, but she was certain that he was not the kind of rogue who would kiss another woman when his fiancée slept only a short distance away.

She would not allow herself to be jealous of the other girl. If Harry had wished to marry her, he would not have spoken to Susannah. Her mind clear on that point, she wondered about the situation between Jenny Hazledeane and her lover.

Should she speak to Harry or keep Miss Hazledeane's

secret? A meeting at a teashop in Bath was one thing, but secret meetings in the moonlight were quite another. Miss Hazledeane was Lady Elizabeth's ward and she ought to behave circumspectly while living here. However, Susannah could not be certain of what she had seen. It would seem spiteful if she accused the woman of doing something she hadn't—besides, it really was not Susannah's place to spy on her.

She sighed and put the problem from her mind. She had problems enough of her own. She was still sure that she loved Harry, even though he appeared to have a temper when roused, but she was having doubts about the future. She had promised to wed Harry and it was what she truly wanted in her heart. Yet how could she ever be mistress of a house like this—the first lady of an illustrious family whose ancestors had entertained and even married with minor royalty? She was, as Lady Ethel had said, the daughter of a country nobody. In London that small fact had not seemed to matter. She had been swept off her feet by all the adulation she received, but here in this house everything seemed different. She was very conscious that the Pendleton family were watching her—waiting for her to make a mistake? Or perhaps she was judging them now?

Why had Harry asked her to be his wife? Was he marrying her because she was charming and beautiful—a suitable match and mother for his heir?

It would explain his anger in the inn yard, Susannah thought. He had spoken of being concerned for her—but had he also been concerned that scandal would ruin her good name? His own name and family clearly meant a great deal to him. He had still asked her to marry him, but how would he feel if there should be scandal over that incident? She remembered the way the Marquis of

Northaven had leered at her when she was leaving Bath in Toby's curricle. If there should be a stain on her reputation, Harry might wish that he had not spoken! Oh, she was foolish to let silly things haunt her! Harry had intended that this visit should be a pleasure and it would be if she could put her silly fears out of her head.

Susannah hunted for and chose a book of poetry she liked, taking it back to bed with her. She read for a while, then felt sleepy and blew out her candle. As she turned over to sleep, she was aware of a feeling of disappointment. She was not sure that she cared to be married because she was beautiful and would make a suitable wife. She wanted Harry to be madly in love with her. She wanted him to kiss her, not as he had when he proposed, but hungrily with a passion that overtook them both....

Chapter Seven

Susannah ate rolls and honey and drank chocolate in the private sitting room with Amelia; Mrs Hampton had hers in bed, as was her custom. Amelia seemed a little quiet and she looked tired. Susannah suspected she had not slept as well as she might, but she refrained from asking questions. She was not as impulsive as she had been, and Amelia was entitled to her secrets. If she had news, she would tell Susannah, because they were friends.

'What do you mean to do this morning?' Amelia asked, as if making an effort to rouse herself from her reverie.

'Harry is taking me for a drive around the estate,' Susannah said. 'I do not know if he will let me take the reins, though he has promised to teach me.'

'Yes, you should learn,' Amelia said and smiled. 'I learned when I was younger than you. It is a useful skill.'

'What will you do this morning?'

'Miss Hazledeane asked me if I liked to walk. We

may walk later,' Amelia said. 'However, I shall not go down just yet for I have some letters of business to write. I advertised for a companion before we left town. I had several answers, but only one appealed to me. I have decided to ask a Miss Emily Barton to come for an interview when I return to my estate.'

'Oh…' Susannah nodded. 'Yes, you will feel lonely when Mama and I leave you. If—if I should be the mistress here, you will come and stay sometimes, won't you?'

'What do you mean, "if"? You are not thinking of crying off?'

'Oh, no, of course not. I—I was not certain where we shall live. I believe Harry has other houses…'

'Yes, I am certain he does.' Amelia looked at her thoughtfully. 'Of course I shall come to stay wherever you are, dearest, and I hope that you will stay with me now and then. If you were not mistress here, but somewhere else, it would be just the same.' She smiled. 'I know it all seems strange and overpowering at first, my love. You will be surprised at how soon you will become accustomed to living here.'

'I might have known you would see how I feel,' Susannah replied and laughed. 'I still love him, Amelia, of course I do—but this house…all those relatives looking at me as if I might suddenly grow another head! I confess it has made me wonder if I am equal to the position of Lord Pendleton's wife.'

'It really was too bad of Lady Elizabeth to invite them all so soon,' Amelia said and looked amused. 'I am glad you can laugh, dearest. Last night you looked so crushed. I wanted to comfort you, but I did not wish to interfere, for your mama will say everything necessary I am sure.'

'Mama is always good to me, but I know she has her heart set on the match,' Susannah said. 'She wants to see me settled and it is a good match, Amelia. Mama would not need to worry about paying her bills—I am sure that Pendleton would see her comfortably settled.'

'An excellent match,' Amelia agreed. 'But your mama wants you to be happy. Do not feel that you are trapped, Susannah. If you really feel unable to go through with it, you may withdraw—now I have said too much!'

'You could never do that,' Susannah said and got up to kiss her cheek. 'I am feeling a little...*trapped* is not quite the word. I think *unworthy* might be a better one.'

'Susannah, dearest,' Amelia said, 'Harry is fortunate to get you. I have found you quite the kindest, most thoughtful girl. Believe me, this feeling of being inadequate will pass. You will grow into the position, my love—and you will do it well.'

'You always understand. If it were not for you, none of this would have happened for me. I might never have met Harry at all.'

'I am glad to have been of help to you, but I should feel guilty if you married and were unhappy.'

'I think I shall be happy married to Harry,' Susannah said. 'But only if he loves me. I am not so sure that I shall ever enjoy being Lady Pendleton with all that it means.'

'I am certain he does love you, and you will grow accustomed to the responsibility in time,' Amelia said. 'But you must talk to Harry about this, dearest.'

A knock at the door interrupted them, and a maid came in. She bobbed a curtsy and looked at Susannah.

'Lord Pendleton asked if you were ready to join him, Miss Hampton.'

'Yes, I have finished my breakfast. You may tell his lordship that I shall be down in five minutes.' She headed for the bedroom as the maid departed. 'I must get ready, for I do not wish to keep Lord Pendleton waiting.'

Susannah snatched up the bonnet her maid had set ready for her, and draped a light stole over her arms, then pulled on a pair of leather gloves. She would not need a pelisse, for it was a lovely day.

Harry looked at Susannah as she came downstairs to greet him. She was wearing a carriage gown of green striped with white and trimmed with a white band at the hem. Her stole, boots and gloves were white, her straw bonnet trimmed with green ribbons. She looked beautiful and his heart turned over. He wanted to sweep her into his arms and tell her of his love, but before he could speak he saw his nephew coming towards them.

'You look beautiful, Susannah,' Toby told her as she reached the bottom of the stairs. 'Harry is fortunate to have secured you as his bride. I shall be riding to the village this morning, but this afternoon you must allow me to show you the lake from the other side. It cannot be reached except on foot.'

'How kind,' Susannah said and bestowed a warm smile on him. 'I can see it from my window and I shall enjoy the walk—but this morning I am looking forward to my drive.' She looked at Harry. 'May I hope that you will allow me to drive your horses, sir?'

'I have purchased a suitable pair for that very reason,' Harry told her and smiled as her face lit up with pleasure. 'Toby was my agent and he has proved a good judge. They are not mad devils like my blacks, but well-bred creatures that are used to a lady's hand.'

'Oh, then I shall be able to manage them more easily

than his,' Susannah said innocently, forgetting that her lessons with Toby were supposed to be a secret. Harry shot a sharp look at his nephew, who was trying to look unaffected, but failing. 'Shall we go—they will not enjoy being kept waiting, will they?'

'You understand your horses better than I imagined,' Harry said and nodded meaningfully at his nephew. 'I shall see you later, Toby. Would you be good enough to call on me in the library after nuncheon?'

'Yes, of course, Harry,' Toby said, a look of discomfort in his eyes. 'Enjoy your drive, Susannah.'

Harry followed Susannah as she went outside. She had gone immediately to the horses and was patting them, stroking their noses and admiring them. She turned to him as he came up with her.

'How lovely they are! It was so kind of you to purchase them for my benefit, sir.'

'You used to call me Pendleton. I prefer it. Sir makes me feel as if I am old enough to be your father.'

'Does it? Forgive me, Pendleton,' she said, her eyes clear and free of guile. 'I did not mean to offend you, especially after such kindness.'

'It is little enough,' Harry said, feeling cross for no reason. Anyone would think she was talking to a kind uncle instead of her fiancé! He gave her his hand, helping her up and taking his seat beside her. 'Would you like to show me what you can do?' When she hesitated, he looked at her hard. 'I know Toby has been giving you lessons—the young idiot. He drives horses I gave him as a birthday gift and they are far too strong for a lady! Now I understand why they bolted like that! He was not in control of them—you were.'

'Oh…' Susannah looked at him uncertainly. 'Please do not be angry with us, and especially not with Toby. I teased him into giving me lessons, you know. I did very well until the horses bolted and then of course I could not hold them.'

'I am not cross with you,' Harry said, though he did not smile in the way she loved.

Susannah looked at him a little uncertainly. He seemed serious but perhaps he was not angry. Some of the tightness eased in her chest. He had bought these horses to please her, so he must be quite fond of her.

She took the reins he held out to her, holding them lightly in one hand and accepting the whip he presented with the other. Harry nodded his approval. Encouraged, she gave the order to walk on. Immediately, she understood the difference, for Toby's horses had been restive, always impatient to be off. This pair of fine horses behaved perfectly, responding to the slightest flick on the reins.

'Oh, how lovely,' Susannah cried after they had been driving for a few minutes. 'So perfectly matched and such polite creatures. One feels that a society hostess has taught them their manners, for they would not dream of disobeying or doing anything outrageous!'

Harry burst into laughter, causing Susannah to glance at him, a twinkle in her eyes. 'Yes, exactly,' Harry agreed. 'I thought them just right for a lady to drive. I am glad you are pleased with them. One thing I would suggest…' He hesitated. 'If I may? If you place your thumb so, it might be a little easier. I find it better like this…' He placed his hands over hers, positioning them at a slightly different angle.

'Oh, yes, that is easier,' Susannah said. 'I have noticed before that you hold your reins in a different way. It did not occur to me that it might make the control easier, but now I see that it does.'

Harry nodded. 'It is a personal preference. Most of us have our differences. Gerard is a fine whip and Max is perhaps even better. I think Toby is getting there and in a short time he may achieve his desire to join the Four-in-Hand. He has been put on probation and, if he does nothing to arouse censure, will given full membership quite soon, I think.'

'I have driven my horses at a walk and a trot,' Susannah said, glancing at him. 'When do you think I shall be ready to race them?'

'Would you wish to?' Harry studied her face. 'It is not unknown for a lady to race her team on a private estate—but it is not encouraged. Are you brave enough to face the thought of gossip? And who do you intend to race?'

'Oh, perhaps Toby,' Susannah said, then remembered that she was about to become Harry's wife and ought to behave with the proper decorum. 'But perhaps I should not think of it. I would not wish to be thought fast.'

'It would be thought fast if the race took place in public, but some ladies have the courage and the credit to carry it off. Perhaps in a few months you might have sufficient skill to try in private, though I am not sure you would find Toby eager to race you.'

'Why?'

'If he let you win, you would be angry with him, but if he beat you, he would be afraid of being thought a bad sport and it might offend his notions of gallantry. I, on the other hand, would have no such scruples. You will have to work hard to beat me.'

Susannah stared at him in wonder. 'You would race me?'

'When I consider you have the skill,' Harry told her with a wicked smile that made her heart race. 'Now, I think you should give your horses their heads and see what they can do—don't you?'

'Oh, thank you,' Susannah said, her eyes bright with excitement. 'I shall keep you to your word, I promise you!'

Susannah had never enjoyed a drive more! As they approached the front of the house at the end of some two hours, during which she had learned so much that Toby had not thought to tell her, Susannah knew that she had discovered a pleasure that would last throughout her life. Any fear she might have had of handling the horses had fled as Harry put her through her paces, encouraging her to gallop her team for short spaces, showing her how to bring them back to a trot and then a walk. They had spent a long time perfecting a turn, and she had learned how to back her horses up, something she would never have dreamed she could do.

'You are a wonderful teacher,' Susannah declared as a groom came to take the reins and Harry helped her down from the curricle. He stood for a moment with his hands about her waist, his eyes intent on her face. 'I did enjoy myself so much!'

'Then we shall drive out again tomorrow,' Harry said. He smiled in the way that made her breath catch in her throat. For a moment she thought he would kiss her as she longed to be kissed, but he moved away from her and the moment passed. 'We must go in now, for Mama will expect us to nuncheon. I know you are engaged to Toby for the afternoon, and I have promised to keep my uncle Booker company on a tour of the estate, so I shall see you this evening, Susannah. Enjoy your walk.'

'Yes, I am sure I shall.'

Harry was being scrupulously polite, just as he was

in the drawing room in London society. Susannah felt a little bewildered. Was this the way they would always live? Behaving politely to each other, considering their guests and talking as friends, but nothing more? Susannah knew it was the way many couples lived, making the best of their marriages of convenience and taking lovers or a mistress in secret. Discretion was all, the public face everything.

It was not what she wanted! Not what she had hoped for when she dreamed of her marriage—but this was reality, not a dream.

She frowned and turned, walking swiftly up to the house. She must have the smell of the horses on her clothes and needed to change before presenting herself for nuncheon. As she was going upstairs, she met Miss Hazledeane coming down.

'You should hurry or you will be late,' Miss Hazledeane said as she came down. 'You would not wish to keep everyone waiting, I dare say—even if you are going to marry Lord Pendleton.'

Something in her tone made Susannah wonder what she had done to upset Miss Hazledeane. However, she passed by without answering—she had no wish to quarrel with her.

Having changed her clothes, Susannah went down to the dining parlour as quickly as she could. Most of the guests were already there, helping themselves to an informal buffet. Miss Hazledeane was standing next to Harry at the serving table, smiling at him as he filled her plate for her. She gave Susannah an odd smirk as she took the plate to the table and sat down. People were sitting wherever they wished rather than in the places allotted in the more formal dinner arrangements.

Susannah took a plate and joined the line, choosing some cold lamb, green peas and small new potatoes with a little mint relish.

Harry had taken his place at table, sitting between one of his elderly aunts and his friend Max Coleridge. She watched as he listened attentively to his aunt until she turned to the person at her other hand, and then began speaking to Max. Sitting further down the table, Susannah could not catch more than a few words of what they were saying, but she thought it concerned horses.

'How do you like Pendleton, Miss Hampton?'

Susannah turned to her right and discovered that the Earl of Ravenshead had taken the seat beside her. He was smiling at her and she immediately felt at ease, for his look was one of approval.

'I like it very well, sir. Lord Pendleton took me driving this morning, but I do not think we saw the half of it for we kept to good roads so that I could learn to handle my team, and I dare say there are many bridle paths that will be exciting to explore. I am to walk as far as the lake this afternoon.'

'You will enjoy that, I am certain. The lake is natural, though it has been enlarged and landscaped,' Gerard told her. 'Pendleton is a large estate, though not, I believe, Harry's favourite home. He has a smaller estate he favours when he has time to go there. I believe he spends only a few weeks of the year here.'

'Yes, I think he mentioned something of the kind.'

'These large houses are very well for a family gathering such as this,' Gerard told her. 'I would not care to live here all the time, and I do not think Harry does—but no doubt he will tell you about it.'

'Yes, perhaps,' Susannah said. 'I believe you have a fine estate yourself, sir?'

'It is not as large as Harry's,' Gerard told her. 'It was mortgaged, but I have managed to pay my father's debts. However, I am not sure whether it will suit me to live there.'

'You would not sell your family home?'

'Perhaps.' He looked thoughtful and glanced across the table, at Amelia, Susannah thought. 'I have considered living abroad, but as yet my plans are unformed…'

'I am sure all your friends would miss you if you did,' Susannah said and blushed. 'I am too forward, sir. I should not have voiced an opinion.'

'I invited it by speaking my thoughts aloud,' Gerard said. He looked as if he had surprised himself by doing so and proceeded to change the subject. 'Besides, as Harry's wife you are entitled to speak to me as a friend. I hope we shall always be friends.' He smiled at her. 'Now, tell me, Miss Hampton, how are your driving lessons proceeding?'

Susannah told him enthusiastically. She wondered why he had confided as much as he had in her—was she supposed to pass the information on to Amelia? She did not think that she would do so, for he must tell Amelia himself if he wished her to know.

After nuncheon the party dispersed. Many of the older guests had wandered out to the gardens, where chairs had been set under the trees so that they could sit in the shade and enjoy the sunshine. Susannah fetched her bonnet, stole and parasol, meeting Toby in the hall, as arranged. He smiled at her and offered his arm.

'I saw you talking to the Earl of Ravenshead at nuncheon,' Toby said. 'He is one of the members of the Four-in-Hand who will either approve or disapprove my membership. I rather wanted a word with him myself. He has proved elusive so far, but I shall see if I can corner him after dinner.'

'Perhaps in the billiard room,' Susannah suggested. 'Invite him to play and you may have a chance to speak privately.'

'You are always so easy to talk to,' Toby confided. 'I couldn't talk to most young ladies the way I do to you, Susannah. You are a good sport! You understand the way a man feels.'

'I think we are good friends,' Susannah told him with a smile. They were walking at a leisurely pace, leaving the formal gardens and the sound of laughter and voices behind. 'I am beginning to enjoy myself at last. I felt terrible yesterday, but it is better today.'

'You mustn't let the old *crusties* upset you,' Toby said. 'They are curious, that's all, mainly because Harry has never shown an interest in a young lady before. Not one he could possibly marry, anyway.'

'Never?' Susannah glanced at him. 'Not even when he was first on the town?'

'To my knowledge,' Toby said. 'My mother is delighted that he is to be married at last.' He pulled a face. 'I suppose it is time, but I hope Mama does not start making plans for my marriage next.'

Susannah went into a peal of delighted laughter, and then stopped as she saw his face fall. 'My dearest friend! Forgive me, please. It is just that I do not see you tied to a lady's petticoats. I think you enjoy your freedom too much.'

'Yes, for a few years yet. Besides, I dare say I would be lucky to get someone to take me, because I am something of a madcap,' Toby said and grinned. 'I suppose that is why I like you so much. You always tell me the truth and you make no demands. I suppose a wife might—' He stopped and pointed ahead. 'There's the lake—fine, ain't it?'

'Yes, it is lovely,' Susannah agreed, watching the play of sunlight on the water. Two swans were sailing majestically towards the far side. 'Does anyone ever go on the lake?'

'Boating, you mean?' Toby grinned. 'Harry took me when I was a lad, but I don't think the boathouse has been used in years.'

'Oh...' Susannah glanced towards the other side of the lake, at what was obviously the boathouse, though it had been built in a very grand style that looked more like a Roman temple. 'I thought I saw someone leaving as we approached, though I am not certain.'

'You intrigue me,' Toby said. 'Shall we walk to the other side and take a look inside? It may be locked, of course.' He offered her his hand. 'Come, the path is narrow and sometimes a little slippery. Let me help you.'

Susannah took his hand. However, they soon discovered that the path was quite dry and it looked as if someone had walked there recently, for the long grass had been flattened.

'Someone must have been here more often than I thought,' Toby said. 'Perhaps Harry intends to have the boats out this season.'

'Yes...' Susannah's keen eyes had spotted something lying in the tall grasses to one side of the path and she bent to pick it up. She saw at once that it was a woman's kerchief. Toby was just ahead of her and had not noticed, so she slipped the scrap of lace into her pocket. 'What fun it would be to spend an afternoon here. We could have a picnic and take turns on the lake.'

Toby was striding ahead now that he knew Susannah

was in no danger of slipping. He ran the last few steps to the boathouse and tried the door, giving an exclamation of annoyance as he discovered it was locked after all. He found a large stone to stand on and put his face to the window, peering inside. Susannah stood beside him, watching as he rubbed at the glass.

'I would not say anyone has been here for years,' he said as he got down. 'However, I dare say Harry would have it opened up if we asked him.'

'Oh, yes, we must,' Susannah cried, eyes sparkling. 'I should love to go on the lake.'

'We'll ask him at tea,' Toby said and grinned at her. 'I usually find the summer visit rather a bore, but it certainly looks like being more fun this year—and that is down to you, Susannah.'

Susannah laughed and took his arm. 'You are such a good friend, Toby.'

'It is a pity all females are not as easy to please as you.'

They made their way home, arms linked, laughing and talking, in such accord that anyone who saw them together could not doubt the real affection between them.

Standing at the back of the house with one of his grooms, Harry saw the couple and felt a twinge of regret. They looked so young and eager and he felt himself to be too old for Susannah, perhaps too set in his ways. She had promised to be his wife, but he was not certain that her heart was truly engaged. He knew that he could have offered for a dozen young ladies and been accepted, but only one had made him wish for her company on a permanent basis.

Susannah had seen him. She waved and then broke

from Toby and ran to him, her face glowing with health and the fresh air.

'We have been to the boathouse,' she told him. 'Toby says that you used to have boats on the lake, Pendleton—please may we have them this year? I should so like to go on the lake.' Her eyes appealed to him, making Harry's heart lurch. She was so very lovely, so sweet and innocent.

'If you wish it, of course. I shall instruct the servants to make all ready, Susannah—but I think it will take a day or two for them to inspect the boats and make sure they are safe to use.'

'Thank you so much!' Susannah clapped her hands and turned to Toby as he came up to them. 'Harry says we can have the boats. Is that not exciting? You must promise to take me in one as soon as they are ready.'

'We shall have a picnic by the lake as we used to,' Harry told her and smiled, because her enthusiasm was infectious. 'The day after tomorrow.' He offered her his arm. 'Come, we should go in, Susannah. Mama told me that she wished for a few moments with you before tea—if you will oblige her. She is in her private sitting room. I shall take you up to her now.'

'Oh…' She gave him a tremulous smile. 'I have hardly had time to talk to her since my arrival, because there are so many people and they all wish to talk to me.'

'That is why Mama asked for a few minutes alone.' Harry smiled at her. 'There is no need to be nervous. She is already very fond of you…' He hesitated for a moment. 'Susannah…I too have been hoping for a little time alone with you. I know that we went driving this morning, but you needed to concentrate on your horses. I feel we need to talk. Do you think you might come down to the library a little earlier than usual?'

'Oh…' Susannah looked shy, her cheeks pinker than normal. 'Yes, of course—if you wish it, Pendleton.'

'I think we must talk privately,' Harry told her and stopped walking. 'Here we are—Mama's sitting room. I shall take you in and then leave you to talk together.' He carried her hand to his lips, dropping a kiss in the palm. 'Until this evening, Susannah…'

Susannah discovered that Lady Elizabeth was as kind and gentle as she appeared, making her feel at ease and assuring her of her welcome at Pendleton.

'I am sorry the relatives have been so particular with you, my dear,' she told Susannah as they sat together in her elegant sitting room, which was comfortable and pretty, just like its owner. 'You must know that Harry has never asked me to invite a young lady to this gathering before. Now that he has chosen a wife, they are all curious. Our little visit here is usually just for the family and a few of Harry's gentlemen friends. Everyone was excited to meet you, naturally, but Lady Booker does tend to be rather outspoken, and she does not realise how her voice carries. I do hope you were not uncomfortable yesterday?'

'A little at first,' Susannah admitted shyly. 'I was not expecting quite so many people—or such a magnificent house.'

'Ah, yes, the house…' Lady Elizabeth laughed softly. 'It is rather awe-inspiring. When I first came here I was terrified. I almost broke off my engagement, for I did not think that I was suitable to be chatelaine of such a house. However, my husband was madly in love with me and he persuaded me that the house was not important. He promised me that we should spend only a part of our lives here, and he kept his word.'

'You were frightened at first?' Susannah was surprised, for her hostess appeared to have been born to her role in life. 'I have never stayed in such a large house before—and there are so many treasures. I am almost afraid to touch anything.'

'Accumulated over the years and worth a king's ransom in themselves,' Lady Elizabeth agreed. 'Harry is the custodian of Pendleton, Susannah. His duty is to preserve the estate and its treasures for his sons, and he takes such things very seriously. Perhaps too seriously. He was very different as a young man, but he has had much to do to ensure that the estate is in good shape. However, I am very certain that he will not wish to live here all the time.' She gave Susannah a reassuring nod. 'His apartments are in the west wing. I have no doubt he will show you one day. If you wish it, I shall take you on a tour of the rest of the house tomorrow, after you return from driving with my son.'

Susannah looked at her thoughtfully. 'Do you think that I would be a worthy chatelaine of a house like this, ma'am?'

'Please, you must call me Elizabeth in private.' Lady Elizabeth's smile was warm. 'If you make my son happy, that is all I ask, my dear. As for the rest—I shall always be near at hand if you need me. I should not dream of interfering, but if you wish for help I am always ready to give it. I can teach you the things you need to know. Besides, the servants are so well trained that you will hardly need to do anything except keep your accounts and inspect the menus.'

'Oh…' Susannah blushed. 'I shall try, but I am sure there must be much more to marriage.'

Lady Elizabeth smiled gently. 'Harry will teach you, my dear. My son is meticulous in all things.'

'Yes, he is,' Susannah agreed. She could not tell her kind hostess that Harry's attention to detail and preference for perfection were exactly what frightened her. 'I am not certain that I can live up to his example, ma'am.'

Lady Elizabeth went into a peal of laughter. 'Oh, my dear, do not put my son on a pedestal. I assure you that he has his failings, as you will no doubt discover before too long.'

'I know that he has a temper sometimes…'

'He is also very untidy and he can be both arrogant and blind to something that is under his nose. However, he is very dear to me and the kindest of men.'

'Yes,' Susannah said and smiled. She liked Harry's mother very well indeed, and this little talk had made her feel better.

Susannah chose a simple white evening dress, which she wore with a spangled stole and a string of seed pearls. She had some pearl earrings her mama had given her and she chose those to finish her ensemble. She was trembling inside as she left the apartments she shared with her mother and Amelia and made her way to the library.

Entering, she saw that Harry was standing by the fireplace. He was dressed in a coat of blue superfine and pale cream breeches, his cravat a miracle of his valet's art and set off by a magnificent diamond pin. On the little finger of his right hand he wore a diamond ring that sparkled in the light of the candles. He smiled as she entered, his gaze intent as she walked towards him.

'You look beautiful, as always, Susannah. Thank you for coming so promptly.'

'I knew you were waiting for me,' Susannah said and

smiled at him a little uncertainly. 'You wished to talk to me?'

'Yes.' Harry reached for her hand, taking it and kissing it, as he had earlier. Susannah felt a tingle down her spine as she looked up and saw his hot gaze. She could no longer doubt that he had feelings for her. 'I wanted to give you this...' He took her left hand and slipped a beautiful diamond-and-emerald ring onto the third finger of her left hand. 'I ought to have given you a ring sooner, but I had this made specially and it arrived this afternoon.'

'Thank you. It is lovely, but...' She hesitated, gazing up at him earnestly. 'Are you certain that I am worthy to be your wife? I know you offered and I accepted, but... are you perfectly sure that you truly want me?'

'Worthy...' Harry frowned. 'I suppose you mean this wretched house and its treasures? You will discover that they are a liability we have to cope with as best we can. If I could please myself, I should sell them and live modestly, but we are merely the custodians and must preserve them for the future.'

'Your mama explained,' Susannah told him shyly. 'She said that she too felt overcome when she first came here and almost broke off her engagement.'

'Yes, she told me that too.' Harry laughed wryly. He moved closer, reaching out to touch her face. His fingers stroked her cheek lightly, sending little shivers up and down Susannah's spine and making her long for something that she did not understand. 'How can you doubt that I want you, Susannah? I have thought that perhaps it was not fair to expect so much of you. The house is a responsibility, of course, and I am older...'

'But I care for you,' Susannah said impulsively.

'Surely that is more important than any other consid-
erations?'

'My wise little love,' Harry said in voice made deep
by emotion. 'I shall speak to your mama about the date
of the wedding, but we shall not rush, for we need to
know each other better, I think.'

Susannah looked at her ring. The emerald was a
bright, clear green and flawless, the diamonds surround-
ing it brilliant and white.

'It is beautiful,' she breathed. 'I have never seen
anything as lovely. Thank you so much for giving it to
me.'

'It pales into insignificance beside your beauty,'
Harry said. He reached for her, drawing her close and
kissing her softly on the lips. 'I have been wanting to
kiss you all day, but it is difficult to be alone with you
while everyone is here. Perhaps you will allow me to
teach you the ways of love, dearest? You are very young
and I prefer to take things slowly.'

'Do you, Harry?' Susannah's eyes were bright with
mischief. She felt a surge of confidence as she saw the
heat in his eyes. 'I rather think I should like you to kiss
me again, please.'

'Minx!' Harry laughed and drew her hard against
him, kissing her in a way that took her breath and was
very different from the first kiss. She trembled as she
felt a rush of desire, awakening feelings she had not
realised existed. 'You will get more of that if you tease
me, miss!'

'Shall I?' Susannah asked and giggled. 'Then I must
think of ways to tease you, sir.'

'What happened to Harry?' he asked, his eyes on
fire. 'You used my name just now and I like it. I think
you will lead me a pretty dance, Susannah, but you have

found the way to my heart and I am never happy unless you are near. I suppose we must go and face them all now, my love. My fond relatives have been eagerly awaiting the arrival of my bride. It is our duty to entertain them.'

'Did you know that Toby calls them the old *crusties*?' Susannah said innocently. She laughed as she saw his expression. 'Yes, it is too bad of him, isn't it?'

'He will lead you into trouble or you him,' Harry said and looked resigned. 'Come along then, Susannah. Dinner awaits us....'

Now that she was wearing the ring, everyone decided that their engagement was official. Before this evening the relatives had been watching her curiously, but now the barriers were down and they all tried to talk at once, wanting to be the first to wish her happiness. Susannah thought she would drown under the weight of congratulations. Everyone came to kiss her and the gentlemen shook Harry's hand. Lady Elizabeth presented her with a small gift, which turned out to be a beautiful pearl necklace.

'I thought he might give you the ring this evening and I brought this with me just in case,' she told Susannah. 'I am so pleased, my dear. Everyone is happy that Harry will be settled at last. We had begun to think he might never marry.'

Toby's mother, Lady Sinclair, added her good wishes. 'I am very fond of my brother. I have been telling Harry to find a bride for the past two years. He could not have chosen better, Susannah. I am so pleased that you accepted him, my dear. I shall look forward to having a sister.'

Since everyone seemed of the same opinion, Susannah

was carried through the evening on a wave of excitement. Harry's relatives had accepted her; they were willing to give her a chance to prove herself and she knew that she must not let them down.

'I wish you all the happiness in the world,' Toby said and kissed her cheek. 'I have a gift for you. I shall give it to you tomorrow.'

'Thank you.' Susannah smiled and glanced at Harry, surprising an odd look in his eyes. He looked serious… no, there was some other emotion in his eyes, but she was not certain of its meaning.

Toby moved on and she saw him talking with Amelia. Susannah found herself alone for the first time that evening.

'You must be very pleased with yourself. Pendleton is a wonderful catch for a girl like you.'

Susannah turned as she heard Miss Hazledeane's voice. It was clear that she was both annoyed and jealous, her eyes hard with dislike. Susannah wondered if she had hoped to catch Harry for herself.

'I am very fortunate,' she said, keeping a fixed smile in place. For some reason her eyes were drawn to a lace kerchief tucked into the sash at Miss Hazledeane's waist. She knew at once that it was exactly like the one she had found near the lake. 'Have you lost a kerchief? I found one near the boathouse this afternoon. It is in my room.'

'It cannot be mine,' Miss Hazledeane said and, if anything, her look of dislike deepened. 'I do not know why you should think it. I have never been there.'

'Oh…' Susannah frowned—she would swear that the kerchief matched the one Miss Hazledeane had and her perfume was the same as that which lingered on the kerchief. 'I must be mistaken, then.'

'Yes, you are. Besides, my kerchief is a gift from Lady Elizabeth, so if you found one it is most probably hers.'

'Perhaps…' Susannah was thoughtful as the other woman moved away from her. It had been clear to her from the beginning that Lady Elizabeth's ward did not like her. However, why stress the point that it was not her kerchief so strongly? There could be no harm in her having dropped it near the boathouse.

'Well, dearest,' Harry said, driving the thought from her head. 'We must go into dinner or my chef will hand in his notice and that would be a disaster. I have engaged to play billiards with Gerard and Max later—but if I do not see you alone again this evening I wish you sweet dreams.' He pressed her hand. 'Do not forget our arrangement for the morning, my love. I cannot wait to get you to myself again. There are far too many people here….'

Susannah laughed, forgetting the small mystery of Miss Hazledeane's kerchief. She would return it to Lady Elizabeth in the morning and then perhaps the mystery would be solved.

Chapter Eight

Susannah left the kerchief lying on the chest in her bedchamber when she went driving with Harry the next morning. It had slipped her mind in the excitement, for she had found a pile of presents by her plate when she took breakfast with Amelia in their sitting room. Everyone had sent her something—some were small gifts like lace kerchiefs, but there were several gifts of silver, and one that she liked very much was a whip of soft leather with a chased silver grip from Toby.

'Isn't that thoughtful of him?' she said, showing it to Amelia. 'Lady Elizabeth gave me those beautiful pearls last evening—and now all these. I am so fortunate.'

'They are merely tokens of affection,' Amelia told her, giving her a small box, which contained a gold stickpin to wear in her cravat when she went riding or driving. 'I am certain you will receive many more expensive gifts when you marry.'

'But everyone is so kind,' Susannah said. 'You in particular have given me so much, Amelia. I owe everything to you!'

'I have done very little,' Amelia told her. 'It was your own sweet nature that secured you Harry Pendleton's affections. However, I should like to give you a wedding at my estate—unless you plan to marry here at Pendleton?'

'I do not know,' Susannah said. 'I think I should like to be married from your house, Amelia, but I must ask Harry what he thinks. Are you sure you would wish all the trouble and expense of a wedding?'

'It would give me the greatest pleasure,' Amelia said. 'If you would prefer it, I could speak to Harry and ask him if he would be agreeable to letting me give you the wedding as my gift to you both.'

'Yes, perhaps that might be best,' Susannah agreed happily. 'And now I must go down, for I do not wish to keep Harry waiting.'

'No, you must not keep him waiting,' Amelia told her. 'I shall speak to Harry about the wedding this afternoon. Have you any idea of when it might be?'

'We have not discussed it as yet,' Susannah said. 'Perhaps I shall know more when I return.'

'Yes, I am sure you will,' Amelia said. 'I believe I shall go for a walk this morning. The weather has been so lovely of late. I am not sure how long it will last.'

'Oh, I hope it will not break before tomorrow,' Susannah said. 'Harry has promised us a picnic by the lake.' She smiled because everything was so wonderful and nothing could possibly spoil her happiness now.

That morning's expedition proved even better than her first attempt at driving Harry's horses. Harry was solicitous for her comfort and did everything possible to make the outing a happy one for her. They drove through the park and reached a secluded area, well out of sight of the house, and there he suggested they stopped, looping the reins and securing them, before helping Susannah down.

'The horses will do well enough under the trees for a few minutes,' he told her, his smile making her heart race. 'I thought we would walk for a moment, because I cannot kiss you as I would wish to in the curricle.'

'Harry…' Susannah was breathless as he took her into his arms, gazing down at her with such heat that she felt a tingle of something she realised must be desire. Her heart raced as his lips touched hers, her body melting into him, her own lips parting as she felt the touch of his tongue. His kiss made her feel very strange and filled her with longing for things she hardly understood. He caressed her cheek and pressed his lips to her throat, making her whimper his name. 'Harry…I do like that very much…'

'Do you, my dearest?' His hand caressed her breast over the softness of her habit, making her stomach spasm with desire. She wished that there was nothing between his hand and her skin, for she would have enjoyed the feel of his fingers on her flesh, but she did not dare to say it. 'I like it very much too. I want so much more of you, Susannah. I had planned to wait, but would you mind very much if we were to marry as soon as the banns are called?'

'I should like that,' she said and gave him a shy smile. 'Amelia is going to ask if you would permit her to hold the wedding at her home. I was not sure…'

'Is that your wish?' Harry asked, gazing at her. 'We must invite all my relatives and it would be easy here, but if you should like it I will agree to holding it at Amelia's home.'

'I think I should like it,' Susannah told him. 'Could

we not have a small wedding at Amelia's and then hold a large reception here for everyone?'

'Yes, we could,' Harry agreed. 'I think I should quite like a quiet wedding myself—perhaps twenty or thirty of our closest friends and relatives. Mama would enjoy giving a huge reception here a day or so later.'

'Then perhaps you would suggest that to Amelia when she speaks to you?'

'Certainly,' Harry agreed. 'We shall say one month from now—and that will give me time to make some changes to my apartments here. I had them refurbished a year or so ago, but you may wish for changes.'

'Oh, I should like to see them as they are now—will you show me?'

'Yes, of course. You might like to help choose the colours for your own bedchamber?'

'I think that would be fun,' Susannah told him. 'Amelia had made changes to her aunt's home and I thought she had done them so beautifully that I would enjoy doing something similar one day.'

'You may make as many changes to my homes as you please,' Harry said. 'I think perhaps—' He broke off as they both heard screaming and the sounds of a struggle. 'That sounds as if it is coming from over there...look! Is that not Amelia?'

'Yes...' Susannah saw her friend running towards them. She appeared to be in great distress. Without thinking, Susannah ran to meet her, Harry close behind. 'Amelia...what is it? What has happened to you?'

Amelia stopped, gasping for breath and holding her side. Her dress had been torn and it was clear that she was in some distress. Her eyes sought out Harry as she gathered her breath and panted out the words, 'I was attacked...two men...back there...' She pointed in the direction she had come. 'I think they were trying to abduct me, though I cannot be sure it was not just an attempt to rob me. I struggled and I bit one of them. He let go and I managed to escape....'

'My God! Attacked? Here at Pendleton?' Harry was astounded. 'Susannah, take the rig and get Amelia back to the house. I must investigate this and I want you both safe.'

'Harry—what of you?' Susannah cried. 'You should fetch help.'

Harry took a pistol from the pocket of his coat. 'I always carry this in case, Susannah, though I did not expect to need it on my own estate. My apologies, Amelia. A search shall be made. The culprits shall be brought to account, I promise you.'

'Pray take care, Pendleton,' Amelia said. 'I heard them say I was not to be harmed, which is perhaps why I am still alive—but they may not be so scrupulous with your person.'

'Susannah, do as I ask, please. Go now!'

'Yes, Harry.' Susannah took Amelia's hand. 'Do you feel well enough to walk to the curricle, dearest? I should get you home in case there are more of them, as Harry says. I am sure he can manage.'

'Yes, of course I can walk,' Amelia said, recovering her composure. 'I am not harmed, merely distressed. It was such a shock to be attacked like that, Susannah. Had you and Harry not been near by, I do not know what might have happened, for they pursued me—but when they heard voices I think they stopped.'

'I wish Harry had someone with him,' Susannah said. 'However, I am sure we must leave this to him and go home.' She saw Amelia safe into the curricle and then got in beside her and took the reins. 'This is the first time

I have driven without guidance, but I must be capable or Harry would not have told me to take you home.'

Amelia was silent as Susannah put her horses to a walk and then a trot. Her face was white and it was obvious that the incident had distressed her more than she would allow, even though she had tried to make light of it. When they arrived at the house, a groom came running to take the reins. Susannah explained what had happened while Amelia went up to the house.

'Please send someone to assist your master,' she begged. 'He has a pistol, but these men are dangerous and may be armed.'

'Yes, Miss Hampton,' the groom said. 'Some of the men will go immediately. Don't you worry, miss. His lordship is capable of dealing with poachers or the like— and the gamekeepers are in the woods. If they should hear a shot, they will be there in an instant.'

Susannah did not find his words reassuring. In the event of a shot it might mean that it was already too late. However, she hurried into the house and went upstairs, finding Amelia in their sitting room. She was standing by the table and about to pour herself a glass of wine from a decanter set on a silver tray, but her hand was shaking. Susannah took it from her.

'Sit down, dearest. Let me do that for you.'

Amelia obeyed. 'I am very foolish. It was the merest incident, and I am not harmed. I do not wish to make a fuss—but I am sure they meant to abduct me.'

'Why would they do such a thing? Who would wish to harm you?'

'I have no idea,' Amelia said. 'I cannot think of anyone who holds a grudge against me…' She frowned. 'I can only think that they wished to hold me for a ransom.'

'That is horrible,' Susannah said. 'Drink your wine,

Amelia. It may make you feel a little better. If Harry catches those wicked men, he may be able to discover who put them up to it.'

'Yes, perhaps.' Amelia drank her wine and then summoned a smile. 'I am better now. It was quite frightening for a moment. I should not have walked so far from the house alone, but I have always walked alone and it did not cross my mind that something of the kind could happen here.'

'No, I do not expect it would. Harry will be most distressed that something of that nature should occur on his land.'

'It was not his fault. It could have happened anywhere.' Amelia looked thoughtful. 'I suppose it is well known that I am the heiress to a considerable fortune. I shall have to take more care when walking in future.'

Susannah shivered. 'It is a sobering thought that people exist that would do such a thing,' she said. 'I am so sorry that it happened to you, Amelia. You have no idea who it might be?'

'None at all,' Amelia replied. 'We must hope that Harry and his men will catch whoever it is.' She stood up. 'I shall change my gown and then go down. You should do the same, Susannah. We do not wish to make a fuss over such a foolish incident.'

Susannah knew that Amelia was trying to make light of the affair, and decided to take her lead from her. She watched Amelia enter her bedroom and then went into her own chamber. She rang for her maid, looking at the fresh gown that had been laid out for her. It was a pretty yellow silk and she would want her seed pearls or perhaps the pearls Lady Elizabeth had given her. She had placed them in the top drawer of her chest the previous night. She opened the drawer and frowned, for the box was not where she had left it.

'You rang for me, miss?'

'Yes, Iris. I am ready to change for nuncheon. I thought I might wear my pearls. I was sure I put them in this drawer last night.'

'Yes, miss, I saw you do it,' Iris said. 'Are they not there? I put away a scarf when I tidied your room just after you left. They were there then…' Iris looked and pointed to the place Susannah had placed them, which was now empty. 'Right there, miss.' She looked horrified. 'I swear, I have not moved them. Cross my heart and hope to die!'

'Do not worry, Iris. I do not suspect you of taking them. Perhaps Mama moved them for safekeeping. I shall wear my seed pearls for now and enquire…' She frowned as she realised something else was missing. 'Did you take a kerchief to wash it, Iris? There was one on top of the chest and that has gone too.'

'No, miss. I took some undergarments that you had left lying on the chair, but nothing from the chest, Miss Susannah. You do believe me?'

'Of course I do,' Susannah said. 'Mama might have put the pearls somewhere safer, but even if they are…' she could hardly bring herself to say the word '…stolen, I should not dream of blaming you.'

'Please ask Mrs Hampton at once,' Iris said. 'The kerchief might have got in with the laundry without my knowing it, miss—but those pearls are valuable.'

'Yes, they are, and a gift, which makes them more important. However, you shall not be blamed, I promise you.'

'Thank you, miss—but others may not be so inclined to believe me.' Iris looked distressed. She began to look about the room, searching all the drawers without discovering the pearls. 'I swear to you, Miss Susannah—I would rather lay down my life than touch anything of yours!'

'Do you think I do not know that?' Susannah smiled at her. 'I had already decided to ask if you will come with me when I marry—and this does not change my opinion of you.'

'Oh, miss…' Iris held back a sob only by pressing a fist against her mouth. 'I do hope your mama has those pearls.'

'Yes, so do I,' Susannah said, for otherwise it would mean that there was a thief at Pendleton.

Coming on top of the attack on Amelia, she could imagine that Harry would find the news very distressing.

'No, Susannah, I did not touch your pearls or a lace kerchief—why ever would I do such a thing?'

'I thought perhaps…to make sure the pearls were safe.' Susannah frowned. 'I believed they would be safe in my drawer.'

'As they ought to have been,' Mrs Hampton said, looking shocked. 'I do not say that you were careless, dearest, but it is a pity that you did not ask if they could be locked away in the strong room until you needed them.'

'I have never needed to do anything of the sort,' Susannah said. 'I must tell Lady Elizabeth and apologise to her for losing her gift.'

'Yes, you must,' Mrs Hampton said. 'You questioned your maid, of course?'

'I asked Iris at once, for I thought she might have put

them somewhere she thought safer, but she says did not touch them, Mama—and I believe her.'

'Yes, I am inclined to think her honest—but someone is not, Susannah. This is most unfortunate…' She looked anxious. 'And the attack on Amelia too…I think they must be linked, do you not agree? Perhaps they are desperate rogues and they meant to rob Amelia rather than abduct her?'

'Perhaps…' Susannah was unsure. 'We must see what Harry thinks.'

'I shall tell Lady Elizabeth in private,' Mrs Hampton said. 'This is distressing for everyone.'

Susannah agreed.

She felt uncomfortable and uneasy throughout nuncheon. Afterwards, Lady Elizabeth drew her to one side.

'My son will be most distressed to hear of this,' she said. 'You are sure you did not move them somewhere else, Susannah?'

'Iris helped me to search. We looked everywhere. Besides, she saw them in the drawer after I went driving with Harry.'

'In that case, I shall speak to Harry as soon as he returns. I do not know what things are coming to. Miss Royston attacked in our woods—and your pearls stolen.'

'I should have asked for them to be locked away,' Susannah said. 'I have never had such a valuable trinket before and did not realise—'

'Do not upset yourself, my dear,' Lady Elizabeth told her. 'I would have told you they were quite safe in your keeping. I have never known such a thing to happen before. I would swear that my servants are honest.'

'Iris would never take anything of mine,' Susannah said. She considered mentioning the lace kerchief, but decided against it. If she told Lady Elizabeth the whole story, it might seem as if she were accusing the owner of the kerchief—and she did not truly know who it had belonged to.

'I shall ask Harry if he thinks we should make a search of the servants' rooms,' Lady Elizabeth said, looking bothered. 'It really is too bad of whoever did it—spiteful, in fact. I have many jewels of equal value. If they wished to steal from us, why did they not take mine? I shall find something else to give you, my dear.'

'Please do not, at least for the moment,' Susannah said. 'I should feel uncomfortable keeping them in my room—and perhaps the pearls will turn up.'

'Well…' Lady Elizabeth sighed. 'We must hear what Harry has to say on his return and decide then. If those rogues have been caught, they may have your pearls in their possession.'

Susannah agreed. She was feeling uneasy and spent most of the afternoon watching from the window for Harry's return, the idea of a tour of the house abandoned.

It was past four when Harry came at last, and the look on his face told her at once that he had not captured the rogues he sought.

'We found a place in the woods where they had left a carriage, for there were wheel marks, but there was no sign of them. The other side of the woods borders a village and they must have come that way. I have done nothing about fencing that border, for the village forms part of the estate, but I see that it makes us vulnerable. I shall instruct a master builder to construct a high wall.

Nothing like this shall happen to a lady staying under my roof again.'

'I wish that you had caught them,' Susannah said. 'But the estate is so large and you would need to be searching all day to be sure they were not hiding anywhere on your land.' She bit her lip. 'I am afraid you will be angry—but there has been more trouble since I saw you....'

Harry's gaze narrowed. 'Pray tell me at once, Susannah. Amelia is not badly hurt?'

'Oh, no. She was shocked, but not harmed, though her dress was torn. You recall that your mama gave me some pearls last evening?'

'Yes, she had shown them to me earlier.'

'They have been stolen—at least, they are not where I placed them. My maid and I searched the room, but they have gone.'

'Good grief! This is beyond anything!' Harry looked startled, a glint of anger in his eyes. 'I shall have the house searched at once in case anything else is missing. The rogues must have got in somehow during the night and taken them. I dare say they attacked Amelia because she disturbed them in the woods, or they may have had hopes of more loot. Has anyone else lost anything?'

'No one has said anything,' Susannah told him. 'Your mama did not think the servants...and I am sure it was not Iris. However, the pearls were there just after I left to go driving with you.'

'You are sure of this?'

'Iris saw them, she told me so.' Susannah frowned. Again, she was uncertain whether or not to mention the kerchief, but decided against it. 'Could someone have crept into the house unnoticed in daylight?'

'I would not have thought it,' Harry said and frowned.

'However, until earlier I would not have thought it possible for anyone to be attacked on my land. I have doubled the patrols, which will continue throughout the day and night.'

'It is all quite horrid,' Susannah said and shivered. 'It was bad enough that someone attacked Amelia—but for the pearls to be stolen right here in the house is unpleasant.'

'Yes, it is, but I am sure you are quite safe now, dearest,' Harry said. 'The rogues took what they could and fled. I am sure they are long gone by now. You must promise me this will not spoil things for you, Susannah?'

'I am not such poor stuff,' Susannah told him and smiled. 'I suppose it is an adventure in a way—but I would far rather it had not happened.'

The guests were asked if they had lost anything. Lady Ethel said that her silver evening purse was missing, but it was eventually found stuffed down the side of a sofa by one of the servants. No one else thought they had lost anything, and there was a general outcry against the rogues who had sneaked into Susannah's room and stolen her pearls. The servants were not asked to submit to a search, but after some talking between themselves they asked if it could be done as a process of elimination. Nothing was found and the general consensus was that the rogues who had attacked Amelia had somehow sneaked in and taken the pearls.

'It seems odd that just your pearls were taken,' Mrs Hampton said. 'But perhaps they were disturbed and they fled with what they had.'

'That does not explain why they tried to abduct

Amelia,' Susannah said, looking thoughtful. It did not explain the disappearance of the kerchief, either.

It was later that evening that Miss Hazledeane came up to Susannah in the drawing room. Lady Elizabeth was at the pianoforte and Susannah had been intent on the music when the other woman sat next to her on the small sofa.

'All this fuss for a string of pearls,' Miss Hazledeane said, a spiteful note in her voice. 'I dare say you will find them if you look hard enough.'

'Perhaps…' Susannah turned thoughtful eyes on her. 'It was very odd, but the kerchief I found near the boat-house was lying on my chest—and that was taken too, though I have not mentioned it for it was not important.'

'Your maid took it to be washed,' Miss Hazledeane said. 'She has probably taken the pearls too—or you mislaid them.'

'I should be very glad to think so,' Susannah said. 'I should be happy if they were found and no harm done.'

'You have caused an uproar,' Miss Hazledeane said. 'As if they mattered when you will have so much. The Pendleton heirlooms must be worth a fortune, though I dare say they are kept in the bank.'

'And may stay there, at least until we know for certain that no one can walk in and steal them,' Susannah said. 'The pearls matter to me because they were a gift from Lady Elizabeth.'

'Well, I dare say she will give you something else. She has plenty of jewels, she can well spare another trinket.' Miss Hazledeane shrugged her shoulders, got up and moved away.

Susannah stared after her. It was wrong of her to dislike Lady Elizabeth's ward. It was quite unthinkable to suspect Miss Hazledeane of taking the pearls and the kerchief, and yet Susannah had an uneasy feeling at the nape of her neck. Something was telling her that Miss Hazledeane knew more about the disappearance of the pearls than she was saying.

She could not accuse another lady of stealing! Susannah knew it would be frowned upon. Besides, it was too embarrassing. Everyone else had accepted that the mystery was solved. Harry was having all the side doors locked and the windows checked. He had increased the numbers of keepers he employed to patrol his grounds. There was nothing more to be done except put the unpleasant incident out of her mind.

As soon as Susannah went into her bedchamber, she saw that the drawer of her chest was opened a little. She felt a little shiver down her spine and went to look in the drawer. A silk scarf had been disturbed and when she pulled it aside she saw the velvet case. Taking it out, she discovered that her pearls were inside.

How had they come there? She was positive that they had not been there earlier, for both she and Iris had moved everything in their search. The pearls had gone missing, but now they were back.

Why had someone taken and then returned them? Susannah could think of only one reason—to make her look foolish. It was very embarrassing after the house had been searched and everyone made to feel uncomfortable.

However, it was clear to Susannah that she must confess to having found them, even if it did make her feel foolish.

* * *

Lady Elizabeth told her that it did not matter. She was simply relieved that the pearls had been found.

'Perhaps your maid found them and returned them to the drawer,' she suggested.

'It was not Iris, for I asked her,' Susannah said. 'I am sure they were not there earlier, for we all looked—but I suppose they must have been. I am so sorry to have caused so much fuss.'

'You must not let it upset you,' Lady Elizabeth told her. 'The pearls were lost and now they are found. It is all settled and shall be forgotten now.'

Susannah thanked her and went to bed. There was nothing more she could say, but in her own mind she was quite certain who had taken the pearls and then replaced them. The only thing she wasn't sure of was why....

The next morning dawned fine and bright. Indeed, it had the promise of being hot. Most people thought a storm would come before nightfall to break the weather, because it was too sultry.

Harry had decided that the picnic would go ahead.

'We cannot allow an unpleasant incident to put us off,' he declared. 'The boats have been brought to this side of the lake. Those who wish to go boating may join us there immediately, and those who are interested only in the picnic may wander towards the lake at noon.'

'I am so glad you have not cancelled it,' Susannah said and smiled her pleasure. 'I cannot apologise enough for causing so much trouble. I can only say that the pearls were not in the drawer when I looked.'

'No such thing,' Harry told her. 'No lasting harm done. I am more concerned with the rogues in the woods. Miss Royston has forgiven me for allowing such a terrible thing to happen in my woods, and she will leave at the end of the week to arrange our wedding.'

'Then we may forget it and be happy again,' Susannah said, her face alight. 'It was a fright for Amelia, but it is over now.'

Harry commandeered the first boat and rowed Susannah out into the middle of the lake. She smiled at him, leaning back in her seat, her parasol protecting her from the fierce heat as he pulled on the oars. She thought that he was very strong. Glancing back towards the shore, she saw that the Earl of Ravenshead was rowing Amelia and Mrs Hampton, while Toby had taken Lady Elizabeth for a turn on the water. Most of the other ladies and gentlemen were strolling about on the grass, talking and enjoying the sunshine. Susannah caught sight of Miss Hazledeane. She was wearing a white dress, wandering by herself apart from the others.

'Are you enjoying yourself?' Harry asked. 'I think we must do this more often. I had forgotten how pleasant it is to be on the water.'

'I like it very much,' Susannah said. 'Tell me, do you have a lake at your other home?'

'No, I don't—though I recently bought a piece of land for the construction of a small lake. I hadn't given it much thought, but I must set the work in hand. It will make a fine addition to the property.'

Susannah smiled and trailed her hand in the water. She closed her eyes for a moment, enjoying the tranquillity and peace of their surroundings. She was very fortunate to have the prospect of spending her life in such a lovely place.

Harry took them back to the jetty after half an hour or so, handing Susannah out. He then offered to take any other lady who wished for a trip, and Susannah was a little surprised when Lady Booker said that she would like to be rowed about the lake.

She saw that chairs had been set out, and the servants were setting up tables for their picnic.

Toby had brought his passenger to shore. He walked up to Susannah as she stood under the shade of a tree, watching everyone enjoying themselves.

'The picnic was a capital notion of Harry's, was it not?'

'Yes—' Susannah began, but broke off as she saw a woman emerge from behind the boathouse. Her attention was caught because of the way the woman was behaving—furtively, looking over her shoulder as if hoping not to be seen. She turned and ran in the opposite direction. Only moments later a man emerged from the shadows and began to walk away in yet another direction. 'Did you see that man on the far side of the lake? He came from behind the boathouse…' Susannah touched Toby's arm. 'I am not certain but I think…it was the Marquis of Northaven.'

'Where?' Toby turned in the direction of her gaze, but was only in time to see the man disappear into a clump of artistically arranged trees, too far away to be seen clearly without a spyglass. 'It couldn't have been, surely? Here at Pendleton—with all these people around? I doubt it, Susannah. He is not welcome here. Harry would want to know the reason why. It is hardly likely—the grounds are being patrolled day and night.'

'Yes, I know. It does not seem likely,' Susannah said and laughed. 'Perhaps I was mistaken, but it did look like him for a moment.'

'I cannot think he would come here. Northaven and Harry do not get along. I know for a fact that Northaven would not be invited to this estate.' Toby frowned. 'It is odd, for I do not know how anyone could be there… None of the guests are missing and the men have been warned to look out for strangers.'

'I was mistaken,' Susannah said. 'It could not have been he.'

'I should say it was one of the keepers,' Toby told her. 'I know there are a lot of them about.'

'I am sure you are right. It could not have been the marquis. It was just a trick of the light.'

Susannah dismissed the incident, because she did not want to cause a fuss. Yet she was almost certain it had been the marquis—and that the woman leaving the boathouse was Miss Hazledeane! She had seen a flash of white and Jenny Hazledeane was the only lady wearing white this morning. If it were Northaven and Miss Hazledeane, they must have met there by prior arrangement, perhaps when they had tea in Bath. She recalled the incident in the gardens the night she had arrived. She had seen a man and a woman kissing. Could it have been Jenny Hazledeane and the Marquis of Northaven?

Susannah was thoughtful throughout the rest of the morning. She managed to join in the activities and to talk about all kinds of things, but at the back of her mind was a niggling doubt that would not let her rest. If Miss Hazledeane was meeting the Marquis of Northaven here at Pendleton, Harry ought to be told about it.

Susannah knew that Miss Hazledeane had met the marquis in Bath, and she was fairly sure of what she had seen that morning. Was it her duty to tell Harry what she knew?

The question continued to tease Susannah throughout the afternoon. Several times she was on the verge

of telling Harry, but Miss Hazledeane had rejoined the
company, and had joined in a game of cricket. To raise
doubts about her conduct might throw a cloud over the
party, and after the upset of the previous day, Susannah
did not feel like making a fuss. She decided that, if she
got the chance, she would speak to Miss Hazledeane
about it in private that evening.

However, she did not have a chance to speak to Miss
Hazledeane alone until much later, because she was
asked to play the pianoforte for the company when the
ladies retired to the drawing room. When Amelia took
her place, one of the relatives asked if she would join a
hand of piquet.

Susannah found herself drawn into a lively game,
which she enjoyed more than she might have expected.
Harry was not a part of it, however, and when she looked
for him he had disappeared.

'If you are looking for Harry, he and some of the
others took themselves off to play billiards,' Lady Ethel
told her in a loud voice. 'Pay attention, my dear, or you
will lose points. You will have plenty of time to bill and
coo tomorrow.'

Susannah laughed and put her mind to the game. She
managed to win at least one hand and to share another.
When she was finally released by Lady Ethel, she told
her mother that she was going to bed.

'I need to be fresh for my driving in the morning,'
she said. 'Please tell Harry that I said goodnight.'

After wishing the gathered company goodnight,
Susannah went upstairs to her own room. However, her
conscience would not let her rest and she slipped out
again a few minutes later, going along the hall to the
room she knew was Miss Hazledeane's She hesitated,
then knocked sharply.

'Just a moment…' Miss Hazledeane opened the door in her dressing robe, staring at her for a moment. Susannah thought there was a flicker of fear in her eyes. 'What did you want?'

'I have something to say to you—in private, if I may?'

The other girl stood back, a sullen look on her face. 'I didn't steal your pearls…'

'No one stole them; they were mislaid,' Susannah said, though she suspected the other girl had taken them to punish her, not realising that it would cause so much fuss. However, they had been returned and there was no point in holding a grudge. 'I haven't come about the pearls.'

'Why have you come, then?' Jenny's eyes were suspicious, her manner uneasy.

'I thought I should warn you…' Susannah drew a deep breath. 'I saw you leaving the boathouse earlier today and I know you have been meeting someone in secret. I believe it may be the Marquis of Northaven. I think you should know that he is not to be trusted. Harry warned me against him and I think—'

'How dare you accuse me of having a lover? You have no right!'

'I did not say he was your lover…' Susannah saw the guilt and fear in the other girl's face. 'I am so sorry. I should have warned you sooner…when I first saw you with him in Bath.'

Tears hovered on Jenny's lashes. 'It would have done no good. We have been lovers for months, long before my brother died…' She brushed her hand over her cheek, pride in her eyes now. 'Edmund promised to marry me… He would have married me, but my brother wasted my inheritance and he is in debt.' Her eyes glittered. 'Edmund loves me, but he must marry a fortune.

You do not know what it is like to feel hopeless! I have nothing and I love him so much.'

'I am so sorry—'

'I do not want your pity,' Jenny flashed back at her. 'You come here interfering in what does not concern you, so smug because you are to marry into a wealthy family.' She turned away, her shoulders hunched as she fought the tears. 'Tell Lord Pendleton, then—tell Lady Elizabeth what a wanton trollop I am. I know you are dying to be rid of me.'

'No, you are quite wrong,' Susannah told her, her sympathy aroused. 'I do not hate you. I would be your friend if you would let me. If there is anything I can do to help you?'

The other girl turned, her expression desperate. 'Please, do not tell anyone what you saw. I beg you, do not betray me. I have given Edmund an ultimatum. He must wed me or I shall never see him again.'

'I am so sorry…'

'Then keep my secret…please?'

Susannah hesitated. It was her duty to tell either Harry or Lady Elizabeth, but how could she deliberately shame a girl who already had so much to bear?

'I will think about it,' she said. 'I shall not tell them tonight, but you must give me your word that you will not continue to meet the marquis here at Pendleton.'

'I promise. Please—do not betray me.'

'Very well. I shall say nothing for the moment.'

'Thank you,' Jenny said, the glitter of tears in her eyes. 'I wish that someone had warned me long ago.'

Susannah wished her goodnight and returned to her room. She was uneasy, because she was not certain she had done the right thing in promising to keep Jenny's secret.

* * *

Susannah woke suddenly. She was not sure what had woken her, but she got up and walked over to the window. It was almost morning, the dawn light just beginning to creep in through the curtains. She pulled them back and glanced out, catching sight of someone moving furtively through the gardens. Surely that was Miss Hazledeane? Susannah felt a tingling sensation at the nape of her neck. She was almost certain that Jenny was carrying a valise!

Why would Miss Hazledeane creep out in the early hours of the morning with a valise? Unless… Susannah remembered Jenny's tears of the previous night. Jenny had begged her to keep her secret and now…she had run off with her lover.

She must be wrong! Susannah shivered as the idea grew in her mind. She was almost sure that Miss Hazledeane had eloped with the Marquis of Northaven!

Susannah could not rest. She paced the floor of her bedchamber, wondering what she ought to do. She had to confide in someone! She had given her word to Jenny, but on the condition that she broke off her affair. She had made a terrible mistake. Instead of speaking to Jenny privately, she should have confided her suspicions to Harry. She should have told him the first time she saw Miss Hazledeane with the marquis. Now Jenny had run off with him and she would be ruined.

Was it too late to do anything? Susannah fretted as she went through to the sitting room. Who should she wake—her mama, Amelia or Harry?

Why hadn't she told Harry of her suspicions sooner? Susannah was overcome with guilt. She had hesitated, because she did not like to create suspicion concerning another lady, but now she was wishing that she had spoken out. She was on thorns. How long must she wait until she could tell someone?

Susannah decided that the best person to tell must be Harry. However, she could not possibly go to his bedchamber, even had she been sure of its situation. She would go downstairs and see if the servants were stirring and then ask one of them to ask him if he would come down and speak to her. If no one was about, she would take a turn in the gardens to help her summon the courage.

Looking out of his bedroom window, Toby saw Susannah pacing up and down in the garden below. She was so obviously in distress that he dressed quickly and went down. They met just as she was returning to the house.

'Susannah—are you ill?' Toby enquired in concern. 'What were you doing in the garden.'

'Oh, thank goodness!' Susannah cried, clutching at his arm anxiously. 'I wanted to talk to someone. You are just the person. I am afraid Harry will be so angry with me....'

'What have you done?'

'I kept something back that I ought to have told him,' Susannah confessed. 'And now something terrible has happened—at least, I think it may have.'

'Sit down and tell me,' Toby said, leading her to a chair. 'I am sure it cannot be anything very dreadful.'

'But it is,' Susannah said, a sob in her voice. 'You know the man we saw leaving the boathouse yesterday afternoon?' Toby nodded. 'Well, I am certain it was Northaven and that he has run away with Miss Hazledeane.'

'No! She would not…' Toby stared at her. 'She has no fortune to speak of…Northaven would not marry her without…'

'So much the worse,' Susannah said and caught back a sob. 'I saw them in Bath just before she left to come here. They were taking tea and the look on her face said it all. She is in love with him.' Susannah saw the shock in his eyes. 'She has been meeting him here and this morning she ran off. She was carrying a valise.'

'Why did you not tell someone before this?'

'Because… I was not sure and when I asked her she wept and begged me to keep her secret. I told her she must break with him and she promised she would—but very early this morning she ran away.'

Toby was stunned. 'Stay here, Susannah. I shall wake Harry, if he is not yet awake. A maid must go to check whether Miss Hazledeane is in her room.'

'Harry will be so cross…'

Toby was no longer listening. He took the stairs two at a time, clearly in a state of some anxiety. Susannah got up and began to walk about, studying the paintings in the hallway in an effort to ease her mind. However, her conscience could not be eased, for she knew that this calamity was her fault. If she had only spoken to Harry in the beginning, this could never have happened!

Some twenty minutes or more had passed before Harry came striding towards her. His expression was one of absolute fury and Susannah trembled inwardly. He did blame her and he was right to do so, for it was her fault!

'It has been confirmed that Miss Hazledeane's bed has not been slept in and that some of her things have gone.'

'I am so sorry,' Susannah said in a faint voice.

'Did she tell you of her intentions? Did you help her to run away?' Harry's gaze was stern and cold. 'Tell me now. I wish for no more lies.'

'I have not lied…' Susannah faltered. 'I did not tell you what I had seen for I thought it was not my affair… and then she wept and begged me to keep her secret. She said that Northaven would have married her, but he needs money and her brother wasted her inheritance.'

The look on Harry's face made Susannah wish to sink into the ground and disappear. 'Not your affair when you saw a young woman not much older than yourself meeting secretly with a man you know to be unworthy! Miss Hazledeane is my ward! You must have known that I should wish to be informed so that I could protect her? You deliberately went behind my back, to keep a secret you must have known was wrong! You have behaved thoughtlessly…recklessly. I had thought you had more sense!'

'I was not sure…' Susannah could not meet his eyes, because she knew herself at fault. 'She was in distress. I felt sympathy… Forgive me. I know this must pain you.'

'It pains me more that you did not see fit to tell me in the first place, Susannah. It shows a distinct lack of trust on your part, and that is serious. A marriage without trust is not worth having!'

'It was not that I could not trust you…only that I felt awkward. I had almost made up my mind to tell you what I suspected last night, but you… I did not see you to speak to alone. So I asked her for the truth and then…' It was a weak excuse and she saw the disdain in his expression. Her heart sank and she wished that the floor would open and receive her. 'I did not know what to do.'

'I am afraid our driving lesson must be cancelled for the moment,' Harry said curtly. 'I must go after Miss Hazledeane and see what can be rescued from this mess.' He glanced up as Gerard and Max Coleridge came clattering down the stairs, closely followed by Toby. 'Not you, Toby. My sister would never forgive me if anything happened to you. Northaven has done this deliberately to draw me into a fight.'

'I am prepared to shoot if I have to,' Toby declared, looking stubborn.

'Thank you, but it will be settled in the proper manner if I have anything to do with it,' Harry told him. 'Please stay here and look after Susannah. I would not put it past Northaven to arrange something for her once my back is turned.' He glanced at Susannah once more. 'I shall speak to you when I return.'

'Yes, Pendleton.' Susannah watched as Harry and his friends strode towards the front door, which was opened by a sleepy-looking footman who had just arrived at his post. Her throat was tight and the tears burned behind her eyes. She glanced at Toby, her face pale. 'He is so angry…'

'Yes, but you might have expected it,' Toby said, for once unsympathetic. 'Why on earth did you not tell one of us? Something might have been done to prevent them running off.'

'Do you think they will catch them?' Susannah asked. She was filled with apprehension. 'Is it too late? I dare say they may be halfway to Scotland by now.'

'I doubt he will have taken her to Scotland.'

'Not—but surely they are eloping?'

'Northaven will not marry her without a fortune.

Harry told me she has only a few hundred pounds from her brother's estate. Hazledeane was the guardian of her inheritance, but he misappropriated the funds—in short, he robbed his sister of ten thousand pounds. Northaven might make her his mistress, but he will not wed her.'

'But she will be ruined.' Susannah was horrified.

'That is the reason Harry is so angry. She was under his protection and he feels responsible for her. Unless he can force a deal on Northaven, Jenny Hazledeane will never be able to show her face in society again. Indeed, if her elopement becomes known, many will not receive her even if she is married.'

'Oh…that is terrible,' Susannah whispered. 'I am to blame—I should have told Harry yesterday.' The tears were so close now that Susannah could not hold them back. 'Excuse me…' she said and made a dash for the stairs before she could break down and disgrace herself further. Harry was so angry with her. No doubt he thought her careless and unfit to be his wife. He was probably wishing that he had not asked her to marry him.

'You must not blame yourself,' Amelia told her when Susannah spoke to her some half an hour later. She had conquered her tears and washed her face, but she could not ease her sense of guilt and distress. Amelia was still wearing her peignoir, a frivolous confection of white silk and lace, for she had not dressed fully. 'I can understand why you did not wish to tell tales behind Miss Hazledeane's back, Susannah. It is unfortunate that you did not mention it to me. I might have been able to help her—and I could have told her something about the marquis that would have warned her to have nothing more to do with him.'

'What do you mean?'

Amelia hesitated, then, 'I had a friend some years ago. I shall not name her for it is an old story. Suffice it to say that she was young and pretty, and very innocent. She fell in love and allowed herself to be seduced, but when she discovered she was with child her lover left her. Ashamed and distraught, she refused to tell anyone his name. Instead she chose to take her own life in the river...' Amelia paused, then, 'At the time I suspected one of three gentlemen, but I have since ruled out two of them.'

'You believe it was the marquis?'

'He was not the marquis then, but it was known that he would inherit the title from an uncle. My friend was a simple country girl. He thought her good enough for seduction, but not for marriage. Northaven is known to be in financial difficulties and may have lowered his sights since then—but he will not marry without a fortune.'

'That is what Toby and Harry say,' Susannah said, a sob in her voice. 'I am very much at fault, Amelia. I ought to have told someone. Even if I could not tell Harry, I should have asked you or Mama what to do.'

'It is easy to say so with hindsight,' Amelia agreed. 'But many of us face similar dilemmas and are as hesitant as you, Susannah. I knew that my friend was meeting a young man, but I did nothing to warn or stop her. I did not know he had seduced her, but even if I had guessed I should not have gone to her mother. You hesitated to interfere in something that was not your affair, and Harry will understand that once he is calmer.'

'I fear that I have sunk in his estimation. Do you think they will prevail upon the marquis to marry her?' Susannah asked in a subdued tone. 'I did not like her—nor she me—but I would not see her utterly ruined and banned from society.'

'She was a little strange in her manner,' Amelia agreed. 'To me she was quite friendly, but I dare say she was jealous of you. I saw her making eyes at Lord Pendleton, but he gave her no encouragement. I think if he had, she might not have run off with a man she probably knows is a rogue.'

'I am not sure. The look on her face that day was of a woman in love... I think she is in love with Northaven.'

'She may be in love with him now,' Amelia said. 'However, I doubt it will last more than a few months—if that.'

'I feel sorry for her,' Susannah said. 'If she had stayed here I am sure Harry would have given her a dowry. She might have married well.'

'He will probably give her a dowry now,' Amelia said. 'Indeed, I believe that may be her only hope.'

'I hope that he will find her,' Susannah said, her throat tight with emotion. 'But I am afraid something terrible may happen. You did not see how angry he was—and Toby told me that he did not like the marquis. Do you think they will fight?' Susannah's hand crept to her throat. 'If Harry should be killed because of this—' She broke off on a sob. 'Oh, Amelia, I feel so guilty... so responsible...'

'You must not be anxious for Pendleton,' Amelia told her. 'He is a gentleman and will not become embroiled in an unseemly fight. I dare say it will all be settled in the manner of gentlemen. Now, my love, give me a moment to put on my gown, and then I think we should go down and join the others, for everyone will be wondering where you are.'

Chapter Nine

'What makes you think he will have brought her here?'
Gerard asked as the three men dismounted and looked
at the house. It was a country manor of medium size,
modernised some twenty years before when the estate
was more prosperous, to include an imposing portico
of white columns at the entrance. There were no lights
at the front of the house, though there was one in an
upstairs room at the back. 'If he intends to marry her,
he could be on his way to Scotland even now.'

'He does not intend to wed her,' Harry said and looked
grim. 'Believe me, I know his mind, Gerard. Northaven
has been looking for a way to strike back at me for a
long time. A bullet in the back would have been easier,
but too quick. He wants to see me squirm, to make me
beg him to marry the girl.'

'If that is his plan, why did he not strike closer to
home?' Max asked and frowned. 'Miss Hampton means
far more to you than the Hazledeane chit. If his plan was
to destroy you, why not kidnap her?'

'Jenny Hazledeane means nothing to me,' Harry

agreed. 'Except that I gave her brother my word I would protect her from Northaven. I have failed in that, but I shall do what I can to put matters right. Northaven knows that if he laid one finger on Susannah I would kill him where he stood. I imagine he wants money from this....'

'You know he won't be satisfied with a few thousand,' Max said. 'Put a ball through his head and pack the girl off to a finishing school abroad.'

'Yes, the thought had occurred to me,' Harry drawled, anger mixed with amusement in his eyes. 'You do not imagine that I have come here simply to force Northaven to marry the girl?'

'He won't take her without a hefty bribe.'

Harry pulled a wry face. 'I suppose I can afford it, but that is not why I am here. I came to settle the score with Northaven, because I can no longer ignore it. If what Jenny told Susannah is true, he seduced her long before I was involved—but in meeting her at Pendleton, knowing she was my ward, he threw down the gauntlet. If I do not settle this now, he may attempt something further—something that would cause me more grief than I could bear.'

'You mean Susannah?' Gerard said and frowned. 'Good God! You think...the attempt on Amelia was a mistake. They were meant to kidnap Susannah.'

'It is my fear,' Harry said. 'I did think at first that it might simply be opportunist rogues, but now I believe they may have been after my fiancée.'

'Then you have no choice but to challenge him.'

'Exactly.' Harry's eyes glittered like cold steel. 'Shall we take a look at the back of the house, gentlemen?'

'Yes, that might be a good idea. I hardly think this is

something we can redress by calling at the front door and offering our cards.'

The three men ran swiftly across the lawns, keeping to the shadows as much as possible and turning the corner to come up at the back of the main wing. Light was blazing from a downstairs window and the French doors stood wide-open. Harry looked at his friends and made up his mind instantly.

'Wait for me here. I know it is a sultry night, but that open door is an invitation and I intend to answer it—but do not come unless I call or you hear the sound of a shot.'

'It could be too late then,' Gerard protested. 'We are coming with you. I don't trust that devil.'

Harry saw the expression on both their faces and grinned. 'Very well, if I refuse you will follow anyway. Let's see what the marquis has to say for himself.'

He set off ahead, Gerard following and Max in the rear. Harry had not drawn his pistol, but neither Max nor Gerard was taking a chance and each had his at the ready.

At the door of what was clearly a library—the walls were covered on three sides with leather-covered books—Harry paused and looked in. Northaven was sitting at a reading table, his boots crossed as they rested on the leather surface, an empty wineglass in his hand. His eyes were closed as if he were sleeping, but as Harry cleared his throat, he opened them, his lip curling back in a sneer of mockery.

'I have been expecting you, Pendleton.' His gaze went behind Harry to the other men and he smiled oddly. 'The holy trio together again, I see. Did you think it was a trap? Or have you come to be judge, jury and executioner? Should I repent my sins and ask forgiveness from my Maker?'

'Where is she, Northaven?' Harry demanded. 'What have you done to her?'

The marquis stood up, his expression one of amused malice. 'You mean the lady you were so chivalrous as to take into your home and make your mother's ward? How she disliked that, Pendleton. Your dear mama wished to turn her into a model of decorum and teach her how to behave in society,' Northaven mocked, his lip curled back in a sneer. 'Oh, yes, I knew all about that, and I admit that I was tempted to see if you would part with a small fortune to preserve her good name. I cannot say her modesty, for she lost that long ago. She was my lover before her brother died. Had she held out, I might have wed her in the end.'

'You damned seducer!' Harry's hand shot out, slapping Northaven across the mouth with his glove. 'How dare you malign the name of a lady! If you have seduced her, you will marry her!'

'It would be interesting to see if you could force me to do that,' Northaven said, eyes glittering. There was menace and hatred in his tone. 'I might oblige if the sum were large enough. However, I fear that the bird has escaped us both. She demanded that I marry her. I declined and she ran away from me.'

'She ran away?' Harry and Gerard spoke together and Northaven laughed mockingly.

'I dare say she may have gone to her aunt.' Northaven shrugged carelessly. 'Hazledeane did not tell you of her? You were duped, Pendleton. The man was a rogue. He probably hoped you would marry his sister if you thought her completely alone. Jenny has an aunt in the

north of England. I dare say you will find her there if
you try—though she will not thank you for it.'

'It was you he told me to watch…' Harry frowned, a
little uncertain. Had he misjudged the man? 'I am not
fooled by your lies. Where is she—upstairs?'

Northaven laughed mirthlessly. 'I almost wish she
was,' he said. 'I should enjoy watching you play out the
role of avenging angel.'

'Damn you!' Harry cried. 'You ruined an innocent
girl and you should pay for it.'

'Leave it,' Gerard said. He and Max held Harry by
the arms as he reached for his pistol. 'He isn't worth
the bother. The girl isn't blameless, though I dare say
he seduced her.'

'She was willing enough…' Northaven sneered. 'It is
a pity I could not convince the innocent Miss Hampton
to run off with me. I should have enjoyed seeing your
face then.'

'You will meet me for this,' Harry said. 'I shall have
satisfaction.'

'Delighted,' the marquis replied and his eyes gleamed
with malice. 'I have been waiting for this for many years.
I shall send my seconds to Pendleton to wait on you
tomorrow.'

'You were not to blame for any of this,' Lady Elizabeth told Susannah as they sat in her private sitting room
and drank tea. 'I cannot understand why the girl has run
away. She must have known that she would be ruined.'

'It is distressing for you,' Susannah said, forgetting
her own trouble for the moment. 'I did try to warn her—
but she was in love with him.'

'It was very foolish of her, for she has ruined herself,'
Lady Elizabeth said. 'I wish now that Harry had never

brought Jenny here, for I was beginning to be fond of her—and now I feel let down.'

'She has betrayed your trust,' Susannah said. 'It is sad that she should do such a thing.'

'If only she had confided in me. I could have made it possible for her to marry. I would have given her a dowry had she told me the truth.'

'I do not think Pendleton would have permitted her to marry the marquis.'

'No, perhaps not—though Northaven is still received in many houses. It would have been better to do the thing properly than have her run off in such a sly way! I am sure marriage would have been the lesser of two evils.'

'Perhaps if I had told Harry that I saw them in Bath, he might have warned her—prevented her from throwing her life away.'

'Well, you were not to know that the foolish girl would behave so badly. No, I shall not have you blame yourself for this, and I shall give Harry a piece of my mind for upsetting you, dearest.' Lady Elizabeth frowned. 'He is inclined to be hasty at times. I hope you will forgive him. I shall tell him that he must apologise.'

'Oh, no, you must not. Truly, you must not.'

'Do not distress yourself, dearest. Well, if you do not wish it, I shall not scold him—but it was his own fault for bringing the girl here. He should have sent her to finishing school somewhere.'

Susannah did not reply. Harry had been very angry with her for not telling him what she had seen. He had accused her of not trusting him and looked at her so coldly that she had wanted to die. She did not think he could look at her like that if he truly loved her, and she felt very unhappy. Had she not consented to marry him, she would have begged her mama to take her home immediately, but that would cause such a fuss that she could not bring herself to do it. She must speak to Harry when he returned.

However, Harry had not returned by the time Susannah retired for the night. She undressed, but could not rest and sat on a stool in the window, looking out, watching for his return. It must have been the early hours of the morning when she saw the three men ride up to the courtyard at the back of the house and dismount. One of them took the reins of all three horses and headed in the direction of the stables; the other two walked towards the house. Susannah's window was slightly open and she caught a few words as they passed through the door beneath her window.

'You were a fool to challenge him! It is what he wanted, Harry, what he has been itching for these past years—his chance to kill you.'

'He may try...'

Susannah felt a chill trickle down her spine. The rest of their conversation was lost to her as they went into the house, but what she had heard was clear enough. Harry was going to fight a duel with the Marquis of Northaven!

Oh, he must not! Susannah put a hand to her mouth as she realised that Harry could be killed or badly injured. She wanted to scream and shout, but she held the agony inside, because it would not help her. She knew instinctively that if she begged Harry to withdraw he would look at her in that cold, proud way and tell her she did not understand—or he would simply lie to her and pretend that she was mistaken and there was no duel.

What ought she to do? Susannah believed that duels

had been outlawed in recent years. If she told a magistrate, he might put a stop to it...but what could she tell him? She had overheard a scrap of conversation that she believed meant Harry intended to fight a duel, but she had no proof—and she had no idea where or when the duel was to take place. Besides, he would be so angry he might never speak to her again!

Susannah paced the floor of her bedchamber. There must be something she could do... If she knew where and when the duel was due to take place, she would do something to stop them. She must do something—she could not bear it if Harry were killed.

Dared she go downstairs? She might hear a little more if she was bold enough, though it would be dangerous, for it would be thought most improper of her to be wandering about the house after everyone else had retired.

'You must know this is madness,' Gerard said as they took a glass of wine together in the library. Max had joined them after handing the horses over to a sleepy groom. 'The chit isn't worth risking your life for, Harry.'

Harry arched his right eyebrow. 'You don't imagine I am doing it for Jenny's sake? Northaven has been spoiling for a fight for a long time. If I don't settle this now, it will drag on—and who knows what he may try next? As you said, Gerard, it could have been Susannah. Oh, I do not mean that she would run off with him, for she has too much good sense. However, he might try to abduct her. He said as much—and that was why I challenged him. He hates me because of what happened in the war.'

'And you think that by fighting this duel you will put an end to the ill will between you?' Gerard asked and shook his head. 'I dare say it may if you kill him.'

'I hope that will not be necessary.' Harry looked serious. 'It will not suit me to chase after that wretched girl.' He looked at Gerard. 'I know you spoke of leaving for France soon. Could I ask you to see if you can find Miss Hazledeane before you go—make sure that she is with her aunt?'

'And if she is not?'

'Then I can do no more. She has been foolish, but Mama is fond of her—and for her sake, I would settle a small sum on Jenny.'

'Very well,' Gerard said. 'I shall leave in a day or so, and then I have business in France. I do not know if I shall manage to return for your wedding, Harry. If not, give my good wishes to your bride—and I shall leave a gift for her with Lady Elizabeth.'

'That is if there is a wedding after the way I spoke to her,' Harry remarked wryly.

'I dare say Susannah will take you—despite your show of temper,' Max said and grinned. 'I am not sure you deserve her—but she has a kind heart.'

'Thank you,' Harry said and pulled a wry face. 'I think we should seek our beds. I have no idea when Northaven's seconds will call, but I dare say the duel will take place the day after tomorrow at dawn…' He glanced at his watch. 'Good Lord, the time! Make that tomorrow, for it is past one.'

Outside the library, Susannah caught her breath. She had heard only a few words—she had wrestled with her conscience before coming downstairs and knew she had missed much that went before. Instinct had told her that the men would take a last drink together in the library. Finding the door slightly ajar, she had shamelessly listened and she had been just in time to hear Harry say that the duel would probably take place the following morning.

Hearing sounds, which told her the men were about to leave the library, Susannah fled up the stairs. Her heart was beating very fast, for she had been shocked to have her suspicions confirmed. She knew she must not let the men see her, because if Harry knew that she was aware of the duel he would be at pains to keep the location a secret from her.

Susannah knew that it would be useless to plead with Harry to withdraw from this foolish duel. He could not in all honour do so and she knew it would go ahead whatever she said. However, she was determined to discover where the gentlemen were to meet. She would follow if she could and then…

Susannah had no clear idea of what she would do. She was distressed at the thought of Harry risking his life because Jenny Hazledeane had run off with the Marquis of Northaven. Harry had clearly had some feeling for the woman or he would not have reacted as angrily. He had called Northaven out and he might be killed—and if he died Susannah would have no one to blame but herself, for if she had spoken out at the start, none of this need have happened.

Back in her room, Susannah leaned back against the door and closed her eyes, fighting the tears. She could not bear it if Harry died…but what could she do to stop him fighting this awful duel?

Susannah was walking in the formal gardens with Amelia when she saw Harry coming towards her the next morning. It was almost time for nuncheon and the two ladies had decided that a stroll in the gardens would suffice as neither of them cared to go for a long walk after Amelia's unpleasant experience in the woods.

'Good morning, Susannah—Amelia,' Harry said. His expression was serious, but not angry. Susannah felt her stomach spasm with nerves as he looked at her. 'May I ask for a few moments of your time, Susannah? You will excuse us, Amelia?'

'Yes, of course,' Amelia said. 'I am thinking of leaving the day after tomorrow…perhaps we could speak later?'

'Yes, of course.' Harry smiled briefly. 'We must talk. I hope you will allow me to send an escort with you when you leave…to be certain of a safe journey.'

Amelia inclined her head and walked away, looking thoughtful.

'That was kind of you,' Susannah said, trying to quell her nerves. 'Amelia was upset by that incident in the woods.'

'Yes, of course she must have been, for it was most unpleasant. It may have been a random attack with robbery in mind, or something more sinister, therefore I have asked Max and Gerard to accompany Amelia to her home.'

'Yes, that would be ideal,' Susannah agreed and glanced at him uncertainly. 'Your mama tells me that Miss Hazledeane was not with the marquis, but may have gone to her aunt.'

'It would appear to be the case,' Harry said. 'Gerard will journey to the north to enquire after he has escorted Amelia home. I shall do what I can for Miss Hazledeane—despite her foolishness. I would wash my hands of the business, but Mama has a fondness for her.'

'I see…' Susannah bit her lip. 'I am sorry I did not

tell you that I witnessed her meeting with Northaven. It was wrong and misjudged.'

'You did what seemed right at the time, but I dare say you have learned a hard lesson.' Harry hesitated, looking rueful. 'Once again I subjected you to a shocking show of temper. I believe in the heat of the moment I was harsh to you.'

'You accused me of not trusting you. I believe I have lost your trust—and your good opinion?' Susannah could not look at him, for she was too ashamed.

'Please look at me, Susannah,' Harry said in a gentle voice that brought her head up. 'I hope to earn your forgiveness if I can. I was angry because of what had happened, but more than that it hurt me that you did not feel you could trust me with your confidences. Even when you began to realise that Miss Hazledeane might have run off, it was to Toby you confessed your fears. I had hoped that you might feel closer to me, now that we are engaged to be married.'

'Toby saw me walking in the garden. He came down. I would have told you if I had seen you first,' Susannah said. 'Forgive me, Pendleton. It was not lack of trust that caused me to hold back. I felt that it would seem sly or ungenerous to cast doubts on a lady's character. I hardly knew her....'

'Yes, I realise that—and I do understand, Susannah. However, I should prefer it if you were to confide in me in future.' He looked grave. 'Unless anything has happened that has made you think you would prefer to be released from our engagement?'

'Oh, no!' Susannah said and then blushed. 'No, I do not wish to be released, Pendleton—but if you wish it...'

'Not at all,' he said and gave her what she felt was a

rather forced smile. He reached out to stroke her cheek with his fingertips. 'I care for you a great deal, Susannah. If…anything should happen… If anything prevented our marriage…I want you to know that you are the only lady I have ever wished to make my wife.'

'Harry…' Susannah's heart raced as he bent his head. His kiss was light, soft and brief. 'Please do not say such things! They frighten me. What could happen to prevent our marriage?'

'Nothing, of course. I should not have mentioned it,' Harry said and his smile warmed her. 'It was foolish talk. Have you forgiven me, my dearest? The force of my temper has caught you three times now. I hope it has not made you take me in dislike?'

'I could never dislike you,' Susannah told him. She was tempted to tell him that she knew about the duel, to beg him not to go through with it, but she could not find the words. 'I cannot wait for our wedding day.'

'Can you not?' Harry looked thoughtful. 'When you go to Amelia's, I shall take a trip to London, to buy your wedding gift. Tell me, Susannah, what is your favourite stone?'

'I like pearls and perhaps diamonds,' Susannah said. 'My emerald ring is lovely. I really do not mind. The pearls your mama gave me are perfect.'

'There are others of equal merit in the family jewels, but I intend to buy something new for your wedding gift—something that has not been worn by any other Pendleton lady.'

'Thank you,' Susannah framed the words, but she really wanted to say, *All I want is you, Harry. Please do not risk your life by fighting a duel.*

They heard a gong sounding from within the house. Harry turned his head and frowned—he had noticed uncertainty in Susannah and he was not sure what was causing it.

'I think we should go in, for I would not wish to keep Mama waiting, Susannah.'

'Yes, of course,' she said and smiled as they turned towards the house.

It was unlikely that she would get another chance to talk to him alone, for she had been invited to play croquet on the lawn with Lady Elizabeth and some of the others that afternoon. She felt a knot of nerves in her stomach as she wondered how she could prevent Harry fighting that duel!

Wild thoughts of sending a servant for the magistrate or locking Harry in his apartments went through her mind and were instantly dismissed. It seemed that there was nothing she could do—she was certain an appeal to Harry would fall on deaf ears.

Perhaps Toby would know what she could do? She could at least confide her fears in him this evening.

'How do you know about the duel?' Toby looked shocked when she told him she had overheard Harry talking of it with his friends. 'That sort of thing isn't for the ears of delicate ladies.'

'I am not a delicate lady,' Susannah said. 'Harry is going to risk his life to defend *her* honour and it isn't fair. She won't care if he dies, but I shall. It will break my heart, Toby. Can you not do something to stop it?'

'What would you have me do?' Toby asked and shook his head. 'Nothing I said would change his mind, Susannah. It is a matter of honour. Surely you know that?'

'Yes, I know gentlemen have foolish notions, but I do not think it is honourable for two grown men who should know better to try to kill each other!' Susannah was cross with him, for he was clearly on Harry's side. 'Couldn't you make sure Harry went to the wrong place—or persuade them to shake hands and make up their quarrel?'

'Have you tried to persuade Harry not to go ahead with it?'

'No…he wouldn't listen to me.'

'Do you imagine he would listen to me?' Toby made a rueful face. 'Harry would soon tell me to mind my own business.'

'Then you can offer me no help?' Susannah looked at him in appeal. 'Please, Toby…'

'Susannah, I would die for you,' Toby told her. 'But I cannot prevent this duel. Besides, there is no need. I dare say it will end with them both firing in the air.'

'Do you really think so?' Susannah asked. 'I could bear it if I thought it was all some silly nonsense—but I am afraid they hate each other and that the marquis will try to kill Harry.'

'Well, if he does, he will fail,' Toby said. 'I promise you that Harry is an excellent shot—the best. He was given awards for bravery when he fought with Wellington. You don't imagine he will die in a foolish affair like this?'

'There you are—you think it foolish too,' Susannah said and Toby frowned. 'At least keep this to yourself, Toby. If you tell Harry that I know, I shall never forgive you!'

She turned and left him, feeling unaccountably cross. Men were all the same with their talk of honour and their stupid duels! Well, she was going to keep watch from her window in the early hours of the next morning, and when she saw the men leave the house she would follow them. She did not know what she could do to stop the duel, but she had made up her mind that she would do something.

Susannah had lain on her bed, fully clothed, because she had had no intention of wasting time dressing later. She'd rested for a while, because the duel would not take place before dawn, then closed her eyes, but slept only fitfully, and was out of bed long before the first rays of the morning light began to creep over the silent gardens. She saw four men leave the house when it was still hardly light. A groom had horses waiting for them. Susannah waited to see which way they would ride before going quickly downstairs.

She hurried towards the stables and found a sleepy yard boy beginning to sweep the cobbles. Bestowing a brilliant smile on him, she went confidently towards him.

'Good morning, lad,' she said. 'Would you prepare my rig for me, please? I have a fancy to go driving before anyone is about.'

The lad stared at her, lifted his cap and scratched his head, clearly startled by her request, but then he laid aside his broom and went to do her bidding. Susannah waited impatiently for him to get the rig ready for her. She climbed in and took the reins from him, but on an afterthought told him to hop up beside her.

'I may need you to hold my horses for me,' she said and smiled at him. 'You won't mind that, will you, lad?''

'Me name is Tim, miss,' he told her and grinned. 'I should like to hold 'em for you. I like 'orses, but 'ead groom says I ain't fit fer nuthin'.'

'Well, if you take good care of my horses, I shall ask

his lordship to see that you are taught to be a groom. In fact, you can be my groom—if it would please you?'

'You're a good 'un, miss—a rare sport.' Tim grinned at her. 'You handle them 'orses a treat.'

'Thank you,' Susannah said. She was glad to have the lad with her, because otherwise she would have felt nervous of leaving the horses alone. 'Do you know the woods well, Tim? Is there a clearing of any kind in that direction?' She pointed out the direction that the riders had taken earlier.

'Yes, miss. I reckon I could show yer where,' Tim said and looked at her curiously. 'Yer up to somethin'—ain't yer?'

'Yes, I am,' Susannah said. 'It is our little secret, Tim. You mustn't tell anyone else about this.'

'Cross me 'eart and 'ope to die.'

Susannah smiled at him. So far her plan had worked well. She did not know what would happen when she reached the clearing, but if she was in time, perhaps she would think of something….

Harry stood with Max, Gerard and Toby as they waited for the arrival of the marquis and his seconds. A doctor had been summoned to attend and was partaking of a snifter of brandy from a small silver flask. Harry glanced at his gold watch, for it was a minute to the time agreed.

'It seems that Northaven may have changed…' he began and frowned as the sounds of horses arriving made him hesitate. 'I believe this may be he.'

Three men rode into the clearing and dismounted. Northaven walked towards them, inclining his head brusquely to the small gathering. He was immaculately dressed in black from head to toe; Harry wore a coat of blue superfine and cream breeches.

'We are not late, I hope?' Northaven asked. 'We were delayed and this clearing was not as easy to find as I imagined.'

'I believe you are on time, sir,' the physician said. 'I am Dr Barnes, my lord. I trust you are happy to accept my services if need be?'

'Certainly,' Northaven replied in a careless tone. 'My seconds, Mr William South—and Sir John Travers.'

'Pleased to meet you, gentleman,' the doctor said. 'You have agreed terms?'

'Yes, the usual rules apply,' Sir John said. 'I would like to inspect the pistols, if you please.'

'Certainly,' Doctor Barnes said. 'I have looked at the pair and they seem nicely balanced, as perfect a weapon as I have seen. Look for yourself. I can find nothing out of order.'

'Yes, a nice pair,' Sir John agreed after a brief examination.

Doctor Barnes cleared his throat. 'Gentlemen, will the seconds please confer and then we shall choose the weapons.'

Gerard and Sir John agreed. They weighed the pistols in their hands, examined them, checked the barrels and loaded each pistol with one shot and powders.

'Gentlemen, choose your weapon, please.'

Harry waved his hand to indicate that Northaven should choose first, taking his own without appearing to look at it.

'Please take your places,' Dr Barnes said. 'Are either of you inclined to reconcile your differences?'

'Damn it, no!' Northaven said, his eyes glittering.

'I believe we are agreed,' Harry said. 'Pray continue, sir.'

'I must ask you to stand back to back,' Dr Barnes said. 'Take measured paces and do not turn until I have finished the count.' He paused, then, 'Gentlemen, we shall begin. One, two, three…'

It had been darker in the woods and not easy to follow the bridle path in her rig, but the light was gathering now. Susannah could hear the voices just ahead of her. She had left Tim tending the horses after he had told her that the clearing was just through the trees. She had wondered at first if they would ever find the right place, and her nerves were tumbling low in her stomach as she crept nearer to the clearing. She could hear someone counting and she knew that she was only just in time. On the count of ten they would turn and fire at their discretion.

She reached the clearing just as she heard the count of ten. Both men turned, looking at each other. Northaven had raised his arm, Harry still had his by his side. Northaven was taking aim. Harry was not responding. The marquis was going to fire first and his pistol was pointed straight at Harry's heart. She saw him draw back the hammer on his pistol and suddenly she screamed, running from the side of the clearing towards the marquis.

'No…you must not…' she cried and her terror spurred her on, her path taking her between Harry and the marquis just as Northaven pressed the trigger. His ball struck her left arm. Her scream of pain echoed on the still air as she fell forwards on to the dry earth.

'Oh, my God!' Harry cried. He threw his pistol down and ran to where Susannah lay, unmoving. Kneeling on the ground beside her, Harry gently turned her over, looking at the blood trickling from her arm. Her eyes were closed—she had fainted from the pain—but she was still breathing. 'Thank God she is alive. The wound is to her arm…' He looked up to see Northaven standing just a few feet away. Fury erupted within him and he glared at his opponent. 'If she dies, I shall see you hang, sir.' For two pins he would have put a ball through the marquis's black heart, but that would make him a murderer and, as angry as he was, Harry could not forget that he was a gentleman. He lived by his honour, for it was his essence, what made him the man he was. 'Damn you…she is my whole life…' His voice cracked and tears glittered in his eyes. 'I love her….'

'She ran between us,' Northaven said, his face white with shock. 'I meant to wing you, Pendleton. I should not have shot to kill. I wanted to prove I am not what you think me—and I didn't see her until it was too late. I swear, I would not have wounded Miss Hampton on purpose! I may be a rogue, but I am not a murderer!' He hesitated, then, 'This settles the score between us.'

Harry was intent on his love and did not even hear.

'Let me look at her, sir.' Doctor Barnes was there beside Harry. He knelt down to examine the wound. 'She is losing a deal of blood. I must place a tourniquet on her arm until we can get her back to the house.' He reached for his bag and took out the things he required. 'Stand back, sir. Allow me to tend my patient.'

'We need a carriage.' Harry looked about him. 'Someone must go for the curricle—'

'It's just 'ere, sir,' a voice piped up to one side of the clearing. 'Lawks-a-mussy, but I never dreamed she would go and do somethin' like that, sir. She told me ter take care of the 'orses, but when I heard the shot I looped the reins over a bush and come runnin'. She's a proper sport, that 'un.'

'I shall speak to you later, lad,' Harry said and, once the physician had applied the tourniquet, gathered Susannah in his arms. His face was grim as he nodded to Tim. 'Lead on. We must get her home at once.'

He strode away from the clearing, carrying Susannah in his arms, his expression turned to stone.

'Damn you, Northaven,' Gerard said, coming up to the marquis. 'I think you should take yourself off out of the country for a while. If anything happens to Miss Hampton, I shall not answer for your life. If Harry does not kill you, one of us will—that is, if you do not hang.'

'He challenged me.' Northaven glared at him. 'He challenged me, remember? The three of you always believe you have right on your side. Damn you! I'll not run like a coward, though you think me one. If Pendleton wants to come looking for me, he knows where to find me. I am not finished with any of you.'

Gerard watched as the marquis turned on his heel, strode towards his horse, mounted and went off at a pace. His seconds lingered, looking at each other in dismay.

'This is dashed awkward, Ravenshead. Northaven did not intend harm to the lady,' Sir John said. 'I am sorry for what happened—but she ought not to have run between them like that.'

'She is a young woman and she is in love,' Gerard said and frowned. 'There is no telling what a woman in love will do. Harry thought Northaven would miss, for he is not the best shot in the world. He told me he would wait and then fire in the air, for he had no desire to kill the man, merely to put an end to this nonsense.'

He looked at Max. 'We had best get back to the house, though I doubt there is much either of us can do.'

'It is in God's hands,' Max said and looked grave. 'The devil of it is—if she takes a fever and dies, Harry will blame himself.'

'He already is blaming himself,' Gerard said. 'This is the worst thing that could have happened. It beats me how she could have discovered that the duel was to take place and where.' He frowned. 'I hope she did not learn of it from Sinclair. Harry will not forgive him if she dies.'

'I do not imagine he would forgive himself,' Max said. 'We must hope that she recovers—I do not know what Harry will do if she does not.'

'Northaven has a lot to answer for,' Gerard said. 'It is a pity that the feud was not ended today. It has dragged on too many years already. Northaven may not have intended harm to Miss Hampton, but if he wanted revenge on Harry, he has certainly had his way....'

Chapter Ten

Susannah stirred as Harry laid her gently on cool linen sheets. She gave a little cry, a whimper of pain, and a tear trickled from the corner of her eye, but she said nothing, merely staring up at him, as if she were bewildered and did not know quite what had happened to her.

'My foolish little love,' Harry said in a soft voice. 'Is the pain very bad?'

'It hurts a little,' Susannah said, trying not to cry because her arm felt so painful that she did not know how to bear it. 'You are not hurt…he did not kill you…'

'Oh, Susannah…' Harry choked. 'My dearest—'

'Stand aside, sir,' Dr Barnes ordered in a stern voice. 'You would do better to leave the room and let me attend her with the help of this good woman.' He looked at Amelia, who had seen them enter the house and led the way to Susannah's bedchamber. She hastened to pull back the covers on the bed for Harry to deposit his precious burden. She was wearing her peignoir, but made nothing of the fact that their apartments had been invaded by gentlemen before she was properly dressed.

'I am very willing to help,' Amelia said at once. 'Only command me, sir.'

'I cannot leave her,' Harry said, his expression one of near despair. 'Must you cut for the ball? How deep is it?'

'I shall tell you when I have examined the lady's arm further. At least stand aside, sir—and let me do my work.' The doctor looked at Amelia with approval. 'Pray fetch hot water, ma'am. I have everything else I need in my bag. But I may need you again in a moment.'

'I shall be as quick as I can,' Amelia promised and, with a sympathetic look at Harry, went out.

Harry watched anxiously as the doctor examined the wound carefully, prodding around the bloodied area with his fingers. He had removed the tourniquet, but a steady trickle of blood was still issuing from the tear in Susannah's flesh. She whimpered a few times, but did not cry out, and after a few minutes the doctor smiled.

'Well, you are a good, brave girl,' he told her. 'You were foolish to do what you did, Miss Hampton, but it took courage. Now you will need a little extra courage, for the ball is lodged just here and I must cut you a little to remove it and then stitch the wound. Do you think you can bear it? I shall give you a small dose of laudanum to help the pain, but I cannot pretend that you will feel nothing.'

'You must do whatever is necessary...' Her eyes moved to Harry's face, a look of appeal in their depths. 'You will not leave me? Do not let Mama come in until it is done, for she could not bear to see me in pain....'

'I promise I shall not leave you,' Harry told her. 'Shall I hold your hand, my love?'

'Ah, Miss Royston,' the doctor said as Amelia returned with a kettle of steaming hot water. 'Thank you. I shall place my instruments in this bowl. If you will pour some of the water over them, please—and then I must cleanse the wound. Perhaps you would hold the bowl for me? Lord Pendleton, if you are to stay, you may hold Miss Hampton still as I cut, for if she jerks my knife may go too deep and injure her more.'

'I am ready,' Harry replied grimly. Having endured such surgery himself on the battlefield, usually without the benefit of laudanum, he knew that Susannah would suffer terribly. He held her hand tightly as the doctor cleansed the wound. She turned her face towards him as the doctor picked up his sharp scalpel and bent over her arm. Harry was forced to hold her still as she jerked with pain despite the spoonful of laudanum she had swallowed. 'It will soon be over, dearest…and then you will sleep and the pain will ease.'

'There…' Doctor Barnes dropped the ball into a small bowl and looked pleased. 'It came out easier than I thought. You were very brave, Miss Hampton.' He frowned and laid his hand on her brow as he saw that she was lying very still. 'The laudanum is taking effect. I dared not give her too much, but she will sleep for some hours now. She will not feel the remainder of what I do.' He worked swiftly, stitching the open wound and then applying a clean linen bandage. 'The wound will heal and she should not have any lasting ill effects, though she may have a scar—but of course there may be fever. If she wakes with a fever, you must call me and I shall prescribe something.'

'Thank you,' Harry said. He bent down to kiss Susannah's brow. 'I pray that she will not take a fever, but, as you say, it may happen despite all you did to prevent it. I thank God you consented to attend this morning, sir.

Had you not, she might have bled to death before you arrived.'

'Perhaps it may help you to reflect on the evils of such events,' Dr Barnes said with a severe look. 'Had it not been Miss Hampton, it might have been you lying here, sir.'

'I wish to God it had been!' Harry said. 'I would far rather it was I who had been injured. You are right, sir. I let pride goad me into this foolishness. Well, I have learned my lesson. I hope that Northaven is satisfied. He has his revenge more surely than if he had killed me.'

'I shall leave you now, sir,' the doctor said and turned to Amelia. 'Will you walk down with me, Miss Royston? Miss Hampton will need nursing for a few days, and you seem to me a sensible young woman. Will you bear the burden of caring for her?'

'I had intended to leave in the morning,' Amelia replied. 'But I shall not leave now until I know that Susannah is recovered. I would not leave her to the care of servants, and her mama will be very distressed. I shall certainly take my share of the nursing.'

'Thank you,' Dr Barnes said. 'I shall tell you of some signs that you should look out for if she develops a fever....'

Harry bent over Susannah as the door closed behind them. Had the doctor not done so, he would have begged Amelia to stay. He had no intention of leaving Susannah alone, at least until she was safely through the worst, but there were things that only a woman could do for her.

'Sleep well, my precious, foolish love,' he murmured as he touched his lips to her cheek. 'Why did you do such a rash thing? You should not even have been there.'

Harry frowned. He could not think who had told Susannah that a duel was taking place. She must have known—she could not have stumbled upon the meeting place by accident. If Toby had told her, he would feel the sharp edge of Harry's temper—and that stable lad should never have allowed her to take the rig out without permission.

He was angry that she had put herself at risk, terrified that he might lose her—and yet at heart he admired her courage. She had seldom driven her horses without either Toby or himself to help and guide her. To have the rig made ready, drive out to the woods at such an hour and then run between opponents bent on shooting each other showed strength of purpose and courage, if a lack of good sense and decorum.

Harry smiled, his feelings of anger cooling as he admitted that the woman he loved had as much courage and determination as most men he knew. She had taken a wrong notion into her head, but he could not help feeling proud of her for what she had done. He would scold her when he was sure she was quite well, but not too severely. It puzzled him as to why she had thought it necessary. Harry had known that the likelihood of Northaven wounding him severely was small. His opponent had never been a true marksman. For himself, he had been prepared to risk it—he had decided that he would let Northaven fire first, then take his time, give the marquis a fright as he took aim and then fire in the air.

He had hoped to put an end to the feuding between them, but his plan had backfired, rebounding on him, because Susannah was suffering and there was the possibility that she would take a fever and die. Even slight wounds could become infected, and if the poison went inwards there was nothing anyone could do.

Harry prayed that it would not happen. He was not sure that he would wish to live if he lost Susannah now.

'Oh, my poor child,' Mrs Hampton said as she bent over Susannah to kiss her cheek, tears trickling down her face. 'You foolish, foolish girl! What on earth did you mean by it?'

Susannah did not answer. She could not, for the fever they all dreaded had taken hold. Once she had woken from the laudanum, the signs had all been there. She was burning up, her brow damp with sweat as she tossed restlessly and cried out in her delirium for Harry.

'Harry…' Susannah whimpered. 'Please do not die… do not leave me…'

'I am here, my love,' Harry said, coming forwards. He had stood back to allow her mother to take his place, but now he bent over her, placing a hand on her brow and brushing back the damp hair. His heart was wrung with grief, for she was so very ill and he felt so helpless. He did not think he could bear the guilt if she were to die, for the duel should never have been! 'I shall not leave you.'

'It is hardly fitting that you should be here in her bed-chamber,' Mrs Hampton said, looking at him oddly. 'I suppose since you are engaged…but it will be thought very strange if people hear that you have spent so much time alone with her, sir.'

Harry looked apologetic, his face dark with grief. 'Forgive me, ma'am. I know you must blame me for this—indeed, I blame myself. If she dies, I shall never forgive myself!'

'Well, I cannot approve of duels, though I know gentlemen think them an honourable way to solve their differences,' Mrs Hampton said, shaking her head at him. 'However, I do not blame you for Susannah's behaviour. It was foolish in the extreme—and not at all what I have taught her. She ought not to have come near that place if she knew what was happening. It was very wrong of her, Pendleton, rash and most improper.'

'Please do not be angry with her,' Harry said. 'I do not know why she took such a risk, but I am sure that she intended to save me from being killed.'

'Of course she did,' Mrs Hampton replied. 'Can it be that you do not understand how much Susannah loves you? If you imagined that she was marrying you for position or wealth, you are much mistaken. I know my daughter, sir. Once she gives her heart, she does not change, though I know she has been uncertain of your feelings for her.'

'I thought...' Harry looked rueful. 'I believed she might care for Toby. He is more her age and I fear that I am sometimes too severe for her. I have tried to please her, but I was afraid that she might find me dull.'

'Now you are being foolish,' Mrs Hampton said and smiled wisely. 'Susannah would not have accepted you if she had not fallen in love with you. My daughter is far too romantic in her notions to marry for anything but love. I thought she might have a preference for Mr Sinclair at one time, but she told me frankly that she cared for him only as a friend. She assured me that they were much alike and would not suit. She once told me that you would be a good influence for her and help her to be a better person.'

'I think that perhaps she may teach me to be a better person,' Harry said with a rueful look at his love. She looked so flushed and ill! 'I shall admit to having a shocking temper at times, but I must—I shall learn to curb it for her sake.'

'We must pray that she comes through this fever so that you may tell her these things,' Mrs Hampton said in a practical tone. 'And now, sir—I really must insist that you take some rest. I shall not deny you my daughter's bedchamber, for I do not think you would heed me, and I have no desire to quarrel with you. However, you should rest for an hour or so. Leave her to me now. There are things I need to do for her. Amelia will be here to give Susannah her medicine shortly, and we shall call you if you are needed.'

Harry ran his hand over his face. He had not shaved in two days and was in desperate need of some sleep and a change of clothes.

'Very well, ma'am. I have your promise that you will call me at once if…'

'My daughter is stronger than you imagine, sir,' Mrs Hampton said and smiled. 'You have my promise.'

Mrs Hampton sat next to the bed after Harry had left the room. She reached for Susannah's hand as she cried out and called his name.

'He will be back soon, my love,' she said. 'You must be a good brave girl, and we shall soon have you better.' She began to pull back the covers so that she could bathe Susannah's heated flesh. 'I really do think you must get better soon, my love, or the poor man will be ill himself.'

Susannah whimpered as she felt the soreness in her arm. What was wrong with her? Her long lashes flickered against her cheek as she struggled to fight off the cotton-wool clouds that fogged her mind, and then she

260 A Country Miss in Hanover Square

opened her eyes to see someone bending over her. She felt a cool cloth against her brow and sighed.

'That feels good,' she croaked. 'Thank you.'

'You are awake at last,' Amelia said and smiled in relief. 'The fever broke last night. We gave you some medicine, because you were in distress, and you slept soundly. Are you feeling better, dearest?'

'My arm is very sore,' Susannah said. 'I am so thirsty. Could I have some water, please?'

'Yes, of course,' Amelia said and sat next to her on the bed, lifting her so that she could drink from the cup. 'I had this ready, for I knew you would be thirsty when you woke. The doctor told me that you must take only a few sips at first.' She smiled as Susannah swallowed and then closed her eyes. 'You are very tired. Would you like to sleep again?'

'No, not yet,' Susannah said and forced her eyes to stay open. 'How long have I been ill? I cannot think what happened to me...'

'You were in a fever for three days and nights,' Amelia told her. 'Do you not recall what you did—the duel?'

'The...duel...' Susannah stared at her and then memory returned with a rush. 'Oh, yes, of course. Harry was not going to fire and I feared the marquis would kill him. I tried to stop him and...he must have fired. I do not remember what happened next...just that it hurt so very much. I think I must have fainted.'

'I am sure that it was very painful,' Amelia told her with a look of sympathy. 'You were fortunate that the ball did not go deeper. Had it hit your chest or your neck, you might well have been killed. The doctor says we were very lucky that you escaped so easily, dearest.'

'I did not think he would fire at me, but I suppose it was too late for him to stop,' Susannah said and winced as she pushed herself up against the pillows. Her head was aching and she felt weak. 'Indeed, if I am truthful, I did not think of anything other than my fear that Harry might be killed.'

'Toby told me that Northaven is not held to be a good marksman. It was likely that his shot would have gone wide—and then Harry would have fired in the air.'

'But he might have killed him. I could not take that risk,' Susannah said. 'I love him too much...' A little sob left her lips. 'Is he very angry with me? Do you think he will wish to break off our engagement? I know my conduct was not what it ought to have been. I ought to have pretended I knew nothing—but I could not. I love him too much.'

'I do not know how he feels about what you did,' Amelia replied. 'However, I am perfectly certain Pendleton will not wish to break off the engagement. He has hardly left your bedside since he carried you up here.'

'Harry has been here?' Susannah stared at her in surprise. 'Did Mama allow it? It was most improper for him to be in my room. I think Mama could not have been pleased?'

'Your mama knew that if she forbade it, he would ignore her,' Amelia said and laughed. 'If you had doubts concerning his feelings for you, Susannah, you may forget them. I have never seen a man more in love than Harry Pendleton. He was beside himself when he thought you might die.'

'Oh...' Susannah blushed. 'Do you think so? I have on occasion thought that my sometimes-reckless behaviour may have given him reason to regret his proposal.'

'Pendleton admits to a temper,' Amelia told her and looked thoughtful. 'However, his own behaviour has shown that he is very much in love.'

'He will still scold me,' Susannah said. 'I have caused so much anxiety and trouble.'

'Yes, you have,' Amelia agreed and laughed teasingly. 'What you did was misguided, Susannah, but I do not think you will find that you are much censured. Indeed, I have heard you spoken of as being plucky and having a deal of spunk. I imagine Harry's relatives believe him to be a lucky man to have inspired such devotion. No one has censured you in my hearing or your mama's.'

Susannah blushed again, picking at the bedcover with restless fingers. 'You had intended to leave before this,' she said. 'I am sorry, Amelia, I have kept you from your business.'

'I wrote to Miss Emily Barton and put off our interview for one week,' Amelia said. 'I could not entertain the idea of leaving while you were still so ill. Miss Barton will understand if she is the person I think her.'

'I have detained you and Harry's friends, for they were to escort you home.'

'Yes, they were. Indeed, Lord Coleridge still intends it,' Amelia said, a strange look in her eyes. 'However, the Earl of Ravenshead has had a letter, which means he must go to France.'

'A letter from France—has he business there?' Susannah looked at her curiously for she sensed that Amelia was holding her feelings in check. 'He spoke to me of that country once.'

'It appears that he has a daughter,' Amelia replied in a tone that was carefully flat and devoid of emotion. 'She has been fretting and unwell and he told me that he must go to her.'

'A daughter? But I thought…' Susannah saw the look on her friend's face. Amelia was struggling with her emotions. 'Harry did not know he had a wife.'

'He does not,' Amelia said. 'It seems that the earl was married briefly during the war in Spain—a French lady, I believe. He rescued her from some troops after her escort had been shot. She had no one and he…married her. She died after the child was born and…the earl put the child into the care of a French family. However, she pines for him when he is absent.'

'Oh…does that mean he intends to live in France?' Susannah frowned, for she recalled his having mentioned something of the kind to her. She could not quite recall what he had said, but thought he might have considered living there for a time.

'I believe he may not return to England for some months,' Amelia told her. 'But we should not be talking of this, Susannah. You need to rest and…it is not our affair after all.'

'No, it is not,' Susannah agreed. 'I am so very sorry, Amelia. Did he say nothing else?'

'What else should he say?' Amelia glanced away, but Susannah could see a pulse flicking in her throat. 'Anything that was between us is long forgotten, Susannah. I shall not allow myself to think of it again.'

'Forgive me,' Susannah said. 'I have said too much. I did not wish to hurt you.'

'You have not,' Amelia replied and turned to face her. 'Nothing has changed—I knew that there was no chance of…' She got to her feet, her expression bleak. 'Excuse me, I must tell your mama that you are awake. Everyone has been so anxious.'

Susannah lay back against the pillows, a single tear escaping to trickle down her cheek. She felt so sad for her friend, because she knew that, despite her brave words,

Amelia was hurting all over again. She was still in love
with the earl, even though she would not admit it.

'Why has Harry not been to see me for two days?'
Susannah asked when her mama visited her that morning. 'He popped in to say he was glad to see me recovered from the fever, but he did not stay and he has not
come to visit me since then.'

'He sent you those beautiful roses,' Mrs Hampton
said, indicating a vase on the dressing chest. 'You must
not expect him to visit now that you are recovering, dearest. While you were in the fever he sat with you, but it
would not be proper for him to do so now that you are
over the worst of it.'

'Then I shall get up,' Susannah told her. 'I want to
see him, Mama. I need to talk to him.'

'The doctor says that you must stay in bed for at
least another week, my love. Please do not be difficult,
Susannah. You were very ill, and you told me only just
now that your arm is still very sore.'

'Yes, it does hurt,' Susannah agreed, 'but if Harry
will not come to me, then I must go to him.'

'You know that it is extremely improper for a gentleman to visit an unmarried lady in her bedroom, do you
not?'

'Yes, Mama, I know,' Susannah replied, her mouth set
stubbornly. 'But if he does not come to visit me today,
I shall get up.'

'Well, I believe he is out on estate business at the
moment,' Mrs Hampton said and sighed. 'However, I
shall tell him when he returns. It really is most improper,
my love.'

'Please do tell him, Mama,' Susannah urged. 'If

he does not come, I shall dress and come down this evening.'

'You are a troublesome girl at times,' her mama said and shook her head in frustration. 'But I suppose you must have your way.'

Susannah looked through the book of poetry that Amelia had given her before she left Pendleton, tossing it aside restlessly. It was almost teatime! If Harry did not come soon, she would be forced to carry out her threat and go down, even though she did not truly feel well enough. She was about to ring the bell and summon her maid to help her dress when someone tapped at her door.

'Please come in,' she called and sat up expectantly. 'Harry…I am so glad you came!' She smiled at him as he hesitated near the door. 'Pray do come in. I am quite decent, for I have my dressing robe on.'

'You are better, Susannah,' Harry said as he walked towards the bed. 'You know I ought not to be here now—though I dare say any damage was done before this. It is just as well that we are engaged, otherwise I should have had to propose if only to save your reputation. Your mama was very cross with me, you know.'

Susannah saw the gleam in his eyes and knew he was teasing her. She laughed and shook her head at him. 'It is such a bore having to sit here, Harry. I have had lots of ladies to visit me, but I wanted to talk to you.'

'Well, I am here now—what have you to say to me?'

'I think I must apologise for all the trouble I have caused.'

Harry arched his right eyebrow. 'Must you? Perhaps you should, for everyone was very anxious for you while the fever raged. We thought we might lose you. I must tell you that several of my family have severely reprimanded me for placing you in danger—and I could not blame them. I should never have forgiven myself if you had died.'

'Would you have minded very much?' Susannah looked at him, an unconscious appeal in her eyes.

'I cannot tell you how much,' Harry said and looked stern. 'Why did you do such a foolish thing? Was it that you were afraid I should be killed?'

Susannah nodded, her cheeks on fire. 'I know it was wrong of me, Harry—but I do love you so.'

'I adore you, my brave, foolish darling,' Harry said. He advanced towards the bed, sat on the edge and took her hand. 'I was not sure if you liked Toby better, but he assures me that you are merely friends—and that he refused to tell you where the duel was. Tell me, how did you discover it, Susannah?'

'I heard you say something as you came in that night—and then I listened at the library door, which was very bad of me, I know. I watched the direction you took that morning, and I asked Tim if there was a clearing in the woods. He told me which trail to follow and—' She bit her lip. 'Why did you not fire at once? I thought you would be killed and I could not bear it.'

'So you risked your life for mine,' Harry said. He carried her hand to his lips and kissed it, his look tender. 'I am not sure that I deserve such devotion, Susannah. I must ask you to promise me that you will not take such a foolish risk again.'

'I shall promise—if you promise not to fight another duel.'

'I had to fight him, Susannah—not for Miss Hazledeane's sake, but because he was my enemy and he might have tried to harm you if I had not challenged him.'

'Oh…' Susannah's eyes widened. 'I did not know—but I still do not wish you to fight again. I should not want to live if you were killed, Harry.'

'Then I must give you my word—the word of a gentleman,' Harry said. 'For I feel much the same, my love.'

'We are agreed,' Susannah said. She tipped her head to one side, a gleam of mischief in her eyes. 'When do you think I shall be ready to drive my horses again? You promised to give me a race. I trust you have not forgotten?'

'No, I have not forgotten,' Harry replied and laughed softly. 'It will be some weeks before you are ready for such a mad adventure, my love. Your arm will be painful and stiff for some time. I think the race should wait until after the wedding—do you agree?'

'Oh, yes,' Susannah said and gave him a wicked look. 'How soon can we be married?'

'Amelia is making all the arrangements. We shall go down as soon as you are able to travel and the last banns may be called when we can attend the church.'

'I cannot wait,' Susannah said. 'I shall get up tomorrow and perhaps we can go down next week.'

'If you are well enough to get up tomorrow, I shall show you my apartments at Pendleton,' Harry said. 'I would like to set any work in hand before we leave.'

'Yes, I should like that,' Susannah replied. She looked at him thoughtfully. 'Tell me, do you think the Earl of Ravenshead will come back from France for our wedding?'

'I do not know,' Harry said and frowned. 'I know what you are thinking, Susannah—but I cannot help you. I had no idea that Gerard had a daughter until a few days ago when the letter came summoning him to France. He will need to settle his daughter—and he will try to find Miss Hazledeane and make sure that she is safe, as safe as she can be in her circumstances. I doubt that he will find time to make the trip back for our wedding. We can hardly expect it.'

'I see…' Susannah sighed and looked wistful. 'I just wondered. I do not mean to interfere, Harry. I have learned my lesson, and I know that there is nothing I can do.'

'If they are destined to be together, they will,' Harry said and leaned forwards to kiss her on the lips. 'However, I am more concerned about you—about us, Susannah. Have you forgiven me for all the things I have done to hurt you?'

'Yes, of course,' she said and laughed. 'You have done nothing but treat me kindly. It was my own fault that you were angry. I should have told you what I knew concerning Miss Hazledeane, for I should have known that you would treat her fairly. I think I must be a very troublesome girl to you at times, Harry.'

'Oh, indeed, you are,' he agreed. 'But I would not have you otherwise.'

Susannah's arm was still sore when she went downstairs the next morning. It was bound with a fresh bandage, but she wore a stole to cover it. Her appearance in the drawing room just before nuncheon caused a stir. None of the gentlemen had seen her since her unfortunate accident, and they rushed to set a chair for her, offering to bring her drinks and making such a fuss that Susannah laughed. Her fears that she might be censured for her rash behaviour were quite forgotten as she heard herself hailed as a plucky little thing and just what this family needed.

'Harry is fortunate to have found a gel of the right mettle,' Lady Ethel said in a voice that carried to everyone. 'In my day we were not so mealy mouthed and I've known ladies to fight their own duels, my dear. In fact, I once challenged a man to a duel, but the coward would not meet me!' Her eyes gleamed. 'I was a whip in my day, you know, and a good shot. I raced Harry's father round the park here once and I have sometimes shot pheasant with the gentlemen.'

'Oh, I did not know,' Susannah said, amazed at the revelations. 'I do not think I should be as brave as you, ma'am, for I should not dare to challenge anyone to a duel—but I should like to race my horses once my arm is healed.'

'You'll be as fit as a fiddle in no time,' the lady said with a nod of approval. 'I'd wager a few guineas on you against almost anyone, m'dear.'

'Really, Ethel, you are outrageous,' Lord Booker said, but winked at Susannah. 'She is quite right, m'dear. Harry kept us waiting a long time, but he certainly knows how to pick a bride!'

Since most of the relatives that still remained at Pendleton seemed to feel the same, Susannah was able to enjoy her lunch without embarrassment. However, every time she glanced across the table at Harry, she felt like laughing, so she was obliged to desist from glancing his way. However, once nuncheon was over, he claimed her for himself before anyone could ask her to play cards or sit in the gardens.

'If you feel up to it, I should like to show you where we shall stay when we visit here, though you know that

I have other houses where we may stay. I do not expect you to live here all the time, Susannah.'

'It is a very beautiful house,' Susannah said. 'I found it overwhelming at the beginning, but it has begun to grow on me. I shall not mind visiting several times a year.'

'Really?' Harry's brows went up in surprise. 'Well, perhaps we shall in that case. If our own apartments are comfortable, it will be somewhere to escape to if we choose.'

'You mean from the *crusties*?' Susannah asked and laughed. 'I think they are rather sweet, Harry.'

'You have not been on the receiving end of their displeasure,' he said and looked rueful. 'They have each and every one of them told me that it was my fault you were hurt. I have been thoroughly scolded for bringing you into danger by taking part in a duel—and risking the future to boot. I believe they know that without you there would be no heir for Pendleton.'

'Poor you,' Susannah said and giggled. 'I was praised for my courage and spirit.'

'It seems that you can do no wrong,' Harry replied and grinned. 'If I ever beat you or run mad, you will only need to tell my relatives and they will have me confined in an asylum!'

'Oh, Harry...' Susannah laughed, for this was the gentle, teasing man that she loved. 'You are wicked, truly you are.' How could she ever have thought him dull?

Harry smiled again, but said nothing until they arrived at a pair of imposing double doors. At their approach a footman sprang to throw them open. Susannah looked about her as she entered, feeling surprised at how comfortable and charming the décor was already.

'But this room is lovely, Harry,' she exclaimed,

looking round at the blend of greens, blues and cream that gave it such a restful air. 'The furniture is so pretty—and modern.'

'It is the work of Mr Adam,' Harry said and looked pleased. 'I commissioned it when I found these rooms needed refurbishment. The furniture in here is mostly satinwood, inlaid with fruit woods—and also porcelain plaques in the French style.'

'I think it beautiful,' Susannah said. 'The furniture is so light and elegant and the colours are perfect. I should not want to change anything here at all...' She ran her fingers over the top of a pretty desk, opening a cupboard to exclaim over the inlay on the tiny drawers inside. Everything was so beautifully made! A display cabinet was set with exquisite pieces of Sèvres porcelain, and some Meissen figures, which were similar to those that had amused her in the guest chambers. 'May I see the rest of your apartments, please, Harry?'

'Of course—go where you please, Susannah.' He followed behind as she ran ahead, exclaiming over the next room, which was another sitting room, furnished this time in highly polished walnut, the décor rose pinks and creams, and clearly intended for Harry's wife to be private when she chose. From there Susannah went to the bedrooms. Harry's own room was furnished in crimson, gold and touches of black, which gave it a masculine feel.

Susannah inhaled the scents of cedar and leather, lingering for a moment. Harry's valet had tidied everything away, but she imagined it with his things lying on chairs and the stool at the foot of the bed and smiled. The next room was intended for her—and Susannah stood for a moment, looking at the décor of pale yellow, gold and white, thinking how attractive it was, and how comfortable she would be in such a room. The furniture here was satinwood, again inlaid with fruit woods and porcelain, elegant and, Susannah thought, utterly charming. Letting her gaze travel round the room, she saw that Harry seemed to have thought of everything.

'This is lovely,' she told him. 'Once I have a few of my own things about me, it will be perfect. I do not think we need to change anything at all, Harry.'

'Are you sure?' he asked and came to her, gazing down at her lovely face. 'If there is anything at all, you have only to say.'

'I love it all,' she told him. 'I am quite content, though one day I may want to make changes elsewhere in the house.'

'You must tell me when you decide,' Harry said and reached out for her, pulling her close to him. He bent his head, kissing her on the lips. At first soft and tender, his kiss intensified, becoming passionate, demanding. Susannah leaned into him, her body seeming to melt into his as she gave herself up to the pleasure of the moment. 'Anything you wish for is yours....'

'Harry...' Susannah breathed, her lips parting on a sigh of content. 'You will spoil me.'

'I fully intend to,' he replied. 'Since you have nothing to complain of here, I think I shall take you for a drive about the park until it is time for tea. Otherwise one of the relatives will capture you and I shall not have you to myself again for an age.'

For the next few days Harry took Susannah driving each morning, and she spent the afternoons sitting at home in one of the parlours. Sometimes she played cards or simply conversed with the relatives. A few of them had gone home in order to prepare for the journey to Amelia's home for the wedding, but some lingered and she discovered that she enjoyed their company. Her feelings of being unequal to the task that lay ahead as Harry's wife had faded to the extent that they no longer worried her. She had much to learn before she could truly take her place as the chatelaine of a great house like this one, but she was learning and she knew that Harry and Lady Elizabeth would help her. Indeed, with such well-trained servants, she need only give her orders and keep her accounts, just as Lady Elizabeth had told her.

It was towards the end of the week that Harry let her take the reins again when they were out, and she managed to drive for half an hour before she was obliged to hand them back.

'I am afraid that my arm still aches,' she said and frowned because she did not like to give in.

'It will take time to get the full use of your arm once more,' Harry told her. 'I was out of action for at least two months when I was injured in Spain.'

Susannah looked at his profile, noticing the little pulse flicking at his temple. 'It is because of something that happened in Spain that you quarrelled with the marquis, was it not?'

'Yes.' Harry frowned. 'We were on a dangerous mission and the enemy were waiting for us. Northaven cried off sick that day and we believe that he betrayed us, though he has always sworn that he did not. He resented it when we accused him of loose talk. Since that time we have not been friends, though until recently we managed to be polite to one another in public.'

'You will not quarrel with him again, Harry?'

Harry looked at her, his expression serious. 'It shall

not come from me, Susannah. I give you my word. I cannot promise that the feud is at an end, but I shall not go out of my way to court trouble. Jenny chose her own fate. I was unwise to promise her brother so much, for I knew nothing of her. However, that is at an end. All I want now is to live happily with you, my darling.'

'And I with you,' Susannah told him, eyes bright with love. 'I cannot wait for our marriage, Harry.'

'We shall go down to Amelia's estate tomorrow,' Harry said. 'The banns have been called twice in our absence. They will be called for the third time next Sunday and we shall be in church to hear them called— and then we can be married.'

'Oh, yes,' Susannah said, her heart swelling with love. 'I can hardly wait to be your wife.'

'I can hardly wait to claim you,' he replied and the look in his eyes burned her. 'I never thought that I should ever find love like this, my darling. When you risked your life for mine, you proved yourself beyond doubt. I am humbled by such love and I shall try to make you happy for the rest of our lives.'

'Susannah, my love. I want you to meet Miss Emily Barton,' Amelia said when she took Susannah into her parlour two days later. 'Emily has been kind enough to become my companion and I think we shall suit very well.'

'Miss Barton…' Susannah studied the young woman's face as she came forward to greet her. Miss Barton was very near Amelia's own age, an attractive woman, but with an air of sadness about her. Her dark blonde hair was pulled back into a tight bun, as if she wished for no sign of softness in her appearance. Her dress was pale grey, offset by a collar of heavy cream lace and pinned

with a gold cameo. She wore no other ornamentation and
her manner was as gentle and self-effacing as her dress.
'I am pleased you are come to keep Amelia company.'

'I am very fortunate that Miss Royston was pleased
to give me her trust,' Emily said with a gentle smile.
Susannah noticed that even when she smiled the air of
sadness did not leave her and she wondered what had
caused it. What tragedy lay in Miss Barton's past? 'I
hope to be all that she expects and needs. I know that
she is fond of you and your mama and will miss you.'

'Oh, but we shall all see each other often,' Susannah
said. 'Harry is to take me to his house in Devon for a
week or two and then we may go to Paris to buy some
clothes. After that we shall return to Pendleton, and I
shall be giving a ball. It will be a grand affair. I do hope
that you will both come.'

'Of course we shall,' Amelia told her. 'I would not
miss it for the world. I am so relieved to see you happy
and recovered from your…accident, Susannah.'

'Thank you, dear Amelia,' Susannah said and kissed
her cheek. 'I do feel much better.'

'We are looking forward to your wedding—are we
not, Emily?'

'Yes, we are,' Emily Barton said and smiled her gentle
smile. 'Very much indeed.'

The morning of the wedding was hot. Susannah was
awake early. She went down and slipped out into the
gardens before anyone was stirring. It felt delicious to
walk in the shade of the trees at this hour, though she
could already feel the heat building. She wandered as far
as the rose arbour and sat there for a while, inhaling the
perfume of musk roses and feeling her happiness seep
through her.

It was only as she left the shelter of the rose arbour and began to walk home that she was aware of someone behind her. A trickle of fear ran down her spine and she spun round, hardly knowing what she expected. What she saw was a man in the clothes that a gamekeeper might wear, a long gun over his shoulder. He nodded to her, but did not smile. Susannah had the oddest feeling that he had been watching her—or rather keeping watch over her—which she felt a little strange.

Was Harry concerned that the marquis might try to harm her? The thought made her a little uneasy, but she put it from her mind as she went into the house, running lightly up the stairs to her room. Harry had spent the night at the inn so as not to spoil the traditions of not seeing his bride until they met in church. Susannah had just regained her room when someone knocked at the door and then Amelia came in.

'I brought you a wedding gift,' Amelia said and handed her a small leather box. 'It is just something to bring you luck today.'

'Thank you.' Susannah took the box and opened it, gasping with pleasure as she saw the gold bangle set with pearls and diamonds. 'This is beautiful, Amelia. It will go so well with the necklace Harry has given me as a wedding present.'

'I did ask him what he would give you,' Amelia said. 'He told me it would be diamonds or pearls and I remembered the bangle left to me by my mother, which I thought would match perfectly.'

'You have been so generous to me,' Susannah said and hugged her, suddenly emotional. 'If it were not for you, I might never have met Harry. I shall never be able to thank you enough, my dearest of friends.'

'If it was meant, you probably would have met

somehow,' Amelia said and smiled a little oddly. 'I shall miss you, dearest, but I wish you all the happiness in the world. Indeed, I know you will be happy, for Harry Pendleton is a good man.'

'Yes, I know. I am very lucky.'

'He is lucky to have you, as I am sure he knows. You will both be content in your marriage, for you are well suited.'

'I wish you to be happy too,' Susannah said but did not elaborate, for she did not wish to hurt Amelia's feelings. 'Did you know someone has armed guards walking the estate? I saw one of them when I went for a walk earlier. He was dressed like a gamekeeper, but I think he was keeping watch over me rather than your pheasants.'

'Yes, I gave permission,' Amelia said. 'They have been here for the past week or so. Lord Coleridge said that he and Ravenshead discussed it—Pendleton too. Apparently, it is as much for my benefit as yours; after what happened in Pendleton Woods they feared I might be the victim of another attack, but I do not think it myself. At first I thought it was a kidnap attempt, but since then I have been inclined to think it merely a random attack, perhaps for whatever of value I happened to carry. After all, no one could have known I would walk that way.'

'Unless you had done so before?'

'Well, I have always enjoyed walking in woods, though for the moment I am content with my garden— and, of course, we shall go to Bath soon, for I intend to live there for most of the year.'

'Yes, I dare say you will be happier there,' Susannah said and frowned. 'Please be careful, Amelia. I should not wish anything untoward to happen to you.'

'Well, I am sure it will not,' Amelia said. 'I shall allow the guards for the moment, but I am certain nothing will come of it.' She shook her head, as if to dismiss the idea. 'We shall not talk of this again, dearest. This is your wedding day and I want you to be happy.'

'I am very happy,' Susannah said, and then the door opened to admit her mama. 'Isn't it a beautiful day, Mama?'

'Very warm,' Mrs Hampton replied with a look of approval. 'I do not think we could have had a better day for it, my love. I have brought you a present—just a lace kerchief of mine and a garter of blue lace. You have your wedding gown, which is new. Amelia's bracelet is old and now something borrowed and something blue. You should have lots of luck, dearest.'

'I am the luckiest girl in the world,' Susannah said and kissed her. 'I have Harry—what more could I want?'

The wedding ceremony went smoothly. The sun warmed the old church, its rays sending showers of colour through the stained-glass windows. Susannah stood beside Harry as they took their vows, her heart filled with so much joy that she thought she might burst with happiness. When they came out of church to the bells pealing and a shower of rose petals from friends and villagers, she stood for a moment on the steps looking about her, her arm through Harry's.

It was as her gaze was drawn towards some trees to her left that a shiver of ice went through her. A man was standing just at the edge of the trees, watching them with an air of menace. She shaded her eyes against the sun, sure that it was the Marquis of Northaven. What was he doing here? Had he come to try to ruin their day?

For a moment she was tense, fearing that he might

suddenly dart forward and pull a pistol. As if he sensed her tension, Northaven suddenly looked at her. For a moment she felt some intense emotion, perhaps hatred or anger—and then he inclined his head to her. For a second longer he lingered before turning and walking into the trees.

Susannah breathed again. His bowed head had reassured her—she sensed that he was showing her respect, telling her that neither she nor Harry need fear him. He might still resent his old friends, but she believed he would not try to harm her or her husband.

'Is everything all right, my love?' Harry asked, turning his head to look at her.

'Yes, perfect,' she replied and smiled at him. 'Even the weather is smiling on us.' There was no need to tell him that she had seen the marquis, no need to cast a shadow over their special day. 'I have never been happier.'

'Then we must leave for the reception,' Harry said. 'Otherwise we shall keep our guests waiting and that would never do.'

Susannah nodded, taking his hand as they ran to the waiting carriage.

'You make a beautiful bride,' Lady Elizabeth told Susannah a little later that afternoon. She kissed Susannah's cheek. 'My son was lucky to find you, my dear. Indeed, had you not acted so boldly, he might not be here today. He says that Northaven would not have killed him, but I am not so sure. That man hates him.'

'Why do you say that?' Susannah asked.

'Oh, it is just a feeling I have,' Lady Elizabeth said. 'I have heard that he is in some financial trouble. His uncle left him a fortune, but he has run through it. He must marry well or come to ruin, I dare say—but I do not know if he will find an heiress to have him.'

'Oh…' Susannah frowned. 'He was always well received in town.'

'A handsome man is always good company,' Lady Elizabeth told her. 'However, I should not have allowed a daughter of mine to marry him, had I one of a suitable age. He will probably have to elope if he finds a girl foolish enough to run off with him.'

Susannah was thoughtful as she went upstairs to change into her travelling gown. Northaven had been watching someone before he became aware of her looking at him. Could it possibly have been Amelia? She had thought he was there to see her and Harry married, but she might have been wrong. Could he have been behind that kidnap attempt in the woods at Pendleton?

Susannah felt a trickle of ice down her spine once more. She had dismissed the incident in Pendleton Woods, believing as the others did that it was by mere chance that Amelia had been attacked—but supposing someone had been trying to abduct her? Could it have been the marquis? Was he perhaps hoping that he might force her to wed him so that he could gain control of her fortune?

Susannah was unsure what to do—should she tell Harry she had seen him, or Amelia? Perhaps it was best to say nothing to Amelia. She was being protected and she did not need warning against the marquis, for she had never trusted him.

Susannah would mention it to Harry later, but not until they were alone.

'I am glad that you told me that you saw him watching us,' Harry said when they were in the carriage, having set out on their journey a few minutes earlier. 'However, I was aware that he was in the vicinity. He is being watched, Susannah, and will continue to be for a while. Max, Gerard and I considered the possibility that it might have been he who tried to have Amelia abducted. We have no proof either way. Amelia is aware that her estate is being patrolled by agents who would not hesitate to shoot anyone who refused to answer a challenge. She does not think that Northaven would attempt it, but is prepared to be careful. When she goes to Bath, she will be more in the public eye and will not need so much protection. However, I have advised her that it would be best to keep one or two of the Bow Street men on for a while.'

'How awful for her,' Susannah said and frowned. 'I do not like to think that anyone would want to hurt Amelia—or to force her into a marriage she disliked.'

'When a woman is unprotected by a husband, especially one as wealthy as Amelia, it is difficult. The property laws may seem harsh as far as women are concerned, but in a way they do protect a woman from rogues and blackmailers. Once she is married, her fortune is under the control of her husband, though in many cases she is given an income and her money secured for her children.'

'Yes, I do see that,' Susannah agreed. 'I should be happier if she were married, but I do not think she has considered it—not truly. At least, she will not marry unless she finds love.'

'Perhaps not,' Harry said and arched his brows. 'Amelia is a capable lady and protected, as much as she can be. That bonnet you are wearing is very fetching, my love—but if you were to remove it, I should be able to kiss you more easily.'

'Yes…' Susannah laughed and untied the ribbons. 'I do not think I need it for the moment—and I have been aching for you to kiss me all day.'

Susannah sat before her dressing mirror, brushing her long hair. She was in the bedroom of her new home, and she was pleased to discover that it was a comfortable house. However, the décor left much to be desired, and the prospect of being given *carte blanche* to set it right was exciting.

Her heart caught as the door opened and Harry came in. He was wearing a long dressing robe of dark blue cloth, and his hair looked damp, as if he had washed it. As he came to her, she caught the fresh scent of soap and cologne.

'You smell gorgeous,' she told him, smiling up into his eyes. 'I am so happy…so very happy.'

'I am glad,' Harry told her. 'I love you so much, my dearest wife. My wife…it seems an age since I first wondered if perhaps one day you would marry me.'

'Yes, it does seem a long time since we first met,' Susannah said. She was suddenly breathless as he put his arms about her, holding her pressed closed to his body. She could feel his heat through her fine nightgown, and she lifted her face in anticipation of his kiss. 'I love you so much.'

Harry moaned deep in his throat. He bent to catch her up in his arms, carrying her to the bed and depositing her gently amongst the silken sheets. Abandoning his robe, Harry lay down beside her, feasting his eyes on her lovely face.

'We do not need this, delicious as it is,' he said and drew her nightgown over her head, tossing it to the floor. 'I want nothing between us, my love. I have waited for this moment so long and now I want to look at you…to touch every piece of your beautiful body…'

'Love me, Harry,' she whispered, looking at him with such longing that he moaned with need. 'Teach me everything I should know to please you.'

'You please me just as you are,' he murmured hotly. 'But I shall show you how we can please each other.' His lips took possession of hers, his hand stroking the satin arch of her back. Susannah gasped as she felt the burn of desire and her body tingled with the new sensation that she knew was need for him, to feel one with him. 'I want you so much…'

Susannah gave herself up to the pleasure of his hands touching her in all the secret places where no one had touched her before, his tongue teasing and tantalising when his hands had done their work. She arched and gasped, moaning as he brought her to fever pitch, before entering her. At the moment of penetration she felt a little pain, but in another moment it had gone as she thrilled to his loving, bringing her such pleasure that she thought she might die.

Afterwards, she lay at peace in his arms, sleeping.

* * * * *